THE PRIORY

JONATHAN WHEATLEY

www.jonathanwheatley.co.uk
Flesh and Bone Publishing
ISBN: 9798641190693

Cover Design by Katrina Scott

DEDICATION

This book is dedicated to my children, Sonny and Harlan, who give me the determination to keep moving forward and to my mum and dad who always let me follow my own path...

To all those aspiring authors I ask you to keep on writing and to all my wonderful readers, thank you for taking the time to read my story.

With hard work and a positive attitude anything is possible... Follow your dreams.

Part One

1 LUCAS

I put my hand down my pants–I'm a man today, that's a start–it's always weird when I'm a woman. Until this all started, I took the simplicity of being a man for granted; the ability to jump out of bed and go to work without brushing my hair, being able to pee standing up, not wearing a bra; the list goes on.

I survey the room. It's just a room, a studio apartment with cream walls and a patchy, well-worn blue carpet. Spiderwebs in the corners of the sash windows wave in the warm breeze that comes through. A cheap-looking IKEA knock-off unit with leftover sticker-marks separates the bedroom and the living areas. Out the window, I see the roof of an old Listed-looking building. I recognize the property style. "Shit, shit, shit." I lay back and pull the covers over myself.

I stayed in a hotel in this town, Westford, after a few too many beers, and ever since, every morning, I've woken up in someone else's body. Today is the 50th anniversary. Fifty days! Fifty new people! What the fuck!

There were no aches or pains today, which is better than yesterday when I was a woman with a shattered ankle. I saw the x-ray on the table next to the bed, and no wonder she had bottles upon bottles of pills next to her. They'd sat her up in bed with her leg raised. Doctors in plain clothes came and went. They cast worried glances towards her from the doorway, and not just because of her ankle. The doctors and nurses treated her as you would a child after a nightmare–reminding her to drink plenty and keep taking the pills. I heard the whispers and saw the glances when they switched over.

That was a dull day, and for once, I was happy to go to sleep and wake up in someone else's body. I was, however, intrigued by what was on her laptop and enamored by her two sons, which was something new for me–they were cute little boys, just the right age before they turn into little shits just like my nephews.

Clothes litter the floor. A grease splattered pizza box and tatty paperback novels clutter the makeshift black coffee table. This is a game I like to play. I look around the room and come up with a picture of the person whose body I'm in. Today's easy. I'm a mid-20s bloke, overweight, nerdy. I imagine slicked-back hair, greasy skin, the kind of guy who wears a man-bag with a clumpy old laptop in it.

I look for the remote for the TV; it's not on the coffee table. I don't dare look behind the cushions on the sofa; two suspicious stains put me off. I can forego TV for the morning this once.

Step on up! It's time to find out who I am. The bathroom smells of ammonia and lemon-scented bleach. A damp, pale green towel lays over the side of the peach-coloured bath. I piss in the yellow-stained toilet and then stand in front of the smeared mirror; I see black stubble in the sink, like a hundred ants scattering to get away. My eyes meet his as I look up and wipe the surface clean. His are nutty brown, with hints of black. He has a strong face, a thick jaw with a couple of days worth of dark stubble that runs high up his front and low down his neck.

"You hairy."

His black hair is cropped short and shaved to the skin at the sides. Large, wild eyebrows frame his face giving him a primitive, uncivilized look. His body isn't six-pack fit, but it is thick and robust. I pump those guns in the mirror. Veiny muscles struggle to escape his arms. The shoulders are round, and he has a slight potbelly. He's the largest guy I've been; not in height, I guess he is 5ft 10 max. What sort of life does he lead on a day-to-day basis, when he hasn't been taken over by a drunken out-of-towner?

I shower, dry myself off and pick up a faded, white Nirvana tee-shirt off the floor, I sniff it, then match it with a pair of ripped jeans and some battered, black Adidas Sambas–I feel good about today.

I have a plan; I've been working on it since yesterday when I was trapped in bed in the woman's body. When I woke her laptop, she'd been on the library website researching the history of this town. It looked as though she'd been searching for a woman called Lydia and something to do with a Priory. Another tab was open full of grotesque images and illustrations of monsters. In the bottom corner of the screen was a camera icon. I clicked it, and CCTV-style footage of the boy's bedroom appeared.

Something caused this. I know it's not normal to wake up in someone else's body every day. It would surprise you after the fiftieth time how you take it in your stride. It hadn't been like that the first ten times, though, trust me. But, today, I would find CCTV footage of that night.

There has to be video of that evening, stored in the cloud. If I follow the trail, I could find myself, or at least trace my last steps. I need access to the CCTV of the hotel and then the town. Simple.

I close the door and go down the dark, web-encrusted narrow staircase out into the blinding sunshine in the middle of the high-street. I trip over my own feet, not expecting to be thrust into a busy crowd so early in my day. "Sorry," I mutter to an old man whose way I've blocked.

Bright colours attack my senses–people wearing floral dresses and pastel shade polo shirts walk past in a blur. The lingering smell of cigarettes mixes with coffee in the air. It's humid, and the high-street is busy. Kids on their school holidays whizz by on skateboards, the plastic wheels rattling on the cobbles. With no breeze, I feel the sweat drip down my back. A heatwave started around the time I arrived in this town and has stayed throughout.

The sunshine brings out scantily clad girls, which is always a perk. They sit on black benches on the high-street, and shiny metal tables and chairs in front of coffee shops. Tall stone buildings loom on both sides of the cobbled road. Half of the street is in the shade, and a few shops are boarded up and empty. The others are expensive-looking women's clothing shops, coffee shops, and charity shops.

I need a computer. I've got this guy's bank card, his name is Jake Dean, but with no knowledge of his pin, the best I can do is use contactless. I could order a laptop—but where would I get it delivered too? I wouldn't be here tomorrow. I walk past the fruit and veg seller at his red and white stall as he shouts, 'Cherries for a pound,' and continue to the library.

The imposing building looks like something from ancient Greece. Four pantheon-style columns hold up the pyramid-shaped vaulted roof with long windows between each. Crumbling grey steps lead to the hexagonal bases of the columns where people sit, smoke, eat their lunch, and people-watch. Contrasting against the yellow-stone to the left of the building, there is a bright red old-school phone box and post box.

There has to be something or someone in this strange yet beautiful town that is causing this. I've searched for my body most days. I questioned the receptionist at the hotel—all she could tell me was that a man (that would be me) had checked out early, but no-one had seen him/me leave; they had assumed he/I had checked out. My body is still missing.

I've been here lots looking through tattered old books trying to find out about the history of Westford and any myths and legends in the area. Anything that might relate to what's going on. So far, I have found nothing. I tried going through the old newspapers, but they made my eyes tired. Why had the woman from yesterday been researching Westford if she lived here? And, what were those illustrations of monsters? Those illustrations weren't suitable for children.

Inside the cool library, I nod at the librarian and walk to the block of computers behind the bookcases to the rear of the high-ceilinged room. Blue fabric chairs sit around a pine table at one end of the room. To the other corner, is an entrance to a small museum with sepia-toned images of Westford. I log onto one of the computers and Google, access local CCTV. Jake's eyebrows raise on the screen when a page loads, offering me access to a public surveillance system in New Hampton, the closest city to

Westford.

There's a link to check a CCTV map which shows live cameras. Westford not being part of New Hampton, I don't hold my breath as I wait for it to load. I hit my hand against the desk when it does and do a little shimmy on my stool. Then look around to check if anyone saw. There are three CCTV cameras that I can access.

I want to share my joy, but the only other person in the library is the old librarian with thinning grey hair and large rimmed glasses. I keep hold of my happiness, but loneliness dilutes it.

The memory of my previous attempts of conversation embarrasses me. I'd tried to chat with someone on the fifth day when I was a shapely blonde woman with a faded tattoo of a rose on her left boob. Her friend looked confused and left after my initial attempts. I remember her face as she looked back over her shoulder as she left.

No one from home misses me, friends, or family. They're used to not hearing from me for months at a time. Maybe, my granddad would have missed me, if he could remember me. I could contact someone, but when I think about it, there is no-one that close to me to convince.

I tap a few buttons on the keyboard and wait for the screen to load. The videos are pixelated. I tap my fingers against the desk. The picture gets clearer, and I see a live stream. I recognize the road—it's Broad Leaf Square, with its cobbles and picture-perfect tourist benches. I see the butchers, the electrical shop, and the hairdressers behind. I can't make out the writing on the windows.

I had stayed at the Cavalier, which was across the road from the square and its shops. A swanky hotel with neon lighting and a black and white tiled floor throughout. Depending on which way whoever had taken my body had gone, this camera stood a 50/50 chance of picking it up.

I click the mouse, grab the time bar at the bottom of the screen, and pull it back as far as it goes. I pray that it will be far enough—the date in the bottom corner ticks over to 05/06/19. I check the calendar on the bottom of the screen; it says 26/07/19. My eyes shut, maths was never my strong suit. That was 51 days ago—the time frame would work.

We went out on Wednesday the 5th of June; I remember the date as it was my mother's birthday. There was a party, and though I was invited, I told them I already had plans (I didn't, the night out was impromptu). I pull the cursor forward and watch the screen darken as daytime fades to evening. My mouth goes dry as I see Billy, John, and I cross the square on our way to the Cavalier. Even though the screen is pixelated, there's no doubting we were pissed. I was in the middle, just ahead of the other two—Billy and John staggered behind, shoulders thrown over one another. I have no recollection of this point of the night.

I forget I'm in the library, lost in the images on the monitor in front of me. I keep pausing the video to look at my magnificent body, my fantastic missing body. Nothing else happens on the screen once I let it play. I grab the timeline with the cursor and drag it across. Still nothing–three hours on the CCTV have passed since I saw myself. A black shape moves behind me on the monitor.

Turning around, I fall from the stool, and I land on the floor with my back against the computer desk. It looks like the old librarian from earlier. but her skin sags like wet flesh, and bulbous wrinkles cry down her face. Her pale white skin is thin like tracing paper, or that stuff sushi gets wrapped in, and a green pus-looking liquid moves underneath as though it will pop at any moment.

The librarian lumbers towards me, her arms splayed forward. Spit flies out of her mouth and into mine. I crawl under the computer desk, forgetting about the CCTV footage on the screen. My butt aches from where I'd landed. I knock over the stool nearby, and it lands with a metallic crash. I scramble over it and along the polished wood floor. My trainer's grip and half standing, I lurch forward and run towards the shelves of books.

She turns on the spot. I run deeper into the library. Covers of Young Adult novels stare at me as I tiptoe through the section. Creeping, I make my way back to the front of the library and towards the exit. I duck and go past the empty librarians' desk. Beyond this is a block of printers and machines. I sit with my back against the printer and catch my breath, listening to the librarian stumbling through the library. The library is still except for her. Time has stopped. The phones are silent. I see a paper sign stuck to the wall; Silence, please! No shit.

The librarian roams the room, slobbering as she moves. I see my exit, but I'm blocked in by a pile of returned books sitting on a wooden trolley with wheels. I poke my head around the edge of the printer, and I see the lumbering feet of the librarian in green pumps and pale blue tights dancing a circular tango on the floor. Watching from my low position, she is moving in slow circles with no rhyme or reason.

I move along the side of the printer against the wall, following it around the edge of the room, trying to be as silent as the sign suggests. I pass the science fiction and horror section; skulls and monsters and flowers watch me from paperback covers as I carry on through to general fiction. The exit is ten yards away. Bright sunlight shines in through the automatic double doors.

I hold onto a shelf with one hand and move into a sprinter pose, waiting for the starter's pistol. I count in my head, 3...2... And then the door shoots inwards.

Two teenagers walk in. They take off their backpacks and sit down around an empty table. They unplug their headphones and rummage through their bags, pulling out thick books, notepads, and pens. A teenager with fluffy ginger stubble in a Guns n' Roses hoodie looks up at me. He kicks his friend under the table and nods in my direction. The other teenager turns to look at me.

"You all right, dude?" he asks.

I stare at him. They stare back. They look at each other; one raises his eyebrows and shrugs. I look towards the librarian. Their heads follow, and they look at the librarian.

"Hi, Mrs. Spencer," they say to the bespectacled librarian.

I grab my bag and run out the door.

2 THE TEENAGERS

The fingernail. That dirty, bent-looking nasty thing. If he mentioned it, would they believe him? His sister, two-years-older, could be a total bitch when hanging out with Ruby. Petey would believe him, wouldn't he? Maybe he should mention it to him first, somewhere private, before telling the girls?

Dappled sunlight lit up the dusty banks of the river. Fast running water sparkled in the sunshine and reflected onto the bright green reeds at the riverbank. Luke stood next to Petey, stone in hand, ready to throw.

Petey's floppy brown hair waved in the breeze and his glasses reflected the sun, and behind him, a battered rope swing rotated lazily in the breeze, its frayed and tatty blue ropes creaked as they tightened around the large branch that hung from the bridge over the river. Would he believe him, he wondered? Petey threw his stone. Something metallic in the dull grey caught the light as it spun over and over in the air. It landed with a splash. Petey turned and saw Luke looking at him. "What?"

They had known each other since the first day of reception class—he shrugged his narrow shoulders. "Nothing." Luke couldn't remember, but his parents' often told him how Petey was his first real friend, and friends are precious. Petey would do anything for you, Luke. He heard his mother's voice in his head.

"You going to throw yours?"

"Sure." Luke pulled his arm back into a pitcher throw and shot his stone past where Petey's had splashed. Luke looked up from the ripples. The opposite side of the river sloped up towards forest and a muddy footpath lining the top of the bridge. A moss-covered stone, the size of a small car, sat halfway up the riverbank leading to the top of the bridge. He watched his sister and her friend sitting, nodding their heads sharing a headphone each, listening to music with their feet dangling over the edge.

Both girls wore baggy black shorts with white stripes down the sides and white crop tops. Their shoulders were turning pink from the heatwave. Under their dangling feet were two cavernous openings.

Each led from this end of the bridge to the other—It must have been a bridge for cattle and farmers decades or centuries ago. Now sharp bushes and weeds stuck out ready to pierce the skin; huge trees with thick branches stretched into the sky, and three fence rails had fallen. The entrances were like twin black holes sucking in all the light from outside. At the other end, Luke didn't know how far away, the light returned. They dared each other to see how far either would go, but neither ever got further than ten yards.

He thought about shouting to them–to tell them about the fingernail. It was a mad itch at the back of his mind, something he knew was important, whether or not they believed him.

"Petey," he said, turning towards him. "I need to tell you something."

"What?"

"Not here, follow me down the stream a bit." Petey frowned, but followed.

They came out from under the shade of the trees, and Luke felt the sunshine burning his flesh despite the factor 50 his mum had rubbed onto his skin only an hour ago. Luke kept on walking, followed by Petey. He glanced across the yellow fields as he dived through a hedge and into the underbrush to their secret place.

A little stream flowed over pretty pink, yellow and blue pebbles. He heard cars on the motorway and the twittering of birds in the hedges. The water was clear. Luke took off his shoes and paddled to a clearing. He sat on a warm rock and waited for Petey to catch up.

Besides Petey, he was sure no one else knew about this place. This was his special place–it was where he came on the days Sam was waiting at the bus stop after school. He watched an ant crawl over the rock and listened to the sounds of the motorway nearby; he found them soothing. A moment later he heard splashes downstream, and he saw Petey.

"So, what's so important?"

"I'm not sure you'll believe me if I tell you."

"Try me," Petey replied.

They sat on large grey rocks opposite each other, their feet dangling in the fresh stream as Luke told Petey about his grisly discovery.

Luke's Mum and Dad had had the decorator in over the weekend. He was a local guy with a good reputation–a recommendation from a friend. During the weeks leading, they argued about the colour of the living room before settling on a mocha colour, which Luke hated. He'd been able to pick the colour for his room though; a pastel shade of blue which made him feel peaceful. The painter finished early Saturday afternoon, and he'd thought no more of it.

Luke sat in his bedroom reading comics on Wednesday morning, chilled as if it was a summer's day at the beach–not that he'd experienced one of those for a while. He looked forward to seeing Ruby later at the river. Luke liked the way her shorts rode up high on her milky thighs.

A shout from downstairs broke his concentration. He walked down the stairs, which led into the living room, picturing pancakes with syrup for breakfast. He brushed his hand down the wall–liking the way the new paint felt and smelled when his hand flashed against something sharp. A pinprick of blood bubbled on his palm. He stopped, backed up, and turned to inspect the area. He rubbed his palm over the spot, feeling the cold roughness until he found it again. There was something there, under the paint.

He picked at it with his fingernail, but the rough scrape turned his spine to jelly. He counted which stair he was on. He repeated the number, seven, seven, seven, over and over again as he went to the kitchen, past his sister who was arguing over loudspeaker about a mobile phone bill with their dad, and found a small, yet sharp, black-handled knife in the utensil drawer.

"We're cutting off your data." He heard his dad say to Lisa on his way back up the stairs.

He sat on the seventh step. The thought that his parents would be mad entered his mind, and then intrigue took back over. He scraped at the spot, wincing when it made a fingernail-down-chalkboard sound. The knife left white scars on the wall, but Luke pried out the object.

It was drenched in mocha colour paint and red brick dust–he had been too heavy-handed with the knife. There was no way his parents' wouldn't notice the chunk missing from the wall. What if the painter left some paint behind, he could repaint the spot? The thing weighed nothing; he rolled it over in the palm of his left hand and saw it was a fingernail. He forgot about touching up the mess he made.

"A fingernail! Are you shitting me?"

"I shit you not," Luke said, he raised his eyebrow. "Do you want to see it?" He reached behind him.

"You have it with you, you weirdo?"

"What would you have done with it?" his hand stopped just above his back pocket.

"Thrown it away, duh!" Petey rolled his eyes.

"Fine," Luke said, as he moved his hand to his front and picked up a stone from the stream. "It's weird, though, right?"

"Yes, Luke, it's very fucking weird!"

"Why would it be in my wall or the paint?" He threw a pebble back and forth between his hands.

"I read somewhere once about a mouse in a bucket of KFC."

"You think it was already in the paint? What, like an accident at the plant–or wherever paint's made?" Luke stopped throwing the pebble.

Petey nodded his head, not agreeing, more like he was weighing up the possibility. "Yes, I think that's exactly what happened, don't you?"

Luke's face dropped, the sparkle in his eyes dimmed, and his shoulders slumped. "I guess you're right, " He tossed the pebble back into the water.

"Come on then, let's get back to the river, you can have first go on the swing–if the girls haven't pinched it from us."

They made their way back up the stream, moving carefully so as not to tread on a sharp pebble or get stung by one of the many stingers that lined both sides.

The girls were still on the rock. They had removed the headphones, and Luke and Petey watched them dance. Their hips gyrated to a Latino pop song. Luke's gaze lingered on his sister's best-friend as she moved to the music. Her straw-blonde hair swung back and forth. Her short shorts rode up high as she crouched down and then in rhythm made her way up again. He felt something stir, a feeling that was becoming familiar, but which he didn't know what to do with.

Ruby looked down and saw him gazing up. She smiled at him, bright white teeth lighting up her freckled face–he turned away, pretending he hadn't been looking. She flicked a piece of hair behind her ear and carried on dancing. Petey hadn't moved; he was standing frozen to the spot, his gaze locked onto Lisa. Luke coughed, and Petey looked around. His cheeks flushed red, and he blushed. Sensing his friend's embarrassment, Luke said, "Race you to the swing." He shuffled on his butt down to the water's-edge. Petey smiled and shuffled after him, thankful that Luke hadn't made a big deal.

They stayed down by the river for the afternoon. The hot sun swept across the cloudless blue sky. Lisa and Ruby sunbathed, their tops next to them, and their short shorts pulled up high. Luke and Petey were building a dam in the river. Luke was topless, but Petey kept his on. Lisa had unplugged her headphones, and music floated down from above.

"Hey, Buttfaces, you ready, or are you still touching each other?" Luke looked up and saw his sister looking down at them.

Petey blushed as he heard the girl's giggling from above.

"We heard you," Luke shouted back and looked at Petey. "Ignore my sister; she's the Buttface."

Petey smiled, and they climbed out of the river, dried their feet, and slipped on their pumps. "Why is Lisa like that? You know, calling us names and stuff?"

"Ignore her; when she's with Ruby, she acts like a spoiled brat, but you know what?"

"What?"

"She's just trying to act cool in front of her friend—I'll tells you a secret though… she still wears character pants," Luke said and laughed. "Barbie ones."

Petey went bright red again, the sunburn from the day covered it up quite well.

The girls walked fifty-yards ahead of them. Not that there was anyone in the fields that would have seen them anyway. To their right, the cut hay had left behind sharp, hollow sticks that stuck up like urchin's spines. Large hay bales, like dominoes, littered the countryside. Tracks of heavy machinery made their way in evenly spaced lines down to where the bushes separated the fields from the motorway.

To the left, through the bracken and stinging nettles, they passed an abandoned cemetery. Crumbling stone graves and carved angels emerged from the grass. The graveyard itself was well-maintained, a large clearing with freshly cut grass surrounded by tall trees and a brown wooden bench. Fresh white flowers lay on a handful of the graves. On others, just the remains of flowers—a dried up petal here, a crusted vase there. They had buried no one there for twenty years. As they got further up the field, they only glimpsed the odd gravestone through the trees.

It was quiet besides the non-stop drone of the cars on the motorway. The boys caught up to the girls. Luke and Petey walked in silence until they were well past the graveyard. Even in the sunshine, dead bodies spooked them. They cut through the break in the bushes and into another larger field. Over the trees and shrubs, they saw the first floors of the red brick houses on the estate. "Race you?" Petey said to Luke.

"Nah, it's too hot, let's walk."

Petey looked down at his feet and continued to walk next to his friend.

Up ahead, the girls had stopped. Lisa stooped over, looking at something to the side of the path; Ruby was crouching. Luke and Petey looked at each other and jogged to them.

"What is it?" Luke asked over Ruby's shoulder when they arrived.

"I don't know." Ruby looked up at Lisa—Lisa shrugged.

It was a hessian sack. It's top, tied with a tatty purple shoelace. Some of the fabric was stained black, and it was stiff as if a pattern or symbol was once printed on it.

"It's probably a dog shit bag," said Lisa, her body pointing towards home.

"Why to go to the trouble of picking up dog shit if you're then going to leave the bag?" asked Petey.

Lisa shrugged. Luke searched in the undergrowth for a twig and found one six inches long and strong. He poked the bag and felt something hard inside. "Definitely not dog shit." He fumbled to get the end of the twig through the hole where the shoelaces tied the bag, missing once, twice, but succeeding the third time. Lifting the bag off the ground, the twig bent in the middle. "It's heavy."

Ruby reached out to the dangling bag. "Ruby, what're you doing?" asked Lisa, turning back to them. A cloud passed over the sunshine, the field turned dark.

"We should open it," Ruby said, looking up at them with glazed eyes.

Petey looked at Luke, his head shaking side-to-side. Luke lowered the bag to the ground in front of Ruby's feet. She reached forward and untied the shoelaces. The bag opened, and Ruby emptied the contents onto the dusty, hay-littered path. It was a dull silver dictaphone. And then something else fell out, a black rock, perfectly round, the size of Luke's fist.

It was a matte-black, darker than anything he'd ever seen. It cast no reflection or glint or shimmer when the sunshine poked back out from behind the clouds. Luke knelt next to Ruby, noticing her sunburnt shoulders and the freckles on the top of her back.

"Should we listen to it?" he asked her. Ruby stared at the rock.

"I think so." She looked up at Lisa and Petey, who were standing to the side. Lisa crossed her arms over her chest. Her feet pointed towards home.

"You and the Hardy Boys can listen to it; I'm going home."

The rock moved. It throbbed twice like a beating heart, then stopped.

"Did you see that?" Luke asked, turning to the group.

Ruby and Luke leaned closer till they were just two inches from the rock. Petey leaned over them, and even Lisa had stepped forward. "What is it?" she asked.

It moved again, another heartbeat-like throb. Luke and Ruby moved back.

"Put it back in the bag." Luke opened the empty hessian sack. Ruby reached down and picked it up. Luke felt the air get warmer around them. Ruby heard birds singing far away. She heard the boys shouting, "PUT IT DOWN! QUICK! GET IT OUT OF HER HANDS…" and a girl screaming.

She opened her eyes and looked up into Luke's scared face. His bright blue eyes swam with worry and fear.

"What happened?" she asked, sitting up. Hay and grass and mud stuck to her back. She saw Lisa behind the boys. Tears ran down her face.

"You had a fit or something," Petey said.

"Are you okay?" Luke held out a hand to help her to her feet.

"I think so–where's the rock?" She looked at the floor where she had been lying.

"We got it back in the bag… but you wouldn't let go, your hand was clenched tight around it." Petey looked close to tears.

"I don't remember that, I remember touching the rock, feeling its warmth and then birds singing and–"

"Birds singing?" Petey looked at Luke.

"Yes, it sounded so peaceful–didn't you hear it?"

Luke, Petey, and Lisa looked at each other and back to Ruby standing in front of them. Lisa spoke first, "Ruby, no birds were singing."

"But I heard the–"

"I promise you, Ruby, no birds were singing, were there guys?"

Ruby looked at Petey and then to Luke. They both shook their heads. "I'm sorry, Ruby," Luke started. "We heard nothing. You just started spazzing out on the floor."

"They were there, I heard them. Where's the dictaphone?"

"Back in the bag," replied Petey.

Ruby turned and crouched down to the bag and reached for it.

"Stop." Lisa stepped in front of Ruby. "We don't know what just happened to you, Rubes; we should just leave that bag where it is."

"We can't–we need to listen to that dictaphone." Ruby looked up to Luke.

"Why?" Luke's eyes narrowed at her.

"I just know okay, we have to listen to it–it's important, please."

"We should vote on it," said Petey.

"Don't be such a square." She shot Petey a dirty-look. "Look, I just want to listen to it once–if it's boring, we'll leave it here, okay?"

"I don't thi–"

Luke cut Petey off, "Okay, just one listen, then we'll go–but don't touch the rock, promise?"

Ruby nodded; a cute smile twisted the corner of the left side of her mouth. He liked that smile and felt the familiar stirring again. Lisa moved out of her way, and Ruby grabbed the hessian sack and turned back towards them. From where she was kneeling, Luke could see down her top and see the forming of her... "Loverboy," said Lisa. "You okay over there, getting an eyeful, haha!"

"Uh–Uh... I don't know what you're talking about, " His cheeks reddened. He backed away from Ruby, and the hessian sack she was emptying onto the floor. The rock tumbled out, and Ruby's eyes wandered over it. The dictaphone landed next to it. Ruby picked it up, and they gathered around her like a rugby ruck. She pressed the button, and a voice started to speak.

3 LUCAS

The cool breeze is pleasant as it blows over my skin. I stand in the sunshine watching the people walking up and down the high street, unknowing of the terror I've just endured in the library. In both directions, I see strangers. Lost and alone, I don't know where to go. I stare off into the distance, my legs quiver like a newborn bird. I want to run, but I can't. I sit down on the steps of the library.

Next to me, a skinny man wearing cut-off shorts and a black tee-shirt smokes a roll-up cigarette. He looks like he's pulled an all-nighter at a shitty strip-club. Green-hued smoke swirls and rises into the air until it gets caught by a breeze and floats away.

"Can I bum one of those?"

He looks at me from behind his dark sunglasses, pondering the question for a moment, as if I've asked him about the Theory of Relativity or the Meaning of Life, and then he says, "Sure. Do you know how to roll?"

I nod my head, and he shuffles over and reaches into his pocket, where he pulls out a battered gold tin with a sticker of a skull on it. He passes me the tin and declares, "You'll have to roach, I don't believe in filters, they take out all the good stuff." His voice is rough, like rolling thunder from a faraway storm.

"That's fine." I'm trying to stop my hands from shaking as I reach for the tin. He looks at me with a wry smile—a grin that suggests, you're one of my kind. Keeping hold of the tin, he opens it picking out the papers and a small pile of dry tobacco. "Thanks," I murmur and watch as he rolls a skinny cigarette with no roach or filter for me. He hands me the roll-up; I pick out the bits of tobacco coming from the end and pop the tip into my mouth. With a stained, tanned hand, (the lines and wrinkles are black with dirt) the man takes out his Zippo lighter and flicks it. I smell lighter fluid, and then the harsh tobacco burns the back of my throat.

I cough once; I guess this kid Jake isn't a smoker; good for him, I wish I wasn't. The tobacco rushes through my body; the invading toxins make my knees feel fuzzy and bright lights flash before my eyes. A sudden need to go for a shit comes over me. I close my eyes and lean back against the column, riding out the nicotine high. My body reverts to some normality, and I look at the man. "Thanks, I needed that."

"No worries, you look like you did. You also look like you're freaking out big time." He slides his glasses down onto his nose, and I see his eyes for the first time. "Care to tell me what happened? I don't share my tobaccy with just anyone, you know."

I turn around and realize I'm still at the library. I need to get away from here, fast. "Yeah, won't hurt, I guess. Tell you what, let me pay you back. Let's go for a beer somewhere–first round's on me."

The skinny man smiles a thin-lipped grin; he has two teeth missing. "Sounds good to me, brother, where do you want to go?" He stands up; his knees are dirty too.

One thing I had become well acquainted with during my 50 days in this town were the local pubs. "I like the Red Lion if that works for you?"

He nods and slides his glasses back up to his eyes. I take the hand he offers me, and he pulls me to my feet. His hand is cold and rough, like a breeze-block. "The name's Bill, but most of my friends call me 'Bug.'"

"Bug, nice to meet ya, my name's Lucas."

Ducking my head as we enter the Red Lion, I notice the bar smells like wet dog and sweat, and my feet stick to the balding carpet. It's dark, even with the sunshine bursting through the windows. A graffitied, oval wooden table in front of the window is free, and I offer Bug a seat. There's no-one behind the bar, but they only opened twenty-minutes ago, and we're the first customers of the day.

"What do you fancy?" I ask

"I'll have a Harp, please."

"A what?"

"Harp, lager?"

"Is that new?" There's rarely a lager I haven't heard of.

"Aww, shit, not Harp too," he says cryptically. "I'll have whatever you're having."

I wait at the bar for someone to appear, and I see Jake smile in the mirror when the brunette with smokey dark eyes from the last time I was in, walks out. "Two Buds, please," I give her a cheeky smile, the sort that if in my own body, would send the girls all aflutter.

A memory hits me; I was here with Billy and John fifty-nights ago. It was early in the night, the sun hadn't set, and I remember flirting with this barmaid. Her name's Laura. "How are you, Laura?" I ask. Her forehead wrinkles and I realize she has no clue who I am. I pay for the drinks using contactless and join Bug at the graffitied table. I sit down and tip my glass to Bug's. "To new friends," He picks his up, and we chink glasses. We sit in silence for a few minutes', both of us watching the world pass us by through the window.

"So, you goin to tell me what happened back at the library, fella? That is why you brought me here, was-it-not?" said Bug, his words joining.

I take a long sip of my pint; the clean bubbles refresh my dry tongue. "You'll think I'm crazy?" I warn him.

"Try me."

I shrug my shoulders. "You asked for it." I tell him the whole story–not just the monster at the library, but the entire god-damn thing; about waking up in someone else's body every day. When I finish, I take another long draught from the cold beer. I bring the glass up to my eyes and watch the condensation trickle down the side.

Bug sits staring at the table; frown lines appear on his forehead and his slim eyebrows furrow. He looks as though he isn't ready to look me in the eye, which is fine with me. The relief of sharing this craziness with someone could make the monkey on my back run away for a while. I pick up a tatty, dog-eared magazine from the ledge behind me and skim through it. The magazine is full of local stuff, adverts for businesses, etc., not adequate to hold my concentration. "So…" I enquire after the silence gets too much. "What do you think?"

"I think you should order another round."

I don't flirt with Laura this time. I tap my fingers on the bar as I wait and keep turning to check that Bug is still at the table. He sits there, a skeletal, tanned man. He's looking out the window, sunglasses still on even though we're inside, I vision him pulling out a skull and crossbones bandana any moment. How many people walk past him every day I wonder, and pay him no attention–does he have any friends?

I guess he is a loner, maybe by choice. He reminds me of a crazy hippy dude back in my local in Cambridge. That guy belonged to the 1960s. He had no right or reason to be alive now, and you could tell he felt the same way. He was often in the room's corner, always on the periphery, looking at other people in the bar like they were aliens.

Bug reminds me of that guy, and I feel sad and ashamed that I never once asked that guy's name. I promise myself that will be something I fix when I get out of this mess. Add it to the list. I chuckle.

The girl puts the drinks down on the bar; I flash Jake's card over the contactless reader–making a mental note to find the inventor of contactless card machines if I get out of here. If it weren't for contactless, I would be a penniless, hungry stranger in someone else's body!

Bug looks over his sunglasses at me as I approach the table with our beers. Once I sit down, he takes a swig of his beer, and he starts, "So, you're not you–I mean you are you, but not the owner of this body," He gestures with his hand at me. "Is that right?"

I nod and lean forward on the table.

"Ok, so you're Lucas, and you're from Cambridge. fifty days ago, you woke up in someone else's body, and you've been stuck in Westford, waking up in a new body every day since." I nod again, and he continues; he isn't calling me crazy or running away, yet, I have hope. "And, today, in Jake's body, you were attacked by a weird, melting, zombie librarian," I lay my head on the table as the words come out his mouth–Bug's voice lowers to a whisper, "I believe you, Lucas."

My head shoots up from the table, and I feel a crick in Jake's neck. "You do? Why?"

"Let's just say, I have some experience with weird in this town, and I've seen shit that makes it easy for me to believe your whacked-out story..."

Bug

The man and woman had a reputation around Westford, but for all the wrong reasons. They were often seen in doorways of shops with a battered rug in front of them. He was gaunt and wore a black baggy hoodie no matter the weather–his hair was matted and clung to his head. She had long, dank, greasy brown hair and wore faded dungarees with a purple, stained vest that would have shown plenty of side-boob, if she'd had any.

This morning they met a regular up the dog-piss-smelling alleyway near the library. The regular achieved a not-so-subtle handover of the goods– they doubted if they had done their business on the high street, anyone would have cared, but old habits died hard. The girl stuffed the baggy in one of the front pockets of her faded denim dungarees, and they went their separate ways.

They were meant to meet at the meadows ten minutes later. She waited on the white bridge for him, watching the ducks in the shallow river on Bath Row. The water shimmered as it rippled when the ducks bobbed for food. The old bathing houses looked over the quiet car park and the twin grass areas. A selection of brown metal benches sat on each side of the path, which ran through the middle. Suited commuters rushed past from the far side of the meadows where the train station was. She looked across towards the larger bridge at the deeper side of the river; Kids jumped off that bridge in the summer. The commuters strode across the path; The men with briefcases and women with handbags. For a moment, she envied them as much as she despised them. Her fingers found the baggy in her pocket, and she grew impatient waiting for him. The old sensation of ants crawling up her skin came back. She picked at a scab on her forearm.

"Where the fuck have you been?" she said, as she watched him stroll down the road towards her. He passed the raised, set into the wall, castle doorway and empty black metal bench beneath it. Bug shrugged at her as he approached, his slumped shoulders rose higher than his head.

"I dunno," he muttered. "You got the stuff?"

She nodded. "Come on, let's go then." He led her by the elbow to the weeping willow on the far side of the meadows.

The weeping willow stood as tall as a three-story building. It's dry and dusty base was littered with rusty fish hooks and discarded cans of beer. From the base of the tree, you could see down the mouth of the river where the streams joined. The bridge that connected one side of town to the other was empty; a dark line stained the brickwork, a reminder of how deep the river got when it flooded. The branches and leaves of the weeping willow created wriggling snake-like shadows on the ground, which withered and moved as one, making the grass seem to undulate and breath.

They sat just away from the thick trunk with their backs to the path and the road. Bug removed a battered gold tin, opened it, and removed a pack of blue king-size Rizla. He licked a line across the thin, almost translucent paper, and motioned for the woman to sprinkle some white powder onto it. Bug held it in his palms, like a newborn kitten, shielding it from a non-existent breeze as he waited for it to dry.

He carried on his operation, sprinkling dry tobacco into the paper along with some stinky weed. Holding it like fresh pasta, he rolled it into a joint. The woman retrieved a battered, silver Zippo from one of her pockets and raised it to the end of the joint. Bug inhaled and felt the immediate rush of the drugs into his bloodstream. He lay back on the hard floor, a root stuck into his back, but he didn't care.

The joint sent up a thin line of yellow smoke into the sky from his outstretched hand. The woman leaned over him and plucked it from his fingers, taking a long hit and flopping down beside him. They passed the joint back and forth between themselves until neither could move anymore. It went out as they lay next to each other, watching the weeping willow's leaves breathe and sigh.

Bug opened his eyes. He sat up, hearing his back crack. He looked to his right, and Eve was gone. The shadow of the tree was shorter now. He arched his neck and saw groups of people sat, enjoying their lunches in the sunshine.

Shit, that was good stuff. He looked around for the end of the joint, but he couldn't see it anywhere. You bitch, he thought, but then he saw her stuff sprawled on the floor next to him. She would never leave that shit lying around.

Where are you? He stood up; it was his knees turn to crack. With his hands on his hips, he surveyed the surrounding area. He felt for his tobacco tin and found it in his hoodie pocket; he pulled it out and opened it. Their stash was still there, as was his dry tobacco and Rizla. A glint of light caught his eye. He looked at the willow's trunk, and it shimmered as if it was a smoke-filled bubble. The lines in the bark started to move. Shit, what was in that weed? The swirling pattern was hypnotizing.

"What the fu–" he started before trailing off as he got lost in the pattern. Without control, he moved towards the trunk. A drop of drool fell from his mouth, and it fell in slow motion, tumbling over and over itself. Bug reached out with one nicotine-stained hand and watched as it dissolved into the tree. The rest of his arm followed up to his shoulder. He stood glazed eyed with his nose less than an inch away from the trunk of the willow. He couldn't feel his arm. From far away, he heard birds singing. He stepped forward and melted into the tree.

"And then what?" I ask, looking up from the table. Bug is staring off into space.

"And then I was on the steps of the library, smoking a roll-up, 20-years older–and you know the real kicker? I can't feel the old sensation, that niggling at the back of my mind–I think I'm clean."

"Come again. So you disappeared 20-years ago and today reappeared just as I came running out of the library?" I down the last of my pint.

"That's the long and short of it, I guess." He knocks back the dregs of his pint. "Now you see why I was so ready to believe you, don't ya? Another one?" he says, putting his glass in front of me.

I nod my head; I've been holding onto the table so tight the tips of my fingers are white. I stand and turn to go to the bar. I stop and ask him, "What about the woman?"

At the question, Bug's face collapses, his already gaunt cheekbones sink further into his face. He scratches his nose with a nicotine-stained finger. "I'm sorry," I say.

I return to the table with two full pints and two packets of crisps. Bug's rallied himself and looks eager to talk.

"Look at me, how old would you guess I am?" He moves his head from side to side.

I look at his face, the wrinkles that fall from his forehead down past his eyes are deep, and his eye sockets are sunken with sagging skin.

"Late forties.".

He laughs. "When I woke up this morning, I was twenty-seven, and it was 2001. Tell me, Lucas, what year is it? I don't recognize half those shops on the high street."

"Um… it's 2019." I shake my head. "Have you really been missing since 2001? That makes no sense, where have you been?"

"I don't know; I keep on expecting to wake up under that Willow tree any moment, I just don't know." He sits back in his chair, his arms wide open.

"And you reappeared at the exact moment, when I was getting chased in the library. I don't know about you, but that seems like a bit too much of a coincidence."

Bug looks at me with his big blue, heavily bloodshot eyes. "That's what I was thinking."

We sit in silence for a few moments' listening to the jukebox on auto-play–a song I know well comes on, and I mumble the words to myself. Bug looks at me, "Who's this?"

"Maybe we should stay for one more, and I can tell you about what you have missed, hell I'll even put on a special playlist for you." Bug grabs me by the wrist and squeezes. "Thank you, Lucas; I don't know what I would have done if I hadn't bumped into you." I hold his gaze. "Same back at ya, buddy."

Over the next hour, I fill Bug in on what he's missed, starting with 9/11 and finishing with Brexit, and fitting in as much in between as possible. Bug's mouth opens wider as I inform him about Donald Trump, and he thinks I'm lying when I tell him Manchester City are Premier League Champions. We listen to everything from The Darkness to the Killers through to Linkin Park, avoiding Justin Bieber and Beyonce; He's been through enough without having to put him through that shit! We have two more pints, and the bar starts to fill up with locals. The clock above the bar says 3.15 pm.

"What do you say? You ready to head down to that Willow tree?"

"I can't think of anything better to do," he replies.

We pick up the few things we both own and duck our heads as we leave the pub through the front entrance. The afternoon's bright and humid. Heavy clouds amble across the sky, never blocking out the dazzling sun for more than a few seconds. The usual traffic sits along Broadgate; exhaust fumes, and the smell of cigarettes lingers on the air–the traffic lights at the crossing slow everything to a standstill.

"I guess some things never change," Bug says with a smile, I look at him confused. "Shit, sorry, forgot you're not a local. This road has been like this forever; one thing Westford wasn't built for is cars." I nod–over the past fifty days, I'd picked up on the crazy drivers and constant traffic in this otherwise quaint and quiet town. We cross at the lights and walk single file down the thin pavement. A truck, too big for the road, brushes against my arm going thirty, I pull it in with a yelp, even though it didn't hurt.

On our left, the massive tower of St. Michan's church overlooks the centre of the town. It's as grand looking as any cathedral I've seen with its gothic architecture and raised gravestones. Stone steps lead to the entrance, which is surrounded by graves. Walking next to the tall stone wall, it's disquieting to think we're the same depth as the bodies buried there. Are human bones still in the ground? Could an arm or a pelvis one day poke through the stone and out into the road? It looks like a setting from Bram Stoker's Dracula.

We're dawdling, both of us in no hurry, both deep in thought about what we might find. We cross over in a little run, just avoiding getting hit by a white Land Rover. Bug gives the driver the wanker sign. I like this guy.

We walk down the hill past the old Post Office–Bug's taking everything in, his eyes wide as he sees the changes in his hometown. A tall spire thing made of yellow-stone stands outside the Pink Flamingo pub. His neck cranes up as he follows it to the top. "What the fuck is that?"

"Not a clue," I say, staring up at the spire. "None of the locals seems too keen on it either, though, if that helps?" It looks like an S&M dildo.

We're approaching the meadows now. Just down the hill, and we would arrive. Bug expects it to be busy, full of groups of teenagers sitting around and a hint of marijuana on the air. He sounds disappointed when we turn up, and it's empty. "What's happened to this place?" he asks. "It looks the same, but it feels different."

"Bug, man, I could have told you something was wrong with this place all day long." I tap him on the shoulder, and we cross the bridge and stand on the path, eyeing the willow tree at the far end.

"You ready?"

"Let's do it." Bug steps off the tarmac and onto the grass. Ducks and geese scatter, quacking as we approach; I do a shimmy-style walk to avoid the goose shit–Bug walks straight through, his head down, yellow smoke flowing from the roll-up cigarette between his lips. This is his mission, so I stay two strides behind him.

The willow tree is fucking huge, one of the biggest beasts I've ever seen, and I can't understand how I haven't noticed it before. The surrounding ground is as Bug described it, dusty and full of rusted fish hooks, it looks like the perfect dumping ground for a serial killer, even this many years later. I imagine getting stoned under here; it seems like the ideal place to unwind with the view down the river particularly peaceful. I would probably need a tetanus shot, though.

Bug stares at the tree, I can't even picture what he's thinking. Our next stop will be the library to check the old local newspapers from around the time he and his girlfriend went missing. But, now we're here, and part of me is glad because I don't want to go back to that fucking library.

"Do you believe it's all connected?" I ask from behind him.

He nods. "Yes, do you?"

"As I said at the pub, I think it's too much of a coincidence if it isn't. Do you see anything?"

"I'm not certain, look here." He points towards the bark, and I walk up, so I'm now standing beside him. "Do you see it?"

I concentrate, but I'm not sure what I'm looking at though. The trunk reminds me of the sagging, melting skin I'd seen on the librarian, deep wrinkles and cracks in the grey-brown bark.

"The pattern in the bark has changed–could be the age I s'pose, but… I don't know; maybe I'm seeing what I want t' see."

"What do you mean, what do you see?"

"There, right in the bark." He steps closer and traces a line with his finger. As he does, I see what he's looking at. Amidst the random lines of bark, I notice a figure-eight laying on its side. From where the circles intersect, I see a line extending up, which reminds me of a street post sign, with four arrow-shaped pointers, two to the left and two to the right. The tip of each is spiked, including the tip at the top. "Do you see it?" Bug asks.

"What the fuck is that?" It's obvious; it can't be natural. "Have you ever seen it before?"

"Not a clue. It looks like a symbol of some sort," replies Bug, moving closer.

"Do you see anything else?"

Bug looks at the trunk and around its dusty red base. He shakes his head, "Nothing." He reaches out with his hand, and time slows–both of us expect something to happen. His fingers touch the rough bark. Nothing. I let out a breath I didn't realize I was holding.

Bug turns away from the tree and walks back to me. Behind him, the lines in the bark move. I shake my head and look again. Yes, the lines in the bark are moving; gyrating and swirling together. The symbol in the tree doesn't move, just the surrounding lines.

"Bug…" I point past him at the tree. He turns, and as he does, a tendril-like root escapes from the ground between his feet, wrapping itself around one of his skinny white ankles. He lets out a shriek as another slimy-looking, green-brown root works its way up his left thigh. He reaches out for me, but a thick branch reaches down, wraps itself around his waist and yanks him back off his feet.

"Lucas," he shouts. I jump forward and grab his hand. His grip crushes my fingers like they're being squeezed to death by a serpent, but I hold on. The bright sunshine of the day flashes by. I glance around the meadows hoping to find help. I see two people walking along the path 200 yards away–too far to make them understand that we aren't two people fooling around. "Don't you let go of me." Bug's eyes are begging me to fight.

"I'm not going anywhere." Behind him, I see the lines moving faster as they swim in the trunk. A hole the size of an eyeball opens up from the centre. Inside I see a swirling green-white light. It looks like the northern lights.

The branch gives another yank, harder this time, and Bug flies backward again, pulling me with him. He's less than two feet away from the swirling trunk, and the hole behind him is opening wider, wide enough to swallow a man.

A sound comes from the tree, a hypnotizing bird song that goes deep into my mind. I feel Bug stop struggling; his eyes roll up into his head, leaving just the bloodshot whites looking at me. I jerk back and lose my grip on him. I land on my butt, one ankle underneath me, and watch as it pulls Bug towards the tree. He doesn't scream as his foot disappears into the swirling green-white lights, followed by his knees. Then he's in it up to his waist. I stare open-mouthed as I watch my only friend vanish–the last thing I see is his face and the whites of his eyes. Then he's gone.

4 THE TEENAGERS

The voice from the dictaphone sounded like a 1979 Harley Davidson Fatboy. It faded in and out. They sat in a circle on the path, underneath the hot sun, in the middle of the yellow field while the dictaphone played in the centre.

"Lucas... Lucas, Oh god, I hope you get this. It's okay–what happened? It's okay. I'm okay. It spat me out again, Only this time I went backward–you believe that shit? Not by a lot, but by a few weeks, I think. All sorts of shit's going down. I did some research bro; it's all fucked up, we're all fucked! I don't have long. Listen, find someone, his name is Theo, Theo Whyte. The longer I stay in one place, the bigger the draw is back to that fucking willow… I hear birds singing–you believe that shit, damn birdsong in my head. Find Theo, he's our only hope, I have tried, but I have had no luck. Fuck! I can hear the birds again. When I get sucked through, all gizmos stop working. I will try to get another message to you if I find anything. Remember where we went for a pint? I will leave one in there. It will be in a sealed baggy in the toilet. Lucas. Find Theo, oh, and don't touch the rock, not yet anyway."

The sounds of static filled the air, and a warm breeze blew through the field along with the faraway rumble of thunder, while heavy clouds approached across the bright blue sky. It had been a summer of scorching heat followed by thunderstorms and torrential rain, and today looked the same. Car horns blared from the motorway, and the kids looked up from the dictaphone on the brown path.

"I touched it." Ruby, wide-eyed, looked at Luke. "What did he mean when he said don't touch the rock?" She stood up and paced along the path.

"Why are you asking me?" Luke climbed to his feet, followed by Lisa and Petey behind him.

"He said your name… that message was for you."

"I'm not a Lucas, Ruby, I never have been." Luke looked to his sister. "Tell her Lisa."

"It's true; mum and dad showed me his birth certificate–he's a Luke."

"What should we do?" Ruby opened her arms wide. The static from the dictaphone was still playing, and she started rubbing non-existent dust and dirt from her shorts and legs when no-one answered. "What should we do? I touched that thing. What did he mean? I heard bird song, that's what he said in… in the message?"

"It's probably a prank," Petey said. Lisa and Luke nodded as if they had been offered extra helpings of dessert.

"Yeah, definitely. Someone left this here knowing we'd find it. It was probably Sam Masters, he lives close by and saw us go to the river earlier," said Lisa. Luke looked at Petey at the mention of Sam's name. The static stopped as the dictaphone clicked off.

"He hates me, Ruby, like really hates me." Luke looked up to the sky. "Yeah, I can imagine him doing it too."

"But the birds?"

"It's hot, we've been in the sun all day, Ruby, that's all." Petey and Luke nodded behind Lisa, who had moved closer to her friend. They looked like the nodding dogs from her Mum's car. Ruby glanced past them, and out over the fields at the approaching storm clouds. She marvelled at the way an area that seemed so bright in the sunshine, could look so ominous when the sky shifted to grey.

"Okay, let's go before the storm arrives," she said, and then turned to the dictaphone. "But, we're bringing that with us, put it back in the bag–Luke, can you keep it at your house, in your garage?"

"Why me?"

"Because you're the closest, and me and Petey don't have a garage."

Ruby bent down and picked up the dictaphone. Holding it at arm's length, she dropped it in the hessian sack and then laying the fabric bag on its side on the floor, she nudged the rock inside. She lifted it and tied the shoelace around the top.

The weight of the rock tapped against her calf as she followed the others up the path, through the avenue of trees and past the rusty playground and back onto the estate.

Lisa and Luke's house was a three-bedroom detached red-brick with a white garage and a white front door that stood opposite the path that led to the park. Their dad's silver Zafira was parked on the drive even though the workday wasn't over. The world was still, the tall trees moved silently, and the air felt hot and heavy. They crossed the road as the first spots of rain fell, and thunder crashed faraway. The black-grey sky lit up by lightning soon after.

Luke ran up to the garage that his dad always left unlocked and opened it. It smelled like old man's balls. He flicked the switch and stared in, past the cardboard boxes, bicycle parts, and christmas decorations. He entered the garage, with its exposed grey brick walls, while the others took shelter under the up-and-over white garage door. Luke searched for a place to hide the sack. The pitter-patter of rain got stronger and echoed off the metal garage door, and another crash of thunder, followed by lightning, lit up the sky.

"Hurry, Luke," Lisa called to her brother. "Before Mum and Dad hear us."

"I'm hurrying," he hissed back.

Luke looked around the back of the garage. Behind a box stacked high with tatty paperbacks of old WWII stories his grandad had left him, he found a dark, damp corner to leave the sack. Luke moved a bag and saw live maggots fall onto the floor. Underneath was a bag of defrosted meat that his parents must have forgotten they'd gotten out. He retched as he hid the hessian sack under a piece of cloth from a box. When he turned back to the others, he saw a beam of light extend from the side of the garage, and a voice shouted, "Lisa? Luke? Is that you?" He saw his Mum poke her head around into the garage. Her usual smile disappeared, and she looked at Petey and Ruby. "Ruby, Petey, I think you best get home now."

"But Mum–" Luke started. He lurched forward, trying to avoid the puddle of writhing maggots.

She pointed at him. "But nothing, Luke–your Dad's inside, and he's been waiting for you." Luke's fingers touched his back pocket where he had been keeping the fingernail, he had forgotten about it after finding the sack. His head fell, and he stumbled out of the garage, like a man on Green Mile. He looked up as he passed Petey. Petey shrugged at him and raised his eyebrows.

"You're in so mu–" Lisa started before being cut off by a glare from her mother.

"Ruby, you best get off home too, sweetie."

"But I didn't even do anyth–" Lisa started before being cut off by another glare, stronger than the first. "In. Now." Luke's Mum stood to the side of the door, creating an opening. Lisa followed behind Luke, leaving Ruby and Petey covering under the garage door. Petey grabbed the string and pulled it down, and they both ran through the rain to their separate houses.

5

Luke's Dad sat on the stairs where he had sat this morning. He was staring into space, picking at the carpet. His white shirt had come loose, and his purple and white tie dangled from his neck, half undone. Next to him, Luke could see the mark where he had scraped the fingernail free this morning.

"I don't want to hear any excuses." His Dad peered down at him and stood; his face red. "What were you doing?"

"I found something in the wall," Luke said, standing stock straight.

"Do you know how much this cost?" His Dad waved his arms at the walls.

Luke looked at the painted walls and shrugged. His Dad erupted, taking the stairs two at a time. Luke flinched, and he thought his sister did the same from across the living room. He had never been hit before, not by one of his parents anyway, and he was shocked at how strong the urge to run was. He'd always liked to think if it came to it, he would be brave, the last man standing, fighting on his own against an oncoming horde of monsters. Instead, his legs shook like a sissy as his Dad glared down at him from an inch away. He could feel the heat coming from him. His mum moved to his Dad's side and she slipped her arm around his waist and led him into the kitchen. He glared back at Luke once, and the look in his eyes was murder.

Luke looked at Lisa; her eyes were glazed and teary. She'd thought their Dad would hit him. She walked over to him and said, "Come on, squirt; let's go upstairs."

He followed his sister up the stairs, past the scratches on the wall. All thoughts of the dictaphone were gone and as he climbed the stairs, tears started to fall. They tasted like seawater as they flowed down his face and into the corners of his mouth. He sniffled and wiped at them with the back of his hand. When he got to the top of the stairs, Lisa took him in her arms and cuddled him.

"He wouldn't have hit you, silly," she whispered into his ear. His mind was blank, and his fingers tingled; little tremors rushed through him. She held his hand and led him to his bedroom. They sat together on the edge of his bed. Lisa used her sleeve to wipe away the snot and tears that had accumulated on his face. "I like the colour of your room." She kissed his cheek and forehead and stood and walked to the door. She turned at the doorway, standing next to a full-length Iron Man poster. "Are you going to be okay?"

Luke nodded, holding back the tears and snot. "I've never seen him that mad before, not even when… well, you know."

"He'll calm down soon, and I bet you'll be able to guilt-trip him into a new game or a cinema trip–just don't forget about me, hey?" She winked at him.

He sniffled again as she left him alone and closed his bedroom door. He jumped back on his bed and lay with his head in his hands, not crying, just wanting to sleep.

Luke waited for a knock on his door; waited for the comfort of his mother, but it never came–it was only a fucking wall, he thought.

He lay on his side, looking at the new blue walls of his bedroom. The smell of fresh paint still hung in the air. He didn't want to read any of his comics; he didn't even want to turn on his Xbox.

A dark mark on one wall caught his eye. A spot, the size of a postcard, a darker shade of blue, barely noticeable unless you looked hard, was not his imagination.

Luke climbed off his bed. The dark spot was at the bottom of the wall opposite his door. He kneeled next to it, moved his hand over the spot, and noticed it was raised compared to the rest of the wall. It was wrinkled and smooth. He pressed harder, wiggling his hand back and forth over it. He felt it give a little–it reminded him of an air bubble.

As he created a circular motion with his hand, it loosened further. He bit his lip as he remembered how mad his father was earlier, and then, with a small 'fuck you' shrug, he started picking at the edges with his fingers.

He cringed at the feeling of dry paint against his fingernails but carried on. A speck of red, the colour of the walls before, started to show, and after one more fleeting memory of his Dad's anger, he took the flap of blue between his fingers and pulled.

Later that evening, he sat on his bed, turning the piece of blue over in his hands. Luke still heard the wet, slurping sound it made when he had pulled it off the wall. The blue paint seeped through to the other side; so that one side was dark blue, while the other side was stained light blue, like the paper leftover from a temporary tattoo.

Luke rubbed his index finger over the strip of lighter blue; it felt waxy and dry, like a pair of old leather shoes he'd worn in his first year of secondary school. What caused him worry were the little black hairs less than a cm long that were flattened and embedded into the thing. If he didn't know any better, it looked like a–.

He heard footsteps approaching his door. Luke looked at the red rectangle on the wall and back to the door and the approaching footsteps. It was impossible to miss.

Luke flung the piece of flesh onto the second shelf of the bookcase at the side of his bed, and then he pushed a multicolour set of plastic storage drawers, filled with Lego and other old toys he no longer played with, in front of the mark. The door opened just as he put them in place. He turned to his visitor.

"You coming down for dinner, Luke?" his Dad asked the empty bed. He looked up and saw Luke at the wall. "Having a move around?" His eyebrows raised, and he spotted the Lego sticking out of the drawers.

"What you building, bud?" he asked in a friendly tone. "You remember when we built that massive Minecraft cave last Christmas?" Luke nodded.

His Dad took one step into the room. "Look, I'm sorry about earlier, but you have to understand the decorating cost a lot of money, we're trying to create a nice home here. You know that."

"I know, Dad." Luke relaxed. "I'm sorry." He moved in for a hug. His Dad squeezed his shoulder before kneeling and pulling him closer into a cuddle.

"It's okay; I'm sorry I got so mad, I didn't use too. What were you doing anyway?" They spoke as nothing had happened. Luke smiled.

"I thought I saw something buried in the paint."

"And did you find anything?"

"No. I'm sorry dad." Luke touched the fingernail in his back pocket and glanced at his bookcase.

"It's okay; it's done now–do you want some dinner? Maybe one night this week we can go to the cinema; you can pick the film?"

Luke smiled. "Sounds good to me, Dad, I know a film." He looked out into the hall. "Can Lisa come too, please?"

His Dad kissed him on his forehead, "Of course she can. Now let's go down for dinner–you can tell Lisa."

Luke looked over his shoulder at the bookcase one last time and then followed his Dad down the stairs.

Luke spoke to Petey later than night. He was sitting on a blue and yellow Fortnite beanbag on his bedroom floor looking up his 32 inch TV. They were playing online on the Xbox. Luke told him about the piece of flesh. He described it to him through his headset while it sat on the floor next to him.

"Do you know who the decorator was?" Petey asked.

"Yes, it was some local guy; his name was Duncan Fuller."

"Never heard of him."

"Why would you have?" teased Luke.

"No reason. What about the rock and the dictaphone, are they still in your garage?"

"I haven't moved it, and I doubt Lisa has."

"Has she said anything?"

"No, why?"

"No reason," said Petey.

"I hope Ruby's okay."

"Why wouldn't she be?"

"She touched the rock, didn't she."

"That was weird–it's all a bit weird, isn't it?" Luke put his controller down and picked up the piece of flesh. "Fancy some detective work tomorrow?"

"I don't know, Luke. I was kinda hoping to leave weird behind for a bit, you know, forget about it all."

"No way, Petey, what about that message, we need to try and find Lucas–then we need to find Fuller."

"I don't know, Luke."

"I'll talk to my sister and Ruby, see if they want to come with us?"

"Do you think they will?"

"I think Ruby will. I'm sure she can talk Lisa into it too."

"Okay, one day, though–no longer, understand?"

"One day and one day only–now you ready to die on Fortnite?"

"Not on your nelly," said Petey and laughed.

Luke spoke to Lisa once he'd finished killing Petey on Fortnite. It surprised him when she was open to the plan. Maybe she still felt sorry for him. She was lying on her bed, her finger scrolling down the screen of her phone so fast he wondered how she never got dizzy. She was tapping and liking things so damn fast that he didn't think she was even reading or looking at anything. After she said okay, he stood in the doorway, hovering she'd have called it, wondering whether to tell her about the fingernail and the strip of flesh.

Her room was lime green and also smelled of fresh paint. His eyes moved over the walls looking for patches of darker or lighter green. She looked at him and raised her eyebrows? Luke shrugged his shoulders and left, shutting the door behind him.

He didn't think he'd sleep, but he did. His eyes twitched, and he muttered in his sleep, turning over and over and over all night long. Sweat stained his pyjamas as he dreamed of thunderstorms and rain and a frayed and tatty rope swing floating away in fast-running water, leaving behind sinewy strings which turned the water red. Twisted and gnarled roots slunk out of the water and slithered up the river bank towards where Petey, Lisa, and Ruby stood. He tried to scream as the roots started to wrap themselves around his friend's and sister's ankles. They turned around, and their faces were empty. There were no eyes, noses, mouths, or any features. A hollow 'O' opened up where their mouths should be, and they screamed as something tightened around his ankle. A slimy, knuckled root coiled itself around his thigh, and like a snake being charmed, it floated in front of his face, swinging from side-to-side before launching itself, with such thrust it knocked him onto his back, down his throat. He woke in the dark and sat upright, trying to control his fast, rasping breathing. Laying back down, he fell back to sleep and forgot about his dream when he woke the next morning.

6 LUCAS

I sit watching the tree as the lines in the trunk stop moving. The figure-eight has moved and now sits further down the base of the trunk. I don't know how long I've been sitting here; my right-hand draws a swirling pattern in the dust. Has it been hours or minutes' since the tree took Bug?

I snap out of my reverie when I hear a car horn honk from across the river. Looking up and around the meadows, I'm alone, and the sun is getting low in the sky; it has taken on a faded orange wispy glow. I look at the pattern in the dirt; it's deep and bold–I must have been here for hours. A silence sits over the town; all I can hear is the rustling whisper of the leaves of the willow tree.

I stand, my knees aching from the position I've been sitting in. I shake out the tingling sensation from both legs and make my way towards the path and across the bridge. The town's quiet, families at home having BBQs and playing in the back garden I suppose as opposed to being in town.

There's an A4 piece of paper taped onto every streetlight, and on the window of every car, I pass, which I hadn't noticed earlier.

MISSING, Ben James, aged 4, please call the emergency line if you have seen my grandson. Underneath, a black-and-white picture of a blonde-haired little boy with chubby cheeks and pale skin stares back at me. He's wearing a Teenage Mutant Ninja Turtles tee-shirt and is smiling a big goofy grin at the camera. He looks happy, as all little boys do, content with his life surrounded by people who loved him. Perhaps this is why the streets are so quiet.

A missing little boy in a town like Westford is a rare occurrence I guess, and I can imagine all the la-di-dah parents I've come across over the past fifty days keeping their precious little angels inside, and who can blame them. In my mind, I see the two little boys from yesterday. I don't have a watch, but I guess it's around 8pm; the library's shut.

Without access to the internet and no internet cafes in this town, my only option would be going back to Jake's flat, watching TV alone and waiting to wake up in someone else's body tomorrow or the pub. I choose the pub.

As I walk, I hope Bug has jumped through time again; I don't like the other option. Somewhere, I hope Bug has found his fiancee, and they're living together.

Focus, that's what I need to do. I need somewhere quiet, to have a beer and think. The willow tree has changed everything. I'm sure something is happening in this town, maybe, hopefully, it isn't just me.

I walk up the empty high street, past the banks, charity shops, and coffee shops lost in my thoughts, my legs on autopilot, leading me to a quiet pub. At the end of the high street, I see a little boy crying on a bench. His little legs dangle, not quite reaching the floor. He isn't much older than four or five, and he bears more than a passing resemblance to the child in the posters.

I duck into the alleyway right before the library, where the postbox stands, and I stop and watch to see if a parent is around. The alley smells of urine, and I hear voices from the top. After waiting for a few moments', I walk out onto the high street; the orange lights have just turned on, giving it a haunted, gothic look. He doesn't look up as I approach. I hear him sobbing and sniffling. The bench is still warm from the day as I sit down next to him.

"Hiya, you okay?" I ask, turning to him

He doesn't look up or react to my question. "Hey kid, are you okay?" He's staring straight ahead, his legs swinging back and forth from the bench. "Is your name, Ben?" I shuffle closer to him, and he turns and smiles. His teeth are tiny, pointed white-crystal daggers. He seems to throb outwards, and then the kid melts in front of me, turning into a purple bubbling puddle of goo on the floor.

I fall on my arse for the third time today and land on the cobbled street, shuffling backward to getaway. The melted puddle of the kid burps in big fat stinking bubbles and then rises in front of me. It blocks out the light from the streetlamp and casts me in its cold shadow.

Three pairs of snake-like yellow eyes form on top of the viscous mess, which then blinks sideways at me, followed by two forked black tongues which flick out tasting the air. Fuck this. I've had enough of monster trees and melting people for one day. I scramble to my feet, bending back a fingernail on a cobble and run.

I fly past shop windows and straight over the road. A blue Volvo honks at me as I pass in front of it, my hand hitting its bonnet. From behind, I hear the driver wind down his window and shout at me. Still, I run. I don't look back until I'm halfway up the next road and in front of the pub.

Breathing heavy, I put one hand on the black pavement sign, and with the other, I grip my side. I risk a glance over my shoulder. The thing isn't behind me. Maybe it didn't chase me? I haven't run far, but my shirt is damp, and I wipe the sweat from my brow. Still taking deep breaths, I head down the steps and through the dark doorway into the pub.

It's cooler in here; The old stone walls keeping the inside of the building fresh despite the rising humidity outside. A mumble of chatter, recognizable in any pub, makes me smile. The air is full of fresh hops and roasted basil.

Dirty, red, heavily worn carpeted stairs lead to the first and second floors, but I make my way to the room on the left. The cold cobbled-stone floor makes me want to take off my shoes and feel the chill on my feet. Two middle-aged couples sit in dark-wood chairs deep in conversation. Oil paintings of countryside scenes adorn the walls with exposed, grey stone blocks jutting out in random places. Bottles of wine and finished meals sit in front of them—my stomach growls.

Following through the room and ducking under a low exposed stone doorway, I enter the bar. It's even darker in here. Comfortable looking leather armchairs sit empty in a cozy snug to the rear. It looks like a room from a gentlemen's club. Behind the solid oak bar is a young guy in a crisp white shirt. Four old-style brass hand pumps sit on the bar alongside the more modern faux-ice beer taps. A mini chalkboard completes the side of the bar with a list of the selection of real ales.

I order the most potent ale on the menu and pay for it with shaking hands. The barman smiles, and I take my beer back the way I came and go up the stairs. The floor creaks as I enter the landing area. I duck my head through another low doorway and find an empty room with high ceilings and exposed wooden beams with rusted-metal horseshoes dangling precariously off dull nails. I take a seat in the corner, looking towards the door, and slink down into my seat, breathing out a loud sigh that echoes off the cold, white stone walls.

The condensation on the beer glass is too good to refuse, and I rub it along my forehead, enjoying the cooling sensation before taking a large gulp that half-empties the glass. It's hoppy and fruity, and my stomach gurgles again. The last thing I ate was those crisps with Bug.

Bug; a sadness comes over me. Closing my eyes, I lean my head back against the chair. "I'm sorry, Bug." It had been a brief friendship, but I feel connected to him. I couldn't save him. I can't save myself. Almost enjoying this moment of self-pity, I tip myself over the edge and think about my grandad back in Cambridge sitting in a sterile care home, the last of his memory fading forever. Has my grandad faded away yet, I wonder?

I open my eyes. Whatever is happening in Westford, Bug and I are a part of it. The room's quiet, the small windows allowing only a little dusk light in. I stare into space, thinking over the day's events. There might be more people like us. Maybe the woman with her leg in a cast? Something is trying to get me, hunting me even. Damn, I wish I had another cigarette. Where is Jake right now? Is he in this body, trapped in the back of my mind watching everything like a passenger in a car? The handful of people I'd encountered whose body I had been in hadn't seemed any different. What did they remember? How did they explain the missing day? I remember once; I had tried not waiting till night time to go to sleep.

I had been in a man's body; I think it was the twelfth or thirteenth day. The man was about sixty years old, and he lived alone in an old bungalow on a quiet cul-de-sac. Upon waking, I'd searched through his cupboards and found a stash of Co-Codamol and a bottle of Glenfiddich. There were four inches of liquid at the bottom of the bottle, more than enough.

His house had been neat. The flower-print fabric furniture clean; if a little dated. The fluffy carpets crumb-free and the wooden surfaces in the kitchen spotless. I had guessed, correctly, that he was a recent widower. Gold framed pictures on the white mantlepiece showed him with his not-unattractive wife and an old golden retriever. I felt sad for the man—the black and white spotty dog bed, just like his wife's side of the bed, looked unslept in for years. I read the instructions on the pill packet; I didn't want to kill him, just knock myself out early.

I took the green bottle and the pills and went through the double patio doors out onto the red brick patio. The garden was impressive; a long lawn with a vast amount of purple, white, pink, and blue flowers in raised borders that led to crumbling stone steps. It led to a shady, secluded spot where a striped blue and white fabric recliner sat on its own, with a battered paperback sitting on a white metal table to its side.

The recliner was comfier than I expected. Putting the bottle of whiskey on the table to the side, along with the pill packet and the paperback, I lifted the plastic armrests and reclined. The sun was high in the sky, and this spot would get it all day, which explained the man's deep tan and wrinkles. I laid my head back and soaked in the warmth. This is how my grandad should be living.

In the hot sun with the whiskey dulling my senses, I thought I might not need the pills. I glugged whiskey out of the bottle and listened to bees buzzing around the flowers. The paperback had yellow pages and bent corners; I read the back cover. It sounded like a trashy, noir detective novel, and I thumbed through reading a few lines on random pages. It seemed better to get lost in someone else's story than the fucked-up situation I was in. I slugged the whiskey back, enjoying the warmth down my throat and read through the first twenty-seven pages of the book.

It wasn't too bad, full of suspicious characters and a brooding detective with a drinking problem. The whiskey was working, and I struggled to keep track of the story; the lines blurred together, and in the afternoon heat surrounded by old people flowers and the smell of whiskey, my chin started to fall to my chest.

Each time I shook myself awake before my eyes closed one last time, and I woke up in a new bed. In a new body.

Back in the pub, I'm staring at a painting on the wall opposite. It's dusty with a freckled, gilded frame, and the colours are faded so the once bright green leaves on the trees are now a muddy brown. I don't recognize the location.

A stone-built house stands surrounded by fields and farmland in the foreground on the left. In the bottom right-hand corner obscured by a great grey Oak tree is the symbol from the willow tree.

I stand up, relieved that my legs no longer shake and walk towards the painting. As I approach, I see the symbol clearly. I lean forward, my nose touches the painting, and it is the symbol. A figure eight on its side, as I first thought, and the line coming from where the circles intersect does look like a signpost with a short bar across the top and a longer one lower down. Not a symbol I'm familiar with, then again, I'm not familiar with many logos except those from beer bottles. Could it be something religious?

My eyes wander over the painting, looking for anything else. There's something scrawled in black oil paint in the bottom left corner. I squint to read it, 'The Village of Nether Hambleton 1926,' and underneath I see a scrawled signature–T.R. Whyte.

I trace my finger over the writing and feel the little bumps on my skin, raised and smooth. Who's T.R. Whyte? Where is Nether Hambleton? I've heard of other villages surrounding Westford during my research, but never Nether Hambleton.

For the first time since the library, I'm optimistic–a clue. I need sleep, though, and I need tomorrow to come. Jake's body has been great, I'll leave a five-star review. (I feel bad comparing it to a rental car, but that's what it seems like) I feel for the poor guy though, he will wake up with some bumps and bruises I hope he won't remember how he got, when he wakes up.

I move back to the table and down the dregs of my beer and turn to leave. The lights flicker once. A strobe effect that lights up the room once and then it's dark. The only light comes from two six-inch rectangles of blue moonlight from the windows. I freeze, turning my head to the door, listening for approaching footsteps. A rank smell fills my nostrils, and I bring my hand to my face. It smells like meat left out in the heat all day; decayed and maggoty with a metallic odour underneath. Something sniffs, it sounds like a wolf testing the air. I take one step forward and the floorboard underneath the carpet creaks. It sounds like a train hurtling through the night. Now I hear another sound. A shuffling from the corridor outside the room, soft pads of an animal approaching. A question that until now hadn't occurred to me; what happens if I die in this body?

The lights flicker again, and I see the silhouette of a beast on the landing: dead black mottled fur and yellow stained teeth.

The lights come back on, and the corridor's empty. I don't think, I just run, taking the stairs two at a time, easy with how narrow they are, and almost trip over the bottom two steps. I run into the night. A black shape falls on me, and the last thing I see are the stars and the low hanging crescent moon in the sky.

Jake wakes up in a dark room. The cold floor underneath him feels like stone and something spongy and damp. The room smells like a dead animal rotting in a field. There's no source of light. He bum-shuffles back till he hits an icy, wet wall behind him.

Where is he? He'd been in the deepest sleep he'd ever had. He puts his right hand into something sticky and warm and brings it to his face. He sniffs at it and turns his head away in disgust. He dry-heaves to the side of him; all he can taste is bile. What the fuck is going on? He'd fallen asleep like usual in his bed after watching TV And now he's here.

"Hello?" No-one answers, and he hears his voice bouncing off the walls and echoing around. How big is this room, and where is he?

"HELLLOOOOOO! HELP MEE…"

There's no reply in the dark. He hugs his knees and rocks back and forth.

7 THE TEENAGERS

The sound of the front door closing woke Luke. He peeked out from behind his Avengers curtains and saw his mum and dad getting into their separate cars on their way to work. He watched them drive away and then turned on his Xbox and sent Petey a message to come over ASAP. He heard Lisa downstairs and opening his bedroom door; the smell of strong coffee wafted through the house. She had taken to making coffee when her parents left the house (he didn't think they'd let her drink it otherwise), not that she looked like she enjoyed it when she was drinking it.

He sat at the end of the oak breakfast bar and noticed her grimace as she took a sip. Searching through cupboards, he found some chocolate cereal and started to eat it dry, straight from the box. Neither spoke as they sat and waited for Ruby and Petey.

Lisa sat swiping through her iPhone, as Luke sat thinking about the plans for the day ahead. They needed to start somewhere, and a Google search seemed the perfect place. His foot tapped against the metal stool leg, and he knew he didn't have the patience to wait for the others.

He fired up the Mac in the living room, and opened up Google Chrome; in the search bar, he typed Duncan Fuller.

"Who's Duncan Fuller?" Lisa asked from behind him.

"It's our first lead."

"Wait… isn't that the painter who did our house? Why is he a lead?" She leaned over him, looking at the screen.

"Just trust me, okay?"

"Whatever, Well, where is he?" Lisa moved back and crossed her arms.

He looked at the screen, to the right-hand side of the search was a logo and some business information, including an address in Westford.

"Do you know where that is?" he asked, pointing.

"I think so, it's the other side of town, towards the college."

"Okay, so what, about an hour's walk?" He twisted in the chair and looked up at her.

"Give or take, yeah. We'll set off when your friend and Ruby get here."

"Okay, and thanks again, Lisa."

"No worries, you owe me though,. She ruffled his shaggy brown hair and turned to get another coffee.

Luke read through reviews of the painter. They were all positive; all of them said how polite, friendly, and professional he was. Maybe the fingernail and the flesh were nothing? But then again, one of the two finds could be a grisly coincidence but both? He was sure he had to follow his instinct. They needed to check this guy out; maybe he would lead them to answers.

He scrolled down the screen and saw two articles, both from the past couple of days. One about a missing boy called Ben James and one about a missing guy from Westford. He clicked on the article about the boy first.

The little boy had gone missing from the beach at Westford Water, a man-made reservoir a few miles away. He was an orphan. Could it be a lead?

He clicked the other article. It was about a local guy named Jake, 23. He'd been missing since Monday evening; now he thought about it he remembered his mum and dad mentioning it at dinner last night. Jake was last seen on his own in the Baron Burghley, one of the last remaining old-style pubs in Westford. Before this, people reported seeing him with another man (who was also missing) in the Red Lion. They'd identified the other man as 'Bug,' a well-known figure from twenty years ago who disappeared along with his girlfriend. Everyone assumed both of them had died from an overdose far away from there.

Luke skimmed over the rest of the article and landed on a word that made him stop. His finger hovered over the page. The bar girl from the Red Lion had identified the man, but she swore his name wasn't Jake—she said the other man, Bug, had been calling him Lucas.

He clicked print on the computer, and he heard the mechanical whirring start. He got up and ran to the garage to find the hessian sack.

"Hey, where are you going?" Lisa shouted after him.

"The printer," he shouted over his shoulder. "Read it." Luke pointed to the printer.

He avoided the pile of now-dead maggots and found the hessian sack and carried it back into the house. Lisa was sitting on the sofa with the still warm printout; she was frowning.

"Do you think it's him?" Lisa asked.

"It fits, doesn't it?"

"And the man on the tape, what, that's this Bug guy?"

Luke nodded and perched on the arm of the sofa; if his father saw him, he'd be in trouble again. "He mentioned something about, 'It happened again, only this time I went backward...' do you remember?" Luke plucked the printout from Lisa's hands. "Well, the article says he's been missing for twenty-odd years. Then re-appeared last week, only to go missing again."

"Okay, say I buy it—what do we do now?"

Luke stood and looked out the window; he saw Petey and Ruby walking together in the sunshine towards their front door. A spike of red hot anger flushed through him, seeing them together. He wanted to run outside and push them apart. He watched Ruby giggle at something Petey said, and Luke crunched up the printout in his hands.

"Do you still have that fake ID?" Luke asked, not turning from the window. Petey waved, and Luke could have screamed.

8

They put the decorator on the To-do list and made their way to the Red Lion. Luke and Petey led the way–walking excitedly down the long, tree-lined road into town. They passed the garage and the large warehouses and then the large field on their left that led to the quarry. Luke filled Petey in on what they'd found on the computer and hypothesized what it could all mean. Lisa and Ruby followed behind, sharing a headphone each from Lisa's mobile that played more Latino-inspired pop.

The previous night's storm had cleared the air; it was warm and sunny without the horrible humidity of yesterday afternoon. Lazy clouds floated across the sky, and cars flashed past before coming to a stop at the zebra crossing halfway into town. A tall blue signpost stood on a grass verge just past the crossing - Welcome to Westford - Stay awhile amidst its ancient charm, it read in a flowing classical font. A massive spider web crisscrossed from the trees to the sign. Petey and Luke waited underneath it for Lisa and Ruby to catch up.

"What's the rush?" Lisa asked, approaching Luke and Petey, who stood with their arms folded over their chests. "The pub won't even be open yet, dumbass."

Luke was thrilled to see his sister was back to her usual self. He didn't know why he was surprised; her being nice never lasted long.

"Shit, what time does it open?" They all looked at the next person. "Haven't you got 4G on that thing?" Luke asked Lisa, nodding at her phone.

"Mum and Dad limited the data, they said I kept going over my limit, and it was costing them shitloads." She gave a "what can you do" shrug.

"Well, we're halfway there already, they must have a sign on the door–I think we should keep on going," said Petey.

"Sounds like a plan to me–you two?"

Lisa and Ruby looked at each other. "We're here now anyway, and I want to know what's going on. I've felt funny ever since I touched that rock," said Ruby.

"We're still in," Lisa said to Luke.

Lisa and Ruby pushed past the boys and took the lead. Luke and Petey trailed behind and watched how both girls swaggered, their hips moving mesmerizingly side-to-side as they walked arm-in-arm down the path listening to some secret music and giggling in hushed tones. Luke noticed Ruby wore tight camo army shorts today and a white vest; the burn on her shoulders had calmed and left a splotch of freckles on her right shoulder. He saw the profile of her face every time she turned to talk to his sister, and he didn't hear Petey talking to him.

"What? Sorry, I missed what you said."

"I said, what's the plan, Stan? So your sister and Ruby are just going to waltz in, buy a drink, then sneak into the men's toilet and look in the toilet bowls?"

Luke wrinkled his nose; they were walking downhill with the houses. They stretch out on both sides of the road, which seems to raise as if on stilts. "I don't know how busy is a pub on a weekday lunchtime?"

"I think it depends on the pub, sometimes dad takes me to the White Swan to watch the football on a Sunday and that place is rammed."

"Yeah, but that's the weekend, and with football on, during the day, surely most adults are at work, aren't they?"

"I think so,"

"Unless… well, you know…" Luke said.

Petey frowned and looked at the ground. "You mean my mum, don't you?"

"When did you see her last?" Luke didn't want to, but after seeing Petey with Ruby this morning, he was enjoying hurting Petey by talking about his mum.

"Last year, for my birthday."

However, when he saw his friend's face, his stomach started to churn. "I'm sorry, Petey, that was shitty of me to bring it up."

"Don't worry."

Changing the subject, Luke started to speculate what they would find in the baggy in the toilet. Petey didn't join in the speculation. They jogged and caught up with Lisa and Ruby as they were walking past the Shell garage on their left. The Red Lion stood opposite. The smell of diesel and petrol and the fumes of the cars sitting in barely moving traffic filled the air.

They sat in a row on the red brick wall that separated the garage forecourt from the path and stared across at the pub.

Tall, grand houses, the sort of homes that Luke, Lisa, Petey, and Ruby could only dream of living in, flanked it on both sides. They had Juliette windows and gated fronts with views down to the basement levels. Black wrought-iron fencing surrounded the bay windows. Engraved in the stonework above each of the doors were words that they couldn't make out from where they sat.

The stone walls of the pub seemed crooked as did the three windows that ran across the ground floor and the three on the first floor and the three in the roof. The pub looked skewed. The windowsills were painted a moss-green and two doors, one to the right of the farthest left window, and one to the left of the farthest right window were closed. The windows were dark, and there were no lights on inside. Two hanging baskets with pink and white flowers broke up the pale yellow of the stone and bought the front of the building to life.

The sounds of the traffic leading to Milgate was like living in a city, not a small town. They sat and watched and listened to the cars honking and pulling out. A white Land Rover poked his nose blindly out of the Shell garage into oncoming traffic, which caused another loud honk.

"What should we do?" asked Petey, leaning across the group of them.

"What time is it now?"

Lisa checked her phone. "Quarter past eleven, it'll open in forty-five minutes'." She turned to look at Luke. "You know, I bet a pub like this would have a cleaner in before they open. I bet they're in there already. Why don't you knock and pretend you need the toilet? It will save all this fannying around."

"But, what if they say no?"

"Then they say no, nothing lost; nothing gained," Ruby answered. "It's a better idea than us trying to use Lisa's fake ID to buy a drink and sneak into the men's' toilets. Just put on your charming smile and get out your winning personality."

Luke flushed red. Ruby pushed him off the wall. "Go on," she said. "Impress me." She winked at him, a wink he was sure no one saw but him. Luke didn't sense a mean or condescending tone to her voice; he thought she sounded sincere, and her smile was dazzling. He puffed out his chest and flicked a bit of hair out of his face before turning around and crossing the road through the standstill traffic.

Arriving at the front door, he knocked twice and waited. No one answered. He poked his head to the side and peered through the window. Luke turned back to Ruby, Lisa, and Petey and did a charade with his hands, which they guessed to mean he was going around the back. He unlocked the wrought-iron gate and disappeared down the gravel path.

They sat in silence, just the noise from the road and the sound of fuel pumps breaking it. All three of them stared ahead at the gravel path to the side of the pub. Luke had left the gate open, and they stared at the side road with ivy growing up the walls to the side.

Petey jumped down from the wall and paced in front of Ruby and Lisa. "What's taking him so long? Do you think he got inside? Where is he?"

"Petey, calm down; it's only been a couple of minutes'. I'm sure everything is fine," said Lisa, jumping down from the wall herself. He started to pick at some chewing gum stuck to the floor using the tip of his shoe. Then he moved onto picking at his ear with a brown stick he found in his pocket. Lisa and Ruby looked at each other and put two fingers down their throats. As they giggled, Petey looked up from the chewing gum that was now stuck to his shoe.

"What you laughing at?"

"Nothing," Lisa said, snorting through the fingers over her mouth. "Just saw something funny."

"I do wish he would hurry up, do you think he's okay?" Petey looked genuinely worried for her brother, and that touched Lisa.

"I'm sure of it—he's probably got his hand down the back of the toilet right now," Lisa said. "I'm sure he's okay." She put a hand on his shoulder. Petey shook his head and walked away from them, staring at the pub.

"Come on, Luke," he whispered to himself as a man walked into him. Petey turned to shout something, but seeing the size of the man, he decided against it. He turned to the girls; Lisa was sitting on the wall again. Lisa's gaze followed the man, and she shouted, "Hey, watch where you're going!"

The man turned around; his face was podgy and pink, and he sported ugly fluffy stubble that came in patches on his floppy face, a snarl touched his top lip. Lisa stood her ground six feet away from him. Sunlight glinted off the top of cars, and a warm breeze blew. She motioned to move forward, nodding her head as if threatening a dog, and the man flinched.

"Thought so," she said. "Why don't you go back and ask if you can start puberty again, dickhead?"

The man walked off, his shoulders slumped, and a couple watching from their stationary bright orange Fiat 500 wound down their window and applauded Lisa. She walked towards Petey and ruffled his hair as she'd ruffled Luke's earlier. "I ain't got no time for bullies," she said and smiled.

Another car horn made them turn to the road where they saw Luke running through the cars towards them. He held an A4 plastic baggy with an envelope in it to his side in his right hand. He stepped up the curb and joined the others who were standing together silently. "What did I miss?" he asked with a smile, holding the plastic baggy out.

9

They left the wall across from the Red Lion and carried on walking into town. Luke wanted to keep hold of the baggy, but Lisa and Ruby insisted he put it in the hessian sack, so they didn't get arrested for drug dealing. Lisa kept hold of the sack. Petey was quiet and had a serene look on his face as they crossed over the busy crossroads. The beep of the zebra crossing was loud and carried over the revving engines.

Ancient stone walls taller than Ruby and Lisa, who were walking in front, had yellow and pink flowers and shrubs growing over them and blocked any view into the old houses on their left. Across the road, loomed the old hospital and its haunting arches and gardens. Cars pulled in and out of the pay and display car park next to it. As they got closer to the centre of town, more people passed them by on the narrow pavements, and they had to walk in a single file.

"Where are we going?" Petey asked Luke.

"Broad Leaf Square, then we'll come up with the next step."

The buildings got taller as they approached Broad Leaf Square. A plethora of brown and cream townhouses looked down on them as they passed. The tarmac path turned to cobblestones under their fee. Red berries from a tree in the graveyard were squashed into the stones on the trail, and the high spire of St. Michan's church, which could be seen for miles from the surrounding villages, loomed high above them. They stood opposite the square and its wooden benches and peered around the curved, moss-covered stone wall of the graveyard and up All Saints street past its wonky Georgian architecture. When the road was clear, they ran across led by Lisa, who looked like a mother goose crossing with her ducklings.

Broad Leaf Square wasn't really a square. A triangular paved area was bordered by wooden benches and seven-foot-tall rectangular stone monoliths with inscriptions. Beyond these were more curious buildings: An independent, timber-framed, coffee house; a local butchers that had stood here for years and an electrical shop which had plied its trade here for decades. A busy, cobbled road cut opposite these buildings separating the square from the high street and its never-ending sprawl of coffee, charity, and expensive clothes shops. Imposing three and four-story buildings looked down at the square from all sides. Another set of traffic lights controlled the traffic, but when two of the off-roads were as narrow as one car, more often than not, a considerable amount of honking and stand-still traffic occurred.

Luke, Petey, and Ruby followed Lisa to one of the empty benches. They sat in a row, their naked knees touching one another. They bent forward in a huddle and listened as Luke spoke.

"It was in the third cubicle. I lifted the lid at the back, and there it was, just floating. I can't believe it's real. It's an envelope." He lifted his head and looked around the busy square. People were rushing back and forth, women with pushchairs waited at the crossing, while men wearing smart shirts and jeans jogged across the road. "We can't open it here; it's too busy."

"What about the meadows?" asked Ruby.

"Could work; it's close, and if it's busy, we could just walk through to the second or third meadows?" replied Lisa.

Somewhere, far off, but not too far, over the noise of the cars and idle chat from passing pedestrians, Ruby heard the birds singing again. She closed her eyes and breathed in contently. When she opened them, the others were standing over. The worried looks on their faces and their silently moving mouths scared her.

She had tunnel vision; bright lights whizzed by silently at the edge of her sight while the brightness of the world had been turned up high and the contrast down low. As cars drove past, they left trails of light behind. Luke's voice broke through the avian melody, and she turned and looked up at him. His voice started as a whisper, but grew louder and stronger as she watched his lips move.

After a moment of concentration, the light went back to normal, and the birds stopped singing. She stood, but her legs gave out beneath her, and Luke caught her. She held on to him, his clumsy hands held her shoulders, and she moved them down for him into a hug and put her head on his shoulder. Luke held her in his arms, careful not to hug her too tight. She smelled of pineapple and coconut. He felt her tremble once, and then she started to sob.

"What's happening to me?" Her voice came out muffled and choked.

"I... I don't know, but we'll find out, I promise." He held her tight against him, wondering if this would be the only time he ever got to hold her like this? Girls her age weren't interested in boys his age.

She pulled away but kept one arm on Luke's shoulder. She dabbed at her wet eyes with the back of her still shaking hands. Lisa held a hand to her, and she took it. "We will find out what is happening, Rubes, all of us, together." Lisa grabbed Petey's hand and pulled him into the group hug. "I must be going soft or something," she said, and they laughed.

They broke out of the hug; Luke and Ruby held hands for five seconds longer than the rest of them. Lisa smiled at her best friend and said, "Come on, let's go." And she led them down the passage to the meadows. Petey and Luke followed behind.

"What was all that about?" Petey asked.

"All what?" Luke replied, tugging at his ear.

"Umm… how about that hug! Or how about Ruby zoning out again like a mong on us!"

"Shut up; she's not a mong."

"Jeez, sensitive… sorry. But, what do you think, was it that stone again, do you think she heard the birds again?" Petey walked backward, down the passage in front of Luke.

"Maybe. Remember that message; it said something about staying away from the willow. The only one I know in Westford is on the meadows, and then he said about bird song again. Maybe it's calling to her?"

"Shit. Let's go somewhere else then."

"I don't think we can; it was Ruby's idea. I think we're supposed to go there." Luke reached out and grabbed Petey before he walked backward into an A-frame sign on the pavement.

"Thanks," Petey said, smiling at Luke.

They carried on in silence as they passed the spiked monolith at the bottom of the bus station.

"You're crushing on my brother," Lisa said, brushing up against Ruby, smiling. "It's okay; he may be a dork, but he's my dork, and as little brothers go, he's alright."

Ruby interlinked her arm into Lisa's.

"I'm sorry, I didn't mean to. I don't know what's going on. Ever since yesterday, I feel… odd."

"So is that a yes or a no? Do you like my brother? Seriously, I really don't mind if you do."

"He's cute and ni–"

"Knew it," Lisa interrupted. "Do me a favour though, keep him hanging on for a while–It'll be great to watch!"

They laughed and continued arm-in-arm. Luke and Petey watched from behind. Luke turned to Petey and shrugged. He thought they might be talking about him. If they were talking about him, that meant there was something to talk about; he smiled. They crossed yet another zebra crossing onto Castle Dyke and followed the path down to Bath Row and the meadows.

A cluster of newer houses intermingled with the older stone buildings on Castle Dyke, which led to Bath Row. Along Bath Row, tall trees stretched up to the sky, their fingers seemingly touching the few clouds above. An ice cream truck sat in front of the pedestrian bridge where a twisted line of parents, teenagers, and children snaked past the black bollard and out onto the road.

Luke and Petey crossed the bridge; they heard the ducks quacking below. They turned their heads turned towards the massive willow tree at the far end of the left-hand meadow and almost bumped into Lisa and Ruby, who had stopped and been staring at the gigantic tree.

Small groups sat in circles dotted on the grass to their left and their right. Young children giggled and ran after geese and ducks, and parents ran after the children. Other people sat alone, engrossed in books, or swiping through phones. Black metal bins along the path in the centre of the two grass areas were overflowing.

The heatwave had brought out the school holiday crowds. Wispy clouds floated across the sky as the sun-dried the grass from last night's storm. Luke smelled marijuana on the breeze.

"It's a bit busy," Petey said, scanning both sides.

"Come on, let's go to the second meadows." Lisa pointed with her right hand, which still held the hessian sack containing the stone, the dictaphone, and the baggy to the fence at the far end of the grass area to her right. The opposite direction of the willow tree, which Luke thought was a good thing.

They set off down the sloping bank through the middle of the grass, which was getting overgrown after the hot and wet summer they'd had. The river ran on both sides of the meadows, a slow and steady trickle on the Bath Row side but faster on the deeper side where the gate was.

They walked in a line; Lisa and Ruby to the left, Luke and Petey to the right. Ruby and Luke walked next to each other with a slight gap between them. Ruby glanced at Luke, and when he looked back, she looked down at the ground. As his eyes looked at her, she glanced at him, and he looked at the ground. They both smiled.

Upon reaching the gate, Lisa pulled up the metal clamp and opened it, letting the others through. "This way," she said, leading them through a well-trod path in the tall grass. They walked single-file again. Something rustled in the long grass, and Ruby reached back and grabbed Luke's hand.

"Just a grass snake," he said, smiling.

They carried on walking and continued holding hands. Luke grinned as he walked behind Ruby; his eyes flowed over her body, taking in the soft, freckled skin of her shoulders and over her camo shorts and her pale smooth legs. She smoothed her thumb over his palm—the movement sent electricity flowing through his body.

Lisa stopped in front of a tree with low-hanging branches, not unlike those of the willow. Around the tree, the long grass touched the leaves. "Under here," Lisa said, pulling up a branch.

Ruby and Luke bent under the branches, not letting go of each other's hand, and Petey followed. It was like a secret garden. The trees and leaves secluded an area about the size of a living room. It was cool and damp with an earthy smell and roots stuck up and out of the ground. Luke shivered but didn't know why.

"This is amazing; how do you know about it?" asked Petey, looking up at the dappled light that flowed in from the trees above. Spots of light danced on the dark floor.

"I found it last week; I think kids have been using it for drinking and what-not."

"It's perfect," said Luke, still holding Ruby's hand. She looked at him and smiled. "It will be alright, see. Now, let's open that envelope." He held out his hand, and Lisa gave him the hessian sack. Luke emptied it onto the dusty floor, careful not to touch the rock which he kicked back into the sack before Ruby saw it. He opened the clear baggy and pulled out the envelope.

It was an off-white, like it had been in the toilet for a while, and the size of a standard letter envelope with the name 'Lucas' sprawled across the front in big lopsided letters. Luke slid his finger under one end and ripped it open. He pulled out a piece of folded A4 paper and sat under the shade of the trees. The others joined him on the cold floor as he unfolded it.

Lucas,

Sorry for the treasure hunt; however, it is the only way for sure of not getting caught—you must not get caught. At least two of those creatures will be looking for you. They know who you are. There's more to all this than we thought. I have been back through the willow tree again; this time, it sent me way back. I don't think it's evil, Lucas; it's trying to show us something. I was an accident, though; I think the tree was waiting for someone else. The rock, you must keep hold of it. Theo will know what to do with it, but it's so important—DO NOT LOSE IT! You must find Theo; I saw him when I went back in time. I followed him to the old Priory out near Morrison's roundabout. He was painting it, the Priory, but then stopped and disappeared around the back. It's not much to go on, I know, but it's somewhere to start, maybe.

Look after yourself,

Bug

Ps. Listen, Lucas, remember the first time we met? I couldn't remember where I had been, but I had aged. It's happened again. I worry that if you don't find me soon, my time will run out. There's a bigger picture here, and I think you may be my only hope.

Check out the Priory, see what you find, but don't trust anyone—the people in this town don't seem right.

Lisa was the first to speak, "Well, at least we know that article was right–it's Bug, but who's Lucas?"

"I don't know, but Bug needs his help. At least we have the next location," said Luke.

They sat in a circle under the protection of the trees. Petey stood up; his skin was ashen. "Are you guys crazy? We're going to follow the directions of a guy who thinks he's time-traveling through a willow tree? And, what about those creatures he mentioned? This isn't some adventure game!" He paced around the tree trunk leaving fresh prints in the dirt. "Come on, guys, it's the summer holidays. We should be playing, or something, not following clues from a letter hidden in a toilet or a dictaphone in a tatty sack next to a magic fucking rock!"

They looked up at him; he was out of breath and leaned forward and put his hands on his knees.

"Breath, Petey," Ruby said, she stood up and rubbed his back. "I touched that rock, and something is happening to me, I need to know what it is. We've come this far–you're so smart and brave, I need you to help me–will you help me?"

Luke and Lisa nodded and stood and moved towards Petey. "We started this together, we need to finish it together, whatever happens," said Luke.

"I've got your back," said Lisa. "Just like outside the pub."

Strobes of daylight filtered through the dark, creating pinpricks of light on their faces. Petey stood straight, his face was still pale, but his cheeks were flushed. He took off his glasses and wiped them on his shirt.

"We need you," Luke continued. "Whoever this Bug guy is, he needs you. We need to find this Theo he keeps on talking about. Are you in?" He held out his hand to his oldest friend.

Petey shook his head. "You're all dicks; you know that, right?" He took Luke's hand, and they shook like men. "To the Priory, then?" he sighed.

"To the Priory," they replied.

10

They left the safety of the tree and walked across the first meadows, where a football match had started. Sweaty, shirtless boys ran after a Nike football and shouted at each other. As they crossed the game, one boy looked up and shouted something at Petey.

"Ignore them," Lisa said. "They're just jealous you're hanging out with us."

Walking together, they crossed the bridge and along Bath Row; where the meadows were separated from the road by the river. They turned into a large car park full of Land Rovers and Audis and went up an alleyway to the side that led them out onto St. Mary's Hill and some of the oldest shops in Westford. Expensive tailored suits and pictures of grand houses stared out from shop windows. Two days ago, above one of the shops, Lucas had woken up in Jake's body.

They exited the dark alleyway and headed down the hill past an eerie-looking bookstore towards the town bridge. On their left, the town hall stood quiet and ominous. As they checked the traffic to cross the road, they saw the steeple of the great church that sat at the top of the hill. Towards the bottom, just before the bridge that stood over where the river joined at the meadows, they turned left and walked alongside the other side of the river onto Wharf road. They followed the road, newly built houses and apartments blocked their view of the river, but when Petey looked over his shoulder, he saw the light green leaves of the willow tree. They came to a T-junction on St. Wilfrid's road. Cars drove past, bumper to bumper, going too fast for the narrow roads of Westford.

Petey crossed over a small roundabout with faded white paint and onto Priory road. A long row of identical grey and brown houses with fields leading to the river behind were on their right, while on the left, were long driveways leading to the more expensive homes of a private estate. After five minutes', all the houses disappeared and were replaced with a long stone wall and fields beyond.

Hedges and trees were dotted sparingly along the fences in the yellow fields, cut off behind sharp and spiny hedgerows. To the left was the renovated house, which was now a retirement village. It overlooked the Priory, which had stood for at least ten centuries as far as he knew. They stopped on the road-side of the gate and looked in at the building.

Tall trees and a moss-covered stone wall surrounded the dry grassland which circled the Priory. In the middle of the day, with the sun shining, Petey thought it looked peaceful and relaxing; somewhere you could escape from your troubles' and get lost in a good book, maybe a classic adventure like The Adventures of Huckleberry Finn. He could hear the busy roundabout just up the road from them. Now they were here, what were they looking for?

Petey, Ruby, and Lisa looked at Luke. He shrugged. "I guess we best go take a look."

They climbed over the black iron gate, the girls first followed by the boys.

"It feels strange, doesn't it?" Lisa asked. "Colder than when we were on the path outside," She bought her arms up to her chest and hugged herself. "I don't like it." Petey didn't like it either.

"Come on," Luke said, "let's have a look around the building; see if we see anything, if not, we can go."

Petey had been close; the Priory had stood on this spot for over 1400 years. It had five high arches along the side you could see from the road. Under the arches, the stonework was stained from centuries under the elements. The bottoms of the walls were black, like dried blood. Above the second arch from the left was a long slit-like window cut into the stone. It was a thin building, with the length at least three times longer than the width. Against the sun, it stood silent and foreboding.

Luke and Ruby led the way. As they approached, she reached out and took his hand. He was thankful for the warmth of her touch. Luke looked at her and smiled and, for the first time in his life, winked. He looked behind and saw Lisa and Petey walking together. Lisa looked pale, ill, like all the blood had drained from her body, and even her usual shiny brown hair looked dull. Petey was walking to the side of her, glancing at her, ready to catch her if she tripped.

"Guys, I don't think Lisa can go any closer."

Luke and Ruby turned and switched the hands they were holding. They stood in front of Lisa and Petey like a couple about to admonish a child. Then their faces softened, and Luke went to his sister. "You can sit this one out, you know."

Lisa shook her head. "I can make i–" she staggered forward. Petey caught her. He put one of her arms around his shoulder and held her weight. "Okay, maybe this one time," she said. Petey helped her back towards the gate. He struggled because of Lisa's height compared to his. As Petey glanced back towards them, The Priory rose behind Luke and Ruby like a monster from the abyss. Petey gave a thumbs-up using the hand around Lisa's back to Luke, but his face painted another picture.

"Let's go," Luke said, turning back to the Priory. They switched hands again, and Luke gave Ruby's a squeeze.

Petey helped Lisa over the gate and back onto the path just outside the Priory. The warmth hit her like a warm pillow, and the colour flushed back into her cheeks.

"Did you feel that?" she asked Petey, who had his hands on his knees panting. He shook his head, stood up, turned, and leaned on the gate looking into the Priory. Lisa followed him. They stood side-by-side and watched Ruby and Luke disappear under one of the five arches. The shadow swallowed them.

"I hope they're going to be okay."

"I'm sure they will be," she said. The cold sensation was gone. Her inside's had stopped squirming to get out of her body. Whatever had happened to her in there hadn't affected anyone else.

They stood in silence, watching the ancient building, waiting for some sign of the others. A warm breeze rustled the leaves in the trees above, and a loud car smoking heavily from its exhaust drove past behind them, leaving the smell of burning diesel in the air.

There was another entrance to the Priory further up the road closer to the roundabout. One for vehicles, not pedestrians. As Lisa and Petey watched for Luke and Ruby, a dusty white Renault Trafic van pulled up into the entrance. Its once silver hubcaps were now a blood-red rust as was the bottom of the body of the car, which looked brittle to the touch. The windows were tinted black, and on the side, written in italic black lettering were the words, Duncan Fuller: Painter & Decorator.

A man got out of the car; his black paint-flecked boots crunched on the gravel underneath. His dirty dark blue overalls were stained with specks of paint. He wore a black baseball cap and dark sunglasses that hid his eyes. Fuller walked over to the gate, opened it, secured it, and then climbed back in his van. He slammed the door, and Petey and Lisa looked up from their gate.

"I know that van," they said at the same time. They ducked behind the stone wall attached to the gate.

"Shit. Luke was reading about him this morning; said he was on the list of leads," Lisa put her head back against the wall. "He didn't say why, though."

"Well, duh... because of that fingernail and that other thi–" Petey moved his hand up to his mouth.

"What fingernail? What other thing? Petey, what haven't you told me?" She wasn't pale now, and she wasn't feeling the cold.

"Let's talk about this later, huh? Now we need to get Luke and Ruby. Can you see them?"

"Fine, later… but don't think I'll forget Petey." Lisa peeked around the corner of the wall, past the gate and towards the Priory. "No, nothing's moving at all. What do you think he's doing here?"

"I don't know, but it can't be good, and I doubt it's a coincidence."

The van's engine came to life in a plume of smoke, and the exhaust growled and rattled. The black smoke blew down the road and over them. It was thick, and they held back hacked coughs. With another roar of the engine and another burst of dark smoke, the van moved forward towards the Priory. The trees blocked their vision once it was halfway down the access path, but they could see the smoke from the exhaust rising high into the blue sky before dissipating.

"Quick, come on," Petey said, and he crawled towards the gate.

Lisa looked towards the Priory, "I can't, that place did something to me; you've got to go alone."

"What? I don't think I c—"

"You must, Petey. Luke and Ruby are in there."

Petey looked up the road towards the roundabout and the sounds of people carrying on with their normal day-to-day lives. He wasn't a hero. Then he thought of Luke and Ruby; he saw them in his mind holding hands in front of the Priory as it loomed over them like some monster from one of the Greek legends he enjoyed reading. Its five arches looked like the gates to hell.

"Shit." He scuttled in a crab-like waddle past Lisa, careful that his head didn't poke over the wall. She reached out and put an arm around his shoulder. "You can do this," she said into his ear, so close he could feel her breath on his face. "Sneak in, keep low, go around the back and find Luke and Ruby, then sneak them back out to me, okay? Easy-peasey."

"Easy, yeah right, easy-peasey," He peered around the wall. The van was hidden from sight, and he couldn't hear the engine. He climbed over the gate and landed on the other side. Petey kept tight to the wall as he made his way around the edge of the Priory's land. He was keeping in the shadows under the tree-lined fence and wall.

He was at the front of the Priory now, not the side visible from the road. There were three arches on the ground with short columns, like teeth, leading to the rear. The three pitch-black windows above had slit-like eyes, and there was an oval all-seeing eye above. A little further and he would see the side fully blocked from the road; the side he guessed Luke and Ruby were.

A scream pierced the air. It came from inside the Priory. He stopped, and a warm patch spread down his leg. Now he knew how it felt to piss yourself, just like his good old mum. He leaned in tight to the fence and wrapped his arms around a wooden post. The scream came again, longer this time, and he looked towards the entrance, towards Lisa. He could see her peering in between the gaps in the gate. She was motioning with her hand for him to come back to her. He shook his head.

Petey looked around; he saw a picnic bench and beyond it another gate. He sprinted in a crouch and ducked down behind the gate. Who was screaming? He looked past the Priory and to the side leading to the fields; behind a broken stone wall were two black shapes huddled together.

He waved his hands, motioning to get their attention, but they stared straight ahead at the side of the Priory he couldn't see. Petey willed his feet to move, and he scuttled around the fence and bushes towards Luke and Ruby. As he passed the bench, the van came into view again. It was parked under a large oak tree. A branch snapped under his foot, and he heard Luke whisper, "Shhh… come here quick."

Petey moved across the last five yards and hopped over the fence and into the dirt by Ruby and Luke. "I came to find you," he looked down at his shorts. "I pissed myself," he stated.

Luke patted him on his shoulder and showed him the front of his shorts where a dark stain had spread. "Ditto. When I heard that scream."

Petey looked over Luke's shoulder to Ruby–she nodded. "Well, at least it wasn't just me." Petey shuffled in between Luke and Ruby, and looked out at the side of the Priory he hadn't yet seen. It was cool under the shade, and the warmth of his shorts turned cold and uncomfortable.

There were no arches on this side. Instead, five square columns ran from the roof to the floor. Between the third and fourth columns were crumbling stairs that led to a bricked-up doorway. There were no seams, and guessing from the faded colour of the stone, someone had blocked it up a long time. Behind the Priory, Petey saw the van and a man in a black baseball cap and shades.

"What's he doing?" Petey asked.

"We don't know; he's been standing there for a few minutes now."

"He hasn't moved," Ruby added. "But his hands, can you see them? It's like they're throbbing or vibrating. Luke can't see it, can you?"

Petey looked at the man's hands; they looked normal. He followed the arm up the body; a shadow blocked out the man's head. "I don't see anything, Ruby, I'm sorry."

Ruby looked down at the ground, Petey saw tears in her eyes. He nudged Luke's knee with his own and nodded towards Ruby.

"It's okay," Luke said, turning to her. "We'll figure it out, I believe you see it."

He reached out to her, and she took his hand. Luke pulled her towards him and into an awkward crouched embrace with his knee's knocking against Petey's. She took a sharp intake of breath, and Petey had to put his hand over her mouth to stop the scream.

The man moved forward into the sunlight. Petey saw the man in dark shades and the baseball cap for the first time and recognized him from when he joked with him about which football team he supported on Luke's drive just last weekend.

"What?" Luke asked Ruby. "Do you know him?"

Ruby reached up and pulled Petey's hand away from her mouth. "Can't you see his face?"

"What about it?" Petey asked.

"What about it? Look at it."

Petey looked at the man. "I see nothing, just a guy in sunglasses and a cap."

"You don't see... you don't see the rest of his face?"

"What are you talking about, Ruby?"

"His face, his face... it's fucking hideous. That's not a man." Petey and Luke stared at the man, but they saw nothing.

"Okay, Okay. Ruby, what do you see?" asked Luke.

"Oh my god, it's horrible. It's like it's melting." She took deep breaths and held onto Luke's arm. "There are two big orbs, one on each side of its face, they're a ruddy colour, and in the middle, oh, it's gross, there's no nose, it looks like the stitching from a basketball crisscrossing across a silver-white space." She spoke fast, and Petey struggled to understand what she was saying. Ruby looked away, before turning back and peeking through her hands, she spoke slower this time, "And, it's not a normal mouth, it's... there are two pincer type things and bile or slime dripping from it. There's fur too. Fucking hell, Luke, it almost looks like a fly's face." Now she started to cry. She leaned her head against Luke's shoulder. "Why can't you see it? Am I crazy?"

"No, I don't think you are," he said, stroking her hair. "I th–"

"Uh-hmm... guys, sorry to break in, but it's doing something," Petey said, unable to take his eye's off the man.

They leaned forward as a light emanated from the rear of the Priory; pure white light that, like the opposite of a shadow, swallowed Fly-face. A solid silhouette of the man turned into a thousand moths that flew away and disappeared into the sky above. The light faded, and the world returned to normal. Fly-face was gone.

The van was still parked where it had been, but Luke was certain the man they called Fly-face had entered the Priory. He looked around at Ruby, who was still crying, and Petey, who had a blank look on his face. They needed to get out of here.

Why was Ruby the only one who could see the monster? Was it because of the rock? This seemed like their best chance to get out of the Priory and back to reality. They should get back to Lisa, and then the four of them would work this out, maybe call the police? Perhaps Petey was right, they were involved in something dangerous, and shouldn't have come.

Luke stood halfway up in a crouched pose and led them back up and over the gate. Ruby put her hand on his shoulder and pointed towards the van. "What?" he mouthed at her.

"We need to wait," she said.

"Why?"

"Trust me." She looked at Luke with wide hazel earnest eyes.

Luke turned to Petey. "You go back without us, tell Lisa we're okay, we just need to wait, can you do that, Petey?" He ducked back down next to Ruby

"No, Luke, I can't just do that! I am not your fucking messenger pigeon; if you're waiting, I'm waiting too." Petey ducked down next to Luke; he was pink in the face.

Luke flushed at his friend's reaction; he turned to Ruby for backup, but she shrugged her shoulders. "Okay, we all stay. Let's get closer."

They climbed the wall and stayed close to it using the trees as cover. They made their way to the van and the rear of the Priory. Luke went first, followed by Ruby, while Petey pulled up the rear. Every time they took cover behind a tree or a wall, they looked out over the dry yellow-green grass. They passed beneath a low-hanging branch, and a bird took flight; the branch shook above them, and the leaves whistled in the breeze. They froze and waited to see if there would be any movement from the van. There was none. It sat silent and ominous, its smeared headlights and dirty water-streaked windscreen watched them as they passed. Under the cover of thick trees, about twenty feet from the van, they found a shadowed spot. They positioned themselves so they wouldn't be seen and waited. The only sound came from the whispering of the leaves in the trees above. They huddled together; Luke smelled a faint whiff of urine which hung in the air.

He thought about what Ruby had seen. She'd also heard birds that none of them could. It must be the rock. She was the only one who'd touched it. What was it? He thought back to their hand-holding; were they a couple already? It was unexpected, but wasn't that how the great storytellers said love happened? Shit, they hadn't even kissed yet. However, he thought because of a lack of privacy rather than anything else. Could Ruby, with freckles on her pale shoulders and her peach-coloured hair, be his first kiss, maybe his first girlfriend? What would Lisa say; her nerdy little brother dating her best friend? Maybe those glances and smiles over the summer holidays were more than just friendly. He thought he'd imagined the whole thing. Or could what had happened, happened because of the situation they were in; heightened tension causes extreme reactions, he remembered from a video at school. It could've just as easily been Petey she held and cuddled in Broad Leaf Square, or was it more than that? Had she fancied him all summer?

The wind picked up, the leaves flicked, and flipped on their branches. A mini dust-devil formed just in front of the van. A noise, not unlike that of a plane, came from the Priory, and then a black hole no larger than the size of a coffee cup appeared in the solid stone. Luke heard sobs coming from within, and a man begging, "...please don't... I'll do anything, please..."

Luke turned to the others. Both Ruby and Petey stared past him, wide-eyed into the black hole. The wind increased, the rustling of the trees got louder behind and above them. Luke felt like he was standing on a train platform. Ruby's hand found his, and he held an arm back towards Petey, which Petey gladly took.

The hole continued to grow. It was the size of a basketball, then a car window, and then the size of a car tire. Luke stared as first an arm, followed by a head, followed by the upper body, and finally, one leg, followed by the other, stepped out of the black hole. It was Fly-face. From here, he saw the outline of the painter's face. It was normal, just like it had been at his house. His eyes were hidden behind sunglasses. Ruby's grip tightened on his hand.

Fly-face turned towards the hole and reached in with both arms. He pulled out a man's body. First, the arms, which were bound with bloodied rags above his head. The rest of him followed. Luke winced and closed his eyes as the body thudded to the ground. When he opened them again, the hole had disappeared. The body on the floor groaned, and Luke saw a bloody stump with maggots crawling over where his right leg should be.

The writhing maggots brought back memories of fishing trips with his dad and the bag of food in his garage back home. The man's leg was covered in them. He heard Petey retch and squeezed his arm tight. He turned and looked at him and raised a finger to his mouth.

Fly-face walked towards his van and opened the back doors. Luke watched as he grabbed the man under his armpits and dragged him across the dry ground towards the vehicle. The man's face was dirty and covered in dried blood, but Luke was sure it was Jake. Or was it Lucas? The bar-girl was certain his name had been Lucas. One thought ran through his head; we need to rescue him. But as quick as it entered his head, the memory of his angry dad lurched forward. His legs turned weak under him. I'm not a hero.

Ruby pulled on his hand. "We need to follow him," she mouthed.

He wasn't able to save him, not yet, but they could follow him. He settled back to watch once again on trembling legs. Luke wondered where Lisa was and hoped she was safe. His hand brushed over his pocket, and he remembered the fingernail and the lump of flesh. A sudden sickening moment of realization dawned on him. He turned to Ruby and Petey and, more certain than he'd ever been of anything, he said, "He's turning them into paint."

11

I wake up somewhere else again. In my dream, I had been falling in the dark. The shadow had gotten me in Jake's body.

I've got no headache, although I feel I should have. The pastel shades of pink on the walls, make me want to throw-up. Where is Jake, did that thing taken him? What is it, and why is it after me? Can I sit back knowing that because of me, Jake might die–if he is still alive? I sense that he's alive.

I've no time for trivial things like playing 'Guess Who' today. I sit. On the side of the bed are a pink diary and a purple fountain pen. I pick up the diary; it has shiny white petals falling down the front. Well, I guess I'm a teenage girl. I want, no, I need to write everything from yesterday before the memories waver and change.

I write about Bug; I write about the willow tree; I write about the missing boy, and I write the name from the painting in capital letters. T. R WHYTE. I doodle a little picture of the symbol from the tree and the painting at the bottom of the page.

Once I have it all down, I'm relieved. Writing things down always helps clear my mind and put things into order. On the sister page, I write, To do. I scan my mind, trying to remember the name of the little boy on the missing posters. Ben James? Yes, it sounds right, and I can always double-check when I walk into town; those missing posters were everywhere.

Find Ben James. What next?

Bug. At the thought of his name a sadness comes over me, I hadn't known him for long, but we were like kindred spirits. Find Bug.

Jake, he was in this mess because of me. Find Jake.

And, lastly, adding to my amazing unknown skills of finding missing people. Find T. R Whyte.

Shit, that's some list. Where do I start? I know one place I won't start. From today, I am no longer a card-holding library goer. Yesterday was a day of reaction; today I will be proactive. I've changed bodies. Whatever was trying to (and ultimately got me); didn't know about my random body-switching; otherwise, it wouldn't have knocked me out.

I'm in the perfect disguise. Still, some clothes won't go a miss. I'm pretty sure a girl in her underwear asking questions about missing people is a solid way to lose my incognito disguise pretty darn fast. If I wasn't in such a rush to get out there investigating, I might take more notice of this body's silky white skin and toned stomach. I am, after all, a man in a woman's body. Alas, such carnal observations will have to wait until I solve this mystery: find Bug, find Ben James, find Jake, find the artist T.R. Whyte, oh, and find my sweet-ass little body. Fuck!

Luckily, a girl's bedroom is a girl's bedroom (and I've been in a few in my time). I climb out of bed and find all the usual stuff in all the usual places, including knickers, a bra, a pair of faded jeans and a plain white top. Out the window, I see a landscaped rear garden with a lush green lawn that is surrounded by an Indian sandstone patio. At the far end, a white metal table and four chairs sit empty on a raised decking area. A rose-gold iPhone 11 Pro is plugged in on the desk charging. I unplug the cord, and the time flashes up on the screen, 10.11am.

Downstairs, the house is empty. It's decorated in a modern chic-style with a stunning feature fireplace and black marble hearth and a grey-wood polished floor. The brown soft-leather sofas and chairs look like they're worth more than my flat back in Cambridge. Everything is spotless and open plan. The uber-modern kitchen has a massive black granite central island and worktops. A piece of paper lays in the middle of the central island.

Morning Brooke,
I know it's the holidays, and you're enjoying your time away from uni, but please can you load the dishwasher for us this morning and polish downstairs?
Try not to spend all your money at the pub later!
Love you,
Mum and dad.

Bright sunshine sparkles through the black-framed bifold doors that run across the entirety the back of the house dazzling on the polished tiled floor. Brooke; it's a beautiful name, the name of a girl I can imagine dating, although I'm not sure how her obviously successful parents would react to her bringing someone like me home?

A fancy black coffee machine with silver taps and buttons sits on one of the black-flecked granite work surfaces, and next to it is a metal stacker full of Nespresso-style pods. I pick the double espresso pod, find a mug and get out Brooke's iPhone while the smell of brewed coffee fills the air. I think about the symbol, and hum, 'Don't fear the reaper'.

Unlocking the iPhone, using her fingerprint, I open up Chrome and try my best to describe the symbol in the search bar. I type sideways figure of eight with lines. I change the search to images, and the page fills with figures of eight on their sides, but with no lines above. Under one image, I read the figure eight is the symbol of infinity. I search again, sideways figure eight monster—nothing comes up.

The coffee machine beeps. I go back to it, pick up the cup, and bring it to the central island. I sit on one of the wooden stools and take a swig. It's intense and hot. I stare out the bifold doors to the massive garden, and the phone vibrates in my hand. A text! I read it.

Hey, babe, what time you coming over? ;)

Fuck that; I have no intention of getting fucked today more than yesterday. I close the message and re-open Chrome; I type, sideways figure eight with a cross. Bingo! The second photo on the right is it! I click on the image to open the link.

The symbol is the Leviathan Cross. I read through the article. The Knights Templar created it—skilled fighters who protected pilgrims during the Crusades who are also the lead characters in a thousand-and-one conspiracy theories. The symbol is a mix of the upside-down cross and the infinity symbol. The Church of Satan later adopted it as their own. What was it doing on the willow tree and Whyte's painting?

Clicking through article after article only helps confuse me. The history of that time seems to have been lost amongst conspiracies, confusion, and missing pieces. Cross-referencing the search with the name T. R Whyte doesn't help. Although, I see some similar paintings to the one in the Baron Burghley. I click through and find a brief bio of Whyte on a website called Flickr. Nothing useful, though.

I make myself another coffee and search for Ben James. As expected, with a missing child, there are page after page of articles. That thing on the High Street wasn't him, I knew it. But, it was wearing his likeness. I read through the local newspaper article about the boy. He had been on a beach with his grandad, who was also his legal guardian, and had simply disappeared. One minute, he was building sandcastles by the shore, and the next, he was gone. A search party was created, and they went around the entire circumference of the reservoir, some 23 miles, and the reservoir itself was searched by private, public, and rescue boats. Nothing.

I watch a video interview with his grandad, and I'm almost brought to tears. Ben is an orphan; his parents' died in a car accident a year ago, and his grandad, himself a widower, had taken him in.

God, I miss my grandpa. Please, don't let him fade away while I'm stuck here.

I need to visit Westford Water, see where the boy, Ben, disappeared.

It's another warm day; school kids on their holidays ride skateboards and bikes filling the parks, paths, and roads. Good for them; most of the kids I know are going goggle-eyed watching YouTube and playing Fortnite back home. Even my nephews, both seven, spend more time online than outside.

Brooke doesn't have a driver's license or a car, so I approach the bus station from St. Peters' Hill. I walk past a pair of old gates standing alone with no fence. To the side is a podium. I cross over and read the writing. The gates belong to the old priory of St. Peters' that no longer stands there.

The bus station has three dark blue buses parked away from the main bays and the cafe area. People of all ages wait under plastic shelters, taking shelter from the scorching sun. I go from bay to bay, reading the timetables until I find the one for Westford Water. It's due in ten minutes'. I take a seat on one of the wooden benches overlooking the Pink Flamingo pub and the square with the tall monolith. The smell of bacon and sausages and coffee wafts through the bus station from the cafe.

Using Brooke's phone, I research Westford Water. I click on the first link. They created the reservoir in 1975, when six-to-seven square kilometers of the local valley were flooded. The reservoir is the largest human-made reservoir in Western Europe and was created to provide more water for the local area. It engulfed two villages; Nether Hambleton and Middle Hambleton. The former, I remember from the painting in the Baron Burghley. I look up as a man takes a seat next to me on the bench. I carry on reading.

Unpopular with the locals, especially historians, the flooding of both villages was frowned upon as during the original excavations, several Roman settlements with archaeological value were found. I wonder about the villagers who lost their homes and about what was in the ground when the valley was flooded–the idea of families packing up all their belongings and losing their land seems impossible nowadays. What secrets have they buried? Two whole villages flooded, both with Roman remains in the ground, surely they would have seen the historical importance and waited before flooding the area?

The main image used by most websites of the reservoir was of Hambleton Church; the only building saved from demolition because of the public outcry from when they announced they would destroy it too. Originally named St. Matthew's Church, it has been standing since 1760, built on top of the foundations of older buildings dating back to the 14th century. It looks like it wouldn't be out of place in Venice or Athens.

A walkway of jagged rocks and boulders the size of TVs lead out into the reservoir where the church stands. Its bottom half has been swallowed by the reservoir, with the ground floor now starting where I imagine the windows to the first floor had been. From the side, four large windows disperse themselves across the yellow stone building–which looks like the same stone used at the library and throughout Westford.

Another photo shows a bride and groom and helps me estimate the height of the church to be around 20 feet. An unusual tower rises from the end deepest in the reservoir. The tower is taller than the main building. Round columns hold up a roof that looks like it belongs in Rome. At the top of the tower is an egg-shaped stone carving with frills around the middle. At the base of the tower, and across the diameter of the roof, is a short wall with chess piece pawns holding up the stone slab top. As I flick through the pictures, there is one building it reminds me of–the library in Westford. I glance up; the man is staring out over the bus bays. I carry on reading, more interested in history than I've ever been before.

There's no doubting its beauty, especially in the pictures when the church reflects on the still water creating a beautiful reverse image, but there's something else, something not right. I can't believe that people would get married there. If I were to get married, and at this moment in time that looks as likely as Man City getting relegated, it wouldn't be there.

The bus pulls in with a cloud of smoke from its exhaust. I get in line and board the bus paying with Brooke's contactless card and take a seat towards the back. I look out the dirty window. The man is still sitting there. Someone has drawn a smiley face in the dust. Now he's looking at me. The bus pulls away from the station. All the time, the man continues to stare at me.

Stone houses, tall churches, and traffic give way to the green and yellow fields as we leave Westford and into the next county. I'm tapping my leg against the red floor, and a fellow passenger gives me a clenched smile. This is the first time I've tried to leave Westford since my first attempt, forty-nine days ago.

That day I tried to get the train first, but everything went against me, including cancellations because of high winds, and even a live wire on the line. After three-hours at Westford train station, I turned around and headed across the meadows to the bus station. The bus I got on that day broke down halfway up the hill leading past the Monk hotel towards the golf club and the motorway. Today, I was expecting much of the same, but as we got further away from Westford, I stop tapping my foot and enjoy the views.

The bell dings, and a little old lady gets off. I see the Shell garage and the large warehouses behind to my right before we skim through Great Beckton, and turn off before getting on the motorway. An American-style diner sits on the right, looking out of place in the countryside, and then we're on rural roads. We speed up, brake, accelerate, and stop, as other cars approach on the narrow country roads. I bounce off my seat when we go over a bump and then shoot forward, missing the red metal pole of the seat in front of me by an inch, when we brake sharply to avoid a red Fiesta coming towards us in the middle of the road.

Houses appear on both sides as we enter Athelney, a larger-than-average village. Stone cottages with thatched roofs and flowers to the front, sit alongside enormous new properties with large driveways. We pass the pub on the right and onto a busy main road, before leaving houses behind and venturing into the countryside.

I see a brown road sign with the words Westford Water on it as I stare out the window to my left-hand side, waiting for my first glance of the reservoir. We're about to go past the turning the brown sign is pointing towards, as I press the red stop button at the last moment and make my way clumsily to the front of the bus. The bus driver shakes his head at me as he opens the doors with a mechanical whoosh. I get off; he closes the doors and drives off before I can say thanks.

I walk on the grass verge to the side of the road. There's no path. I don't know where I'm going or how long the verge is. I still can't see the reservoir, and I don't have a clue how far away the bloody thing is. After ten minutes of walking, I round a corner and it appears like a mirage as if from nowhere. As I shield my eyes from the sunlight reflecting off the water, I understand why I haven't seen it till now.

The fields running towards the water are ever so slightly raised, like the lip of a cup and only now that I'm higher up, can I see into the reservoir. The views are breathtaking; it looks Jurassic, untouched by man. I exhale at the views over to the other side of the reservoir. To my left, over an up-and-over gate, is a long winding footpath with no end in sight. I follow the original road into a car park. Signs point to a gift shop, play park and the beachfront. This is where little Ben James went missing. Sand has mixed with the dust and gravel from the car park and on a warm day like today, it feels like a shitty Dubai.

As I approach the beach area, I notice the tip of St. Matthew's Church. I round the corner and see its half-submerged body peeking out of the water. Now I'm here, I realize I haven't appreciated just how large the reservoir is. Black and white posters of Ben adorn fence posts, tree trunks and the walls of the buildings. Considering the warmth of the day, the car park is empty besides two cars. The play park sits sad and lonely beyond.

Standing outside a red brick building is a tall old man I recognize; Ben's grandad. He's bigger than I expected from the video. His face is old and friendly, but there's deep grief etched into the lines around his mouth and eyes. I know that look too well.

He looks ten years older than the man in the video. The similarity to my own grandad is creepy. He holds a wad of paper ready to give to anyone who comes past. Now I understand why it's empty; it isn't that the boy has gone missing, although that is part of it, it's because this old man reminds everyone about it every day. People like to get on with their lives and forget the terrible things they see, however, if someone is there reminding them, they disappear pretty quickly.

I walk over to the man and he looks up, his mouth agape. Remembering that I'm a teenage girl in jeans and a short top, I chuckle to myself. His grandson is missing but still, he can't help that old-time libido; maybe a little blue pill is working its way through his system.

My sick sense of humour is how I cope. I remember making a very inappropriate joke (about an old man, a father and a daughter at a park,) once at my grandad's care home. It didn't go down well, except with the residents. The mind works in mysterious ways and mine turns dirty in sad situations.

As I get closer, I see his old eyes are watery, whether from tears or the reservoir air I don't know. He looks pathetic and I feel my guts wrench up and down and then side-to-side.

"Hi." I say.

He smiles at me. "Hi, please, take one of these." He hands me the poster which is already etched into my mind.

"Thank you, I'm so sorry." he looks lost. "You're his grandad, aren't you? I saw you on a video?"

"Yes." he holds out his hand. "Gerry, nice to meet you...?" I shake it, noticing how dry and cold it is.

"Brooke, likewise. I don't mean to pry, but have you heard anything yet?"

His eyes tear up. He dabs at them with one of his dry hands. "You're not another reporter are you?"

"No sir, I'm just a local gu– girl. I'm back from uni, and I saw you on the news and I wanted to see if I could help at all?" He takes a step back from me and looks me up and down before moving forward again.

"Well, that is so kind of you Brooke, it was Brooke, wasn't it? Sorry, my mind isn't what it used to be." He puts two fingers against the side of his head.

"Yes, and you're Gerry, right?"

"That's the one." He smiles. The lines around his eyes and mouth creak. "Ben was such a good boy, his parents would have been so proud, I'm sure they wou–" Tears start to fall. "I'm sor–" He starts before more tears flow down his grey stubbled cheeks. I move forward to stop him from falling to the floor. He lowers himself to the ground, where he brings his legs up to his chin, and wraps his arms around himself and sobs. It reminds me of videos of 9/11 victims.

I lower myself down next to him. To have the chance to talk to Ben's grandad has never occurred to me, and despite the risk of coming off too strong, I decide I can't take the chance to not ask what I know I shouldn't ask.

"What happened? Did you see anything, well strange?"

He turns his head, his watery blue eyes look at me, as if seeing me for the first time. "Who are you?" He shuffles an inch away from me.

"I just want to help."

Gerry looks out over the fields and the reservoir. "He loved coming here, Ben that is." I nod. "He loved building sandcastles, playing near the shore, throwing rocks and watching them splash–never near the ducks or birds though, he would give stern looks to anyone who threw a stone too close to a duck." He chuckled to himself. "Ever since his Mum and Dad, well you know... all I wanted was for him to be happy. He was too young for that to happen and they were wonderful parents. Mary, that was my daughter, I see so much of her in Ben." He stops and looks at the ground between his feet. He shakes his head. "It's not right, a little boy, so happy shouldn't just be gone, and that's what he is you know, gone." He breathes in deeply. "A little boy shouldn't have to be raised by his grandad, it's not fair on him. I do my best, but I wish Mary and Jack were here, they'd be so proud of him, I know they would. He was only four, he'd just started at nursery and if you could have seen the look on his face when he brought home pictures he'd painted. One day he brought home pictures of his mum and dad he'd drawn. I cried myself to sleep that night, but he was so happy."

Jesus, I'm nearly crying myself. I picture the little boy from the photos at nursery; when the teachers say let's paint a picture of your family, and he looks around and sees the other children all drawing pictures of their mums and dads; painting happy smiles and curly hair onto blue-eyed faces, he would have to make them up in his mind and the saddest part is that he has no-one to give it to when he gets home, but his kind grandad. No wonder Gerry comes here every day.

"I really am so sorry," I say, laying a hand on his shoulder. He sobs into his hands and I sit next to him; my hand never leaves his shoulder. I think about my nephews back home, and my sister, and my mum and dad and my grandad whose memory is fading from Alzheimer's. Will he ever be able to tell me a story again?

After a few minutes', he seems to have gotten all the tears out and he turns to me. "Why did you ask if I saw anything weird?"

I look him in the eye. "It just seems like a strange situation, people don't just vanish. Sometimes things happen and can't be explained and it scares people to say anything in case people think they're crazy... trust me, I know," There was something here, something he had told no one else.

"Will you come with me?" he asks. "To the place where he went missing–I haven't been since that first day."

"Of course I will." I stand up and dust off my jeans.

"Give an old man a hand?" Gerry puts his hand up towards me.

I heave him up off the grass and we walk towards the beach. To an onlooker, we would look like granddaughter and grandfather. He offers me his arm and I take it. As we walk, he talks. He tells me about the morning Ben disappeared.

66

12

They had breakfast at home, Ben ate Cheerios and Gerry drank a black coffee with two shortcake biscuits; his favourite. Once breakfast was finished, and the pots were soaking in the sink, they went out into the back garden. Gerry pulled weeds from the flowerbeds—so beautiful when his wife had been here, full of colour with sunflowers, multi-coloured daisies and bougainvillea, but now sad-looking things that the weeds attacked every morning; still, he kept on looking after them, they were hers. Sweat soaked the back of his cotton shirt.

Gerry helped Ben put on a pair of oversized gardening gloves that hung off his little fingers, and filled up a yellow watering can from the rusty outdoor tap under the kitchen window. Ben followed his grandad around the garden and poured water where his grandad pointed. Soon bored, Ben picked up a little blue metal trowel and set about digging a hole in one of the empty flowerbeds.

After their morning in the garden, they went back inside and watched some TV. Gerry made them lunch; cheese and ham white bread sandwiches with the crusts cut off. Ben laughed at a bright cartoon with a talking monster truck and a host of other characters, while Gerry read the paper that the paperboy delivered this morning. He was one of the few people left on his road that still used the paperboy from the village shop. Ben giggled, and Gerry poked his head out from behind his paper. He smiled as he studied his happy little grandson. He marvelled how his eyes were so similar to his daughters, while the silky soft, pink-white skin was so clear, without imperfections. He had a little button nose that he would crinkle just before he laughed.

He laid the newspaper down on his lap and asked, "Hey, Kiddo, what do you say we go to the beach?"

Ben smiled a big goofy grin and jumped up and ran to him.

"Is that a yes?"

Ben nodded and climbed up Gerry. "Yes, grandad, please, please, please." Gerry opened his arms and leaned in for a cuddle. They fell back into the chair, both of them snorting with laughter. Ben snuggled into a loving bearhug, he squirmed and giggled as tried to get away from Gerry who was attempting to tickle him. Gerry let him go and put him down on the floor.

"Okay, where are your sandals?"

Ben looked to the left, and to the right, and then span around in the centre of the room, before falling down on his backside. He looked at his grandad, and laughed again.

"I'll find them then, shall I?" Gerry said.

Sandals found, Ben and Gerry left the bungalow. Ben carried a bright yellow bucket and a blue spade and they left through the path that led between the colourful flowers onto the main road.

They held hands as they walked. Gerry leaned over to peer at the ants and snails that Ben found on the path. The little boy picked up small rocks and sticks and put them in his bucket to keep for later.

Gerry told Ben stories about his Mum as they walked—about how one time she'd chased a rabbit into a field and had scratched her leg on an old fence post and needed a shot, and how another time, she had fallen out of one of the big oak trees and knocked out one of her front teeth.

Ben would listen raptly to the stories. His little face turned up to look at his grandads—looking at him as if he was a shooting star, with his mouth wide open. Gerry hoped he enjoyed listening to the stories about his mum and dad— he thought it was important to let their memory live on and not hide him away from the pain, like they were never here. The stories made him happy, Ben said.

This story reminds me of my grandfather. We had a similar relationship. I remember a bucket and spade and the love of stories shared. It had been six-months ago when mum had called out of the blue. Over the last six months, his memory has gone from bad to worse. Some days he'll be in the room, other days a shell of the man I love. No one else visits him, but I do. I'd take the hours' drive every Wednesday after work. Sometimes he'd remember me, other times he wouldn't.

Gerry lives only twenty minutes' walk from the beach at Westford Water, and it's a lovely walk, full of natural wonder; animals, trees and birds that you rarely see anywhere else. When they flooded the Gwash Valley, they created new habitats for these animals, which is why it's such a unique and wonderful place to live, he tells me. It isn't unusual for crane's, with their long thin necks and skinny legs, to fly over the house or to hear a Cuckoo's call in the evening when sitting on the front porch with a can of beer; Ben tucked up safely in bed. Gerry started talking again.

He and Ben had walked past the cemetery on the right where Ben's nan was buried. Sometimes they sat down on one of the benches and looked out over the fields and cows and horses, but not that day; Ben was in too much of a rush to get to the beach. They followed the path and stopped and looked both ways before crossing the road to the entrance to the lane that led to the car park and the beach.

Gerry hoisted Ben up onto his shoulders, for safety, as the road wound around and a car could appear out of nowhere. Ben reached down with his soft hands and gently stroked his grandad's stubble. Gerry's voice breaks remembering this moment.

"I see the beach," Ben shouted from above. He was so excited, he always was when we came to the beach–that's one reason I stayed here after they were all gone.

The car park was busy that day, there were two large tourist buses and at least fifty cars. You could hear the happy screams of children playing in the park. Young families sat outside the little ice cream shop built into one of the buildings. People milled around the front of two red-brick hexagonal buildings, one was a toilet and the other a gift shop; "If I remember right," he said. "That's where Ben got his bucket and spade from."

"Where first?" Gerry asked Ben, who was looking around wild-eyed. "Park or beach?"

Ben pointed, with a hand that was holding a yellow plastic spade down, to the beach.

"Beach it is."

Gerry let go of Ben's hand, and let him run to the beach while he followed a little behind. The warm sun and the gentle breeze felt good on his skin and the sound of happy children and families made him happy to be alive–a feeling rare at nighttime when Ben was asleep and he was all alone in the big bungalow with only his memories.

Ben had been by the shore picking up rocks and placing them carefully into his bucket; his face a picture of concentration with his nose wrinkled and his eyebrows furrowed. Gerry had sat down a few feet away and stared out over the reservoir at the sailboats that glided around on the water. A stone monolith stood in the middle of the reservoir and he wondered what it was for? Across the shining, glinting water he could make out the tower of Hambleton Church.

"Grandad, look what I've found." Ben skipped to his grandad, and pulled something from his bucket. Gerry took it in his hand and inspected it. "What is it?" Ben asked.

He spread the thing over the palms of both of his hands. It was dry and flaky, an aged-newspaper colour with glassy see-through concentric circles running all the way along. He took hold of it from each end between his forefinger and thumb and stretched it out. He raised it against the bright blue sky. At first, he thought it was a dried up dishevelled condom, but looking at it stretched out, it was something familiar. He brought it up to his nose; it smelled of rotten eggs. He craned his neck and looked at the reptile house at the top of the car park.

"It's reptile skin. Ben, where did you find it?" Ben pointed to a dark hole near where the waves lapped gently against the sand. "It's mighty big though?"

Gerry took Ben's hand, and they walked to the wet sand and kneeled by the hole. There was more reptile skin inside. "Mighty big," Gerry mumbled. "We should report it." Maybe one of their snakes had escaped–but wouldn't they have reported it and closed the beach?

Ben dug deeper into the hole, pulling out the reptile skin as he went. A dry pile of dead skin built up next to him. Gerry thought they looked like a heap of mummy bandages from the old black and white horror films he grew up watching. "Look grandad, something else," Ben said, poking at it with his plastic spade.

"Can I borrow that, please, buddy," Gerry asked, pointing at the spade.

Gerry dug; the sand turned into fine crystallised rocks the size of tiny diamonds. Something large lay flat across the bottom. He cleared away the sand and saw a thin off-white surface, not shiny, but dull.

It ran the entirety of the bottom of the hole, which was at least a two-foot across. It looked like an eggshell with tiny dark spots and imperfections on it. He didn't want to pierce it, worried about what might be inside, so he grabbed Ben's hand and led him away from the hole and the pile of mummy-like bandages, which smelled rank in the hot sun. As they walked, he looked down at the ground afraid of what was below his feet.

"Wait, grandad, I forgot my bucket."

"Okay, run back and get it, I'll be right here." Gerry looked up towards the car park and he saw the sloping grey roof of the bug zoo and the bright green sign that sat on top. "What have you lost?"

Impatient and wanting to get to the zoo, he turned round, "Be–" Ben wasn't there. The yellow bucket lay on its side next to the hole. But Ben wasn't there. "Ben?" he shouted, glancing up and down the beach, shielding his eyes with his hand from the sunlight. "Ben, this isn't funny, where are you?" No answer, except for the giggles of other children… and the sound of the lapping waves on the shore.

"Ben, you get here right now!" People on the beach stood and looked at him. He ran to the bucket and the hole, kicking up sand behind him. The spade lay to the side too. "Ben?" He picked up the spade and studied it stupidly as if it would tell him where he was. He ran down to the water's edge. There was no sign of Ben. Looking back towards the car park, he saw a little boy with the same blonde hair. "Ben!" The mother and child looked back at him. It wasn't Ben. The hole, he thought.

With two great strides he stood over it. He peered down. Did something move underneath that egg shell? Using the spade, he started hammering into the thing. The plastic spade snapped. He knelt, one leg either side, and started hammering at it with his fists. It was hard. A hand touched him on his shoulder and he turned, praying it was Ben.

"Mister, are you okay?" a young boy asked. He looked about fifteen.

"I can't find my grandson."

The teenage boy turned and shouted to his friends; a group of twelve boys and girls all in swimming gear. "His grandson's missing, will you help me look?" The kids in the group nodded and ran over. Gerry felt the first tears coming, but he held them back. "He's four years old, he has dark blonde hair and big brown eyes." he looked up to the sky and blinked. "He was wearing a blue and white horizontal striped tee-shirt and red shorts. Please, he lost his mum and dad… and I'm supposed to look after him."

Gerry stops before we get to the edge of the water, and turns to me. "The original teenager put his hand on my shoulder, 'We'll help, we'll find him,' he said, and looked at another teenager, I remember him because he had bright blue hair, 'Run to the ice cream shop and tell them a little boy is missing,' he said. The kid with blue hair set off straight away and then the teenager turned to me and asked, 'What's your name, sir?' I told him and he introduced himself, damn, but I forget his name, now."

"After that, everyone stopped playing; families, children, teenagers, and even the shop owners shut their shops and came down to help look. The police turned up, and they organised search parties out onto the reservoir using private boats." He looks at me with tears in his eyes as we stand side-by-side at the water's edge. The reservoir is calm. "There must have been over a hundred people on this side of the reservoir, and they told me even more along the whole perimeter. But there was no sign of him. We checked cars before they left, and they checked CCTV–But there was no sign of him." I watch this grandad reliving the worst day of his life all over again.

"I'm sorry."

"The search continued once it got dark. All along the water's edge, for miles torchlights lit up the water. But there was no sign of him." He picked up a rock and absently threw it into the reservoir.

"Eventually the police offered to drive me home. I didn't want to go, but they insisted. The next day about fifty people showed up, including the young man and his friends. The next day twenty and then just me and the police. People wanted to help, but they didn't know what else they could do. I did that video for the local news and the major dailies picked up the story… Liam, yes, Liam, that was his name, and his friends were ever so helpful, they've made me believe in the goodness of people again. Liam and his friend Jonny went around all the villages and Westford putting up posters." He puffed out his chest.

"I saw."

"Good kids. Anyway, I never mentioned to anyone about the reptile skin and that egg. I figured with the amount of people in the search party someone either filled the hole in or it got filled in naturally. I tried to find it again, digging deep with a proper shovel from my garden, but it was gone, same for the reptile skin. That's weird isn't it?"

"It's odd, yes. Did you say you thought you saw it move?"

"Underneath the white shell, yes, something moved."

We stare out over the reservoir, and I think about everything this man has gone through: losing his wife, his daughter and her husband... and now his only grandson. I can't even imagine what he must feel, and it makes me ashamed of my own small insignificant problems.

My family is alive; my mum and dad are at home, probably gardening, much like Gerry did with Ben, and my sister's at work teaching at the same primary school we went to. What have I been doing? Drinking too much after work, not calling or even talking to them, and why? Because they want better for me than to drink my days away in a blur after I finish a job that is conning people for money? Would my grandad be proud of me?

Standing next to Gerry, overlooking the sparkling reservoir in front of us, I make a pact with myself. I will find Ben and return him. If I can do one good thing in my life, this will be it. Then, just maybe, I will be able to make amends with my own family.

Something took Ben, much like something took Bug. I will find both of them, I will keep on searching for as long as it takes. I know where to start: T.R Whyte.

13

Gerry and I walk the winding road, surrounded by fields and hedgerows with nests tucked safely inside, and back towards the main road where the bus dropped me off. It's late afternoon now. I stayed with Gerry down the reservoir handing out flyers to the few stragglers that came by. We walk in silence, another day with no news for Gerry, and I can see it's taking its toll. His hands shake at his sides. He offers for me to go back to his house for a drink, but I tell him I need to catch a bus back to town. I need to think.

There's a link, that much I'm sure. The willow tree, Westford Water, the symbol, Ben, Bug and the artist. I rub my temples as I sit on the bus, trying to put everything into some order. Tired, I lay my head back against the leather headrest on the bus and close my eyes.

PART TWO

1 JESS

These four walls were driving Jess crazy. Cream-coloured walls. It had been two weeks since the Priory. Brown curtains. After she'd been found, her ankle broken and covered in blood, she was put on bed watch, first at the hospital, and now at home. They were officially worried about her mental health–whatever the fuck that meant. All she knew was, if she didn't escape this bedroom soon, she really would go cuckoo.

She was suspicious of each doctor that came into the room–wondering if the creature had changed form and come back to finish her. But perhaps they were right? Maybe she'd had what they called 'A break from reality.' There was her lost day on Sunday. The day after, she'd gone to sleep like normal after watching reruns of Friends on Netflix and woken up, not on Sunday, but Monday. Today was Wednesday. Wasn't it?

She hadn't shared this with her husband, Mike. Jess had guided the conversation with her kids and husband, and they told her about the strange chats they'd had with her on that missing day. They thought she hadn't seemed herself, but blamed it on the painkillers. This morning, she'd flicked through her mobile upon waking and saw two worrying news stories; one about two missing men, and an update on that poor missing boy.

Rosemary had disappeared. Jess wondered if Rosemary Eve was involved with these latest disappearances. Was it Rosemary Eve, or was the real Rosemary Eve wasting away in the creature's bowels–like Lydia? There had been no missing posters or social media posts about Rosemary. She was gone and forgotten. But not to Jess.

Something was very wrong in this town. She had taken the time to do some research while laid up in bed. A laptop lay next to her on the bed-tray that Mike had bought her the day after the accident. It was ugly, with autumn flowers and leaves printed on it, meant for an older person, but she didn't mention that to him; he seemed so proud that he had done something so thoughtful. He had been sleeping on the sofa downstairs for the past two weeks, scared he would roll over and hurt her otherwise. There was an old silver HP laptop next to her, which took forever to turn on. She was surprised Mike hadn't replaced it. She'd been working on a timeline of events and gathering any information she could find of weird occurrences and missing persons in Westford. The list was more extensive than she had expected. A lot of the strange events happened within the last year. Never two as close together as the little boy and the two missing men, though. There'd been a sinkhole near the Red Lion, then the blue algae that closed Westford Water, followed by the disappearance of her friend Lydia, and now these three further disappearances. The more she looked into it, the more Jess was sure they were all connected. She looked at her leg in the white cast raised off the bed with pillows.

She'd hoped she'd be back on her feet sooner than she had been. Next to the door, she saw the matte-grey crutch that awaited her, but she didn't mind that. She'd be able to leave the bedroom, the house even. The severity of the break of her ankle shocked the doctors. Multi-colour doodles now covered her white cast; cute drawings from Hugo and Billy. Both of them had sat on her bed with her, picking the right colour before starting their renderings. More than once, one of them would lean on her leg, and she'd clench her teeth. "Sorry, Mummy," one of the boys would say, and she'd pretend that it didn't feel like her bone was being ripped out through her flesh again.

Jess wanted to kill the creature, something like that couldn't survive. It angered her that it was still out there. If it had moved on from women to children, she would kill it; even if it hadn't, she'd kill it. Her research provided her with a list of creatures from myths that matched Rosemary's description. She'd suspended her disbelief, having seen the creature for herself, and wanted to hunt. She wanted to hunt for the parents' who couldn't or wouldn't.

Hugo and Billy came running into her room, and she smiled.

"Hey boys, come and give Momma a kiss."

They climbed the king-size oak bed. Both boys had the softest skin she'd ever felt. Their smiles were as homely as a blanket and a fire when it was raining outside. Two sets of big brown eyes looked at her as they nuzzled into her chest. She put her arms around both of them and kissed their heads. They smelled of bubblegum bubble-bath and chicken nuggets, and both had sticky red ketchup around their mouths, which she wiped off with her sleeve, ignoring the grotesque flashback of Rosemary's mouth covered with Lydia's blood.

"Mummy's escaping her bedroom this afternoon, boys, are you excited?"

"Yay," they both shouted, bumping against her leg.

"Take it easy with me though." She stroked their heads. "Mummy's still got a poor leg, okay?"

Two sets of chocolate eyes looked up at her. "We will Mummy."

Yeah, right, she thought as she felt more bumps and kicks from them both. "Now, have you both had lunch, where's your daddy?" With that, Mike appeared at the doorway, his face covered in dark stubble and black rings under his eyes. He looked like he'd been up for days'.

"Fed and watered," he said with a smile. Both boys jumped from the bed and ran past Mike out onto the landing. "They're exhausting," he said, not unkindly. She smiled, picked up the tray-table and the laptop. She switched it on, and a picture of two men, one young and one older with dreadlocks, stared back at her. Mike walked out of the room.

"Where are you?"

The pills from the morning made Jess tired. She slept fitfully in the early afternoon; her dreams full of maggots and forked tongues and blood and flesh. She was back at the Priory, only it was dusk, and the sky was full of pinks and reds and oranges and wispy grey clouds. Around the side, she saw a van with a name on the side, but in her dream, she couldn't read it. Another creature was there, alike, but not the same as Rosemary—the same way a Poodle and a Terrier are both dogs. She watched as it pulled two bodies behind it. A silent scream escaped her mouth as her two beautiful boys, covered in maggots with their legs gone, were dragged and dumped into the van. She tried to move, but roots from the ground locked her into place. Her skin itched, and she saw fleas the size of ladybugs crawling over her—stopping and drinking her blood as they went. A black snake, its forked tongue flickering in the air, slithered on the ground towards her. She felt it slide inside her jeans. Its cold, dry scales rubbing against her thighs. Its rattle tail flicked against her crotch, and she tried to scream again; this time, maggots fell out of her mouth, landing in a moving, trifle of foul-smelling decayed flesh. The snake moved up under her blouse; she felt its wet forked tongue snatch at her nipple as it slid under her bra and out the top of her blouse and down her throat.

She woke in the bedroom that had become her home. The curtains were drawn. She looked at her watch; it was 1.13pm. The house was silent. Had Mike taken the boys out? She sat, careful not to use her leg, and grabbed the laptop. The screen lit up the room with blue light. She minimized the pages, which showed pictures of the two missing men and the missing boy, and she opened up a new tab. She typed Westford Priory into the search bar and clicked enter.

Her screen filled with page upon page of answers to her search. She'd done this search before, but she knew she'd missed something. She clicked through article after article, hoping to see what she hadn't seen before. Though her eyelids grew heavy, looking at the glowing screen, she found a scanned in page from an old book. Jess squinted to read the old-script writing.

It spoke about the Priory and St. Wilfrid. She read that St. Wilfrid had founded a monastery on the spot where the Priory now stood. St. Wilfrid? He was a Saint she'd never learned much about.

St. Wilfrid, a well-traveled and controversial saint from the seventh century and his followers, built the original monastery. It was destroyed in a Danish invasion and was later rebuilt, as a Priory, by William the Conqueror to atone for his sins. It is of Norman design and is now a Grade I listed building. It is said that a great secret lies buried.

These were details she already knew, well except the bit about St. Wilfrid, but it was in there somewhere, she knew it; the missing piece.

Maybe it wasn't the body text she needed; perhaps it was something else. She scrolled to find the author, seeing a squiggle of a signature, all loops, and hooks. It looked like T. R Whyte.

She Googled T. R Whyte, Westford, and after scrolling through to the second page, she found an image-list of paintings he had produced of Westford throughout his life. His first name was Theo.

A haunting illustration of the Priory caught her eye. There were no photos of the man himself, only a brief description on Flickr ,where for a small fee, you could use his pictures for magazine articles and blogs. She searched again, trying to find any details about the man himself. Was he still alive? Where did he live? Was he local? Nothing. She tried social media but wasn't surprised when again she found nothing.

Jess lay back in bed, the rush of finding a clue fading and tiredness seeping back into her veins. Those damn pain pills. She clicked on the illustration of the Priory, and it filled the screen. The picture looked like pen and watercolour. The contrast seemed to have increased. Trees and finger-like branches silhouetted against a moody, orange-brown sky. The details in the stonework looked almost photo-quality, and the shadows and the archways were so dark to be near enough black. The grass was a vivid green, jumping off the screen. It contrasted against the brooding quality of the sky and building. She knew it all started and ended at the Priory.

They stood around her bed as she tried to stand using the crutch for the first time. The curtains were open, and afternoon sunshine filled the room. Mike hovered just to the side, ready to catch her if she fell—he had tried to hold her under the armpit to help her up, but she shooed him off. The boys stood at the bottom of the bed, excited little smiles emanating from their faces.

She grimaced at the pain that came from within her doodled-on cast, but continued to slide her right leg off the bed. She picked up the crutch and swung the rest of her body to the side. Both legs lingered in the air. She put the crutch on the floor, followed by her first left leg, and stood.

Jess wobbled and held her right leg an inch off the ground. Mike reached out to steady her, and she let him. Once she had her balance, she looked up at Mike and nodded her head. He let go and followed closely behind as she hobbled out of the bedroom. Her boys followed.

On the landing, she looked down the steep stairs and then back towards Mike and the boys. Mike took a careful step past her and onto the top step. "I'll be right in front of you, okay?"

"Thanks, now if I fall, I'll take out both of us." She laughed.

Ambling, hopping on one leg, while holding the railing with one hand, the crutch in the other, she made her way down the stairs. At the bottom, sweating, she leaned on Mike and put her head against his chest. As tired and breathless as she was, it was nice to have back a bit of independence.

She'd always been independent, having moved out of her parent's house at seventeen with just the clothes on her back. Even as she was walking out the door, all they kept on saying was 'we'll see you later,' and, 'you'll be back,' not realizing that by saying those things, they only strengthened her resolve to make her way in life.

"Coffee?" she asked Mike. "I'm making."

After coffee and a late lunch, Mike took the boys to his parents for the rest of the afternoon so he could make up some time at work. Jess lounged around the living room and even hobbled out into the back garden and up the patio steps to the lawn. It was the first time she'd seen the downstairs of the house for weeks, and she was pleasantly surprised; sure, there were a few things, like the pots in the sink and the toys under the sofa, but otherwise, Mike had kept on top of the housework.

She looked at her mobile again; the time was 2.27pm. The bus came at 2.54pm. She'd promised Mike she would take it easy on her first day on her feet. The bus stop was half-a-mile or so from their house. If she set off now, she thought she could make it. She sat at the table in the kitchen, her good leg tapping away on the floor.

The clock on the kitchen wall ticked away in the background. It was an antique-style wall clock with roman numerals, a gift from his parents one Christmas, and it hung above the matching, metallic red toaster and kettle. All top-end appliances. The tick-tock was loud in the empty house. The minute hand ticked over just as the digital digit did on her phone. She grabbed her bag from the kitchen table, stood up, and made her way out the front door, locking it behind her.

Using her crutch, she made her way off the estate and down the road, passing garages, warehouses, and the quarry on the left. It didn't take long for her forearm to ache, but she could see the signpost and the bus stop just ahead near the zebra crossing across from the 'Welcome to Westford' sign.

Jess hadn't seen the bus go past, so she was sure she hadn't missed it–she hoped not anyway; she wasn't sure she would make it back up the hill. Her forearm pulsed and tensed. Jess reached the bus stop and reached out and held onto it for balance. The metal was warm. Two weeks in bed had made her more unfit than she already was. Although, she was sure she'd lost some weight because of restricting her meal sizes, added to the fact that Mike was a pretty shitty cook.

The bus arrived, and she climbed on and took a seat at the front in one of the disability seats. She couldn't remember the last time she'd ridden the bus, but it had changed little. Maroon faux-leather seats and horrible swirling blue and orange pattern fabric. Speckled light blue flooring and dust-covered windows.

She watched her home-town of Westford, as tree-lined streets and unnecessary SUVs flashed past. The few people she saw wandering the streets just out of the town centre, looked ominous and suspicious. Any one of them could be a creature, she thought. A few turned to stare as the bus passed: An older man with a little white border collie, two kids on bikes who had pulled over to the side of the road, an overweight man in a suit with white trainers, a skinny woman pushing a pushchair and the blonde wild-haired girl inside.

They passed Water Furlong–a thin cobble-stoned road that weaved its way down to the meadows–and approached the bus station from St Peter's Street with its row of terraced stone-fronted townhouses and dark alleyways. On the right, they passed a dollop of green land with a random stone pillar and iron gate with no walls on either side; and to the left, a grand tall building loomed large before they turned into the bus station.

She hobbled off the bus, down the steep hill to the square opposite the Pink Flamingo, with its weird monolith statue in the middle, which stretched high into the sky. To the right, the road flowed down to Bath Row and the meadows. She crossed and headed towards the high street, avoiding the hill up to Broad Leaf Square. She walked along the narrow path leading to the square, past rude people who ignored the fact she had a crutch on the single-file road. She smiled sarcastically at them as they passed.

Jess kept her head down, not wanting to be recognized for her photo in the local paper just after the incident. A couple smoked a cigarette outside the doors of one of the town's many pubs. The smoke she walked through made her crave a cigarette, like a junkie needing a fix; she hadn't smoked for over a year, but the smell still got her. The traffic lights turned red and beeped, and she crossed the road along with the noisy kids enjoying their summer holidays and the nattering women with pushchairs and the men in smart shirts and jeans who were always in a rush.

Entering the High street, it surprised her how little it had changed; sure, it had only been two weeks, but in her mind, that was two weeks for the creature to sink its teeth further into the town. Couples and families walked in groups, while professional-looking people rushed to pick up a late lunch from a shop, ready to go back to work and eat it at their desks. She hated the idea of her sons having a tedious desk job like their father in the future. Sure, it paid bills, but how do you get up every morning and do the same thing over and over again? She wanted more for her boys.

Hugo was an incredible story-teller for his age; she didn't know many three-year-olds who could invent their own stories on the spot. Sometimes when he climbed onto her bed, he would look up at her with those big chocolate eyes and say, "Once upon a time..." then he would be off, making up incredible stories about zombies and vampires. And, Billy... Billy was born to work with his hands. He was building Lego Technic from the age of two. Cranes that moved and whirred, wrecking balls swinging from them, and remote control cars that whizzed around her feet in the conservatory and on the driveway. She wouldn't let a generic materialistic life take over, turning them into 9-5 office drones. They had so much creativity; she didn't want it squashed by the school system.

She reached the T-junction, where only one-hundred years ago, horses and carts would wait before turning and going up the hill of Ironmonger Street. How different were the clothes shops and opticians now from then, she wondered? Market sellers still came to the town every Friday, closing off Almshouse Street that ran parallel to the High street. A fruit and veg stall was set up all week at the bottom of Ironmonger Street and yells of, 'A pound for a dozen,' filled the air as Jess carried on towards the library.

As she approached, she felt a chill come over her. She zipped up her jacket and hugged herself. Her stomach tied itself up in knots. There was a blackness in her mind eating away inside her. It reminded her of that day at the Priory. She hopped over to a wooden bench near the graveyard opposite the library and waited for it to pass.

The pyramid-shaped roof and columns loomed darkly over the rest of the High street. Its windows and limestone pillars reached out at awkward angles, like roots from a tree, and the bright blue sky filled with dense, grey clouds. No one else noticed the metamorphosis of the building, and she pulled her hand up to her mouth as she saw a young woman with two children–a boy and a girl–enter the building through its dark entrance. She almost called out to them, but they were already inside.

After five minutes, with her eyes closed and having gained control of her breathing, she felt herself again. The library appeared normal in the sunshine, but she wasn't going in there, not today. Where else could she go to research and track down Theo Whyte? The museum had been closed for years, and she was sure it was now a dance school or an Indian restaurant, she couldn't remember which.

She pulled out her phone, a new shiny silver Samsung Galaxy (Mike insisted on keeping up-to-date with technology, and she rarely argued if it meant a new phone every year). As she looked up, pondering what to type into the search bar, she saw the gallery opposite—worth a try.

Jess stood, balanced, and hobbled through the path that had been cut between the headstones in the graveyard.

The Gallery was adjoined to a hairdressers, and the women inside stared out at her as she passed the window. The door opened before she could push it herself and a man–not the type she would associate with a gallery–brushed past her on his way out. He turned and said, "Sorry."

She watched him carry on up the road towards the High Street. He wore tight, skinny jeans and a white tee-shirt that clung to his lean body. He was fixing or putting something into his back pocket. A bell chimed as she entered the Gallery, and the smell of oil paints and wood filled her, and she breathed in deep. She hadn't been into an art shop since she'd given up painting five years ago. She'd had talent, but no more than the average college student; mostly, she had painted as a release.

A kind-looking bespectacled man, around her dad's age, welcomed her from behind the counter. He was shuffling through some papers on the desk in front of him. "Afternoon, can I help you, Miss?" He said, looking up.

"Hi… Afternoon, how are you?" she said. Was two weeks enough to turn you into an imbecile when communicating with others, she wondered?

"I'm good, thank you, how can I help?"

Jess leaned on the counter, taking some weight off her crutch.

"Would you like a seat?" The man offered.

"That would be great. Thank you so much."

He pulled a seat from the counter, wheeling it around and through the gap between his desk and the wall. "There you go, Miss, now how can I help?"

"I'm looking for someone," she said as she sat down.

"Oh, well, we sell frames and supplies mostly, but I'll see if I can help. Who is it? A painter or an artist?"

"Yes, both, I believe. His name is, or was, Theo Whyte. I'm not sure if that's his rea–" She stopped talking, the man's face opened into an 'O,' his thin, grey moustache sagging to the sides.

"How odd, you're the second person who's asked about him today. Has he died or something. His paintings aren't exactly well-known or worth much!"

"Who else asked about him?" she asked, sitting forward in her chair.

"That young man, who you met on the way out–between you and me, he was a trifle odd–but he was very interested in Mr. Whyte."

"Did you get his name?"

"Sorry, Miss, he never mentioned it, and I didn't think to ask."

Jess sat back in the chair and looked outside the window. What were the odds? "What did you tell him?"

"Not a great deal, I'm afraid. We had a few of Mr. Whyte's paintings in the Gallery a while back. A collector bought them all at the start of the year." He sat down and leaned back in his chair, crisscrossing his fingers in front of him. "Regarding Mr. Whyte himself, there isn't a lot to know. He was a quiet man, always pleasant, but always on guard if you get my meaning? He always seemed so serious. He would pop in, and I would pay him any profit from his paintings, and then he would go again." He flicked through the dark blue leather diary in front of him. "Thinking about it, it has been a while since I last saw him. He hasn't even collected his money from the big deal earlier this year."

"Who bought his paintings? Can you tell me?" she asked.

"I'm afraid not, Miss, I keep all of those details confidential." He looked over his glasses.

"Could you tell me if they were local, at least? It would be a big help?"

He looked at his desk, fiddling with a pen to the paperwork and the blue diary and then at Jess. "I can't see what harm that would do." He opened the journal and thumbed through its pages. "Let... me... see, yes, here we go... January–" A deep frown crossed his face, and heavy wrinkles appeared on his brow. "–that's odd, the page has been torn out," he said, turning the diary around and showing it to Jess.

She grabbed her crutch and pushed herself up out of her seat. The man was shaking his head. "I don't get it?"

"The man who was here before me, what else did he say?" she asked.

"Not a lot, the same as you? He was asking about Mr. Whyte." His eyes lit up. "Do you think he stole the page?"

Jess tilted her head to the side in an awkward, sarcastic little nod, eyebrows raised. "That would be my guess, yes?"

"Oh dear."

"Yes, oh dear!"

The man leaned back in his chair, took off his glasses, and wiped them with a little black cloth before putting them back on. "What's going on? Why would he steal that page?"

"That's what I would like to know. If he comes back–" she took a pen from his desk and wrote her number on a piece of paper. "–please call me straight away."

"This all seems very clandestine to me, dear."

"Just call me if he comes back." She pulled the door open with one hand, the other holding the crutch, and exited the Gallery.

2

Jess had been in the gallery for five-minutes at most–which gave the guy in skinny jeans plenty of a head start, especially in her current condition. She hadn't seen which direction he had gone once he'd entered the High street.

At the top of the road, towards the graveyard on her left, she stopped to look down the High street. People were ambling along, enjoying a pleasant stroll while others rushed past. But she couldn't see the skinny man. She heard the fruit and veg seller, "Blueberries for a pahnd," he said.

"Fuck," she muttered under her breath, and an old lady with a stroller and white hair looked at her, shocked. Jess glared back. "Fuck, fuck, fuck." She stood leaning on her crutch in front of the library, which stood silent and menacing in the sunshine. "Fuck you too," she said.

Jess looked left; there were more shops that way, and right, which led to the supermarket express and the private school. If the skinny man was looking for Theo Whyte, then it made sense that he would use the internet and anyone else with information on him. Maybe, the man in the gallery hadn't told her everything?

The bell above the door chimed as she entered again. The man behind the counter was where she left him; the diary still open in front of him. Crumbs from a pastry of some sort spilled down his maroon jumper, and he had bits in his greying moustache. He went to move and then saw it was Jess.

"You again, what now?"

"I'm sorry for all of this," she started. "It is vital, though. I need to ask... did you and the young man talk about anything else, anything at all?" She stood in the doorway, holding the door open.

"Well, let me think... he asked about Theo Whyte, I told him about the sale at the start of the year, he seemed interested, and then he stole that page from my diary. That was about it."

"Did he mention where he'd come across Mr. Whyte, by any chance?"

"Of course, when someone comes in asking about an unheard-of artist, it piques one's interest. He told me he'd seen it at the Baron Burghley, the pub." He leaned back; she got the impression he enjoyed regaling people with stories; she bet he was a hoot at a dinner party. "I remember the day the landlord came in; I kept asking are you sure you want that one? It didn't seem to suit the aesthet–" The door shut, and he was alone in the gallery. He shook his head, rolled his eyes, picked up the pastry, and started to eat again.

Jess hobbled the High street; past the library, past the benches outside the supermarket and towards the Baron Burghley. From the front, it looked like an old-style Westfordian townhouse; however, the chalkboard sign outside confirmed it was a pub—the pub where Mike took her on their first date ten years ago. A dark doorway led down lower than street level.

Inside it hadn't changed; there was still the uneven stone tiled flooring and dark exposed ceiling beams. It felt like years since she set foot in a pub, and it was, except for a wedding here and a christening there. She and Mike rarely did anything which didn't involve the children, and they weren't the sort to take them to a pub, not that they saw anything wrong with bringing their children to a pub, it just ended up a stressful experience.

It was mid-afternoon, and a few older couples were on the ground floor, eating lunch. The smell of grilled chicken and wine and beer brought back memories of weekends before children. She ducked her head, avoiding the low ceilings and exposed stone in the doorways and made her way through to the bar area. Her crutch stuck in a hole between the stone flooring, and she had to pull hard to get free. Other patrons watched. The space just past the bar with its leather wingback chairs was empty. She remembered their first kiss, when life was still full of dreams, under the yellow metal sign that said Westford Station.

The bar was well-stocked with a variety of silver, ceramic, and brass hand-pumps offering real ale, and behind was a vast range of multi-coloured bottles on the back shelf. The solid-wood bar and the shelves were a lighter yellow that complimented the painted walls which weren't exposed stone.

Thinking of less busy days, she could have happily whiled away a day here with a good book and a bottle of Glenfiddich and ginger beer.

"Hi, what can I get you?" the bartender asked.

Jess looked around the bar. "It's a bit quiet?" she asked.

"Yeah, it always is at this time."

"I'm meeting a friend here–you might have seen him. A skinny guy, he's wearing a white tee-shirt and skinny jeans."

"Oh yeah, I know the guy. He's upstairs."

Jess sighed. "Phew, thought I'd missed him."

"Not at all, he's only just got a drink." He looked at her leaning on her crutch. "You might struggle with the stairs, though."

Jess looked at the silver piece of plastic and metal. "I think you may be right." She said with a smile.

"I can go get your friend if you would like?"

"No!" Too aggressive, shit. "I mean, no, don't bother him. I'll be fine, but I may struggle to carry a drink."

"What do you want? I'll get a waitress to bring it up to you."

"That's very kind, thank you." Jess pondered a soft drink or alcohol. She couldn't remember if her medication said she could or couldn't drink on it. Fuck it. "I'll have a Glenffidich and ginger beer, please, with a slice of lime and ice."

"Coming right up, go take a seat, and I'll get this sorted for you."

"Thanks." Jess crutched herself back through the front room past the couples enjoying lunch and towards the stairs. She looked up the uneven carpeted staircase. It was taller than she remembered. A white, peeling painted banister ran up the stairs attached to the wall on her right. At least the railing was on the right side for her leg. She hopped on her left leg, trying to find the easiest way to attempt the climb. Jess ignored the glances from the man and woman sat under the window which hadn't helped her earlier. You could come and help instead of staring; it's not like I'm contagious. She let out a sigh, turned around, and sat on the third step. She bum-shuffled up the stairs, using her good left leg to push. Before she rounded the corner, she smiled sweetly at the couple. Fuck you.

On the first floor landing, Jess picked up the crutch she had dragged with her and stood up with the help of the banister. A quaint little room with uneven carpeted flooring and old oak-wood tables and chairs was on her right, which itself led through to a larger room with a high vaulted ceiling and more exposed dark-wood ceiling beams stretching and meeting in the middle. Two long dark-wood beams hung across the room at head-height held up by vertical wooden beams. A row of circular and square tables ran down the right, and to the left, there were three sets of church-style pews, back-to-back with red-leather seats and tables in the middle of each creating private booths.

At the back of one of these sat the skinny man, his head down, reading a piece of paper. He looked up when she entered and then went back to reading. She noticed his shocking blue eyes and short grey-blonde hair.

Jess took a seat at one of the circular tables close to the exit resting her arms on the armrests. She looked around the room: Black and white portraits and faded colour landscapes mixed with the black chalkboards advertising lunch specials. One painting, an old dark oil-painting, stood out. It was one she'd seen before at home on her laptop. A waitress entered the room and put Jess's drink in front of her and smiled.

"Thank you," Jess said. "Interesting painting, who's it by?" She pointed at the painting.

"That old thing, sorry, not a clue... gives me the creeps, though." The waitress laughed, and then left Jess alone with the skinny man.

Jess poured the ginger beer from its green bottle into the golden liquid and squeezed her lime into it, licking her fingers after giving her tongue an electric shock. She had her back to the skinny man and wished she'd brought a book or something. Then again, she didn't expect to end up on a stakeout. She pulled her phone out of pocket; she had two bars but no 4G.

"It is interesting, isn't it?" a man's voice spoke behind her. "I agree with the waitress, though–it is more than a little creepy."

"Definitely creepy," Jess replied, without turning around. She took another sip of her drink. "I don't recognize the area though, is it local?"

"Nether Hambleton," the man answered.

"Never heard of it?" Jess continued to study the painting. "Is that a signature at the bottom?" Shuffling came from behind her. Then the creaking of the floor as a shadow fell over her table. The man pulled up a seat nearby and leaned forward onto the table, the fingers of his hands interlocked. He looked at her as if he knew her. The skinny man was studying her cast, and his eyes lit up when he saw the boy's doodles.

"It is a signature, yes–a man called Theo Whyte painted it, but you knew that already didn't you?" Jess looked up into his blue eyes and nodded. He was a beautiful man. A nice angled jaw, sharp cheekbones, and just the right amount of stubble. "Why did you follow me, you were at the gallery, weren't you?"

Jess nodded, why did she get herself into these situations. The man was blocking her exit from the table, and with her being on a crutch, she doubted she would get very far anyway. He was still looking at her–not like a stranger– but as someone familiar. She thought of the narrow stairs and how easy it would be to make a fall look like an accident, especially with one leg in plaster.

"What do you know about him?" the man asked.

"Nothing, that's why I was following you." She crossed her arms over her chest.

"Why are you interested in him?"

"I like art…"

"Bullshit."

"Why are you interested in him? Why did you steal that page from the gallery?"

"I'm looking for someone," he said.

"Besides, Mr. Whyte?"

"Yes, and I believe Mr. Whyte might be able to help." His eyes grew sad. "Now you know why I'm looking for him, will you tell me who you are?"

"Something happened to me." She looked down at her leg in a cast. "And I want to find answers."

The skinny man rubbed at his chin. "But, how will finding Mr. Whyte help you get answers?"

"My Whyte seems to know a great deal about the local area…"

"I agree."

Jess smiled at him for the first time. "The Priory…" she blurted out, not knowing why.

"The Priory?"

"Yes, the Priory, the one near Morrisons. Something attacked me, it wasn't human."

The man's face tensed. Even though he looked no older than twenty-five, wrinkles appeared on his forehead. His knuckles whitened as he clenched his fists tight. He looked around the room and then spoke quietly to her, "You've seen something, haven't you? Something not... natural."

Jess reached out and grabbed his hand. "You too?" she said. He nodded gravely. "There's something in this town." Jess moved to his side, her cheeks reddening. She leaned back into her chair and puffed out her cheeks. "What's your name?" she asked.

"Lucas." He held out his hand to her. "Jess, will you tell me what happened?"

"How do you know my name?"

Lucas smiled at her. "I love a good story. I'll tell you mine if you tell me yours."

3 JESS (TWO WEEKS AGO)

It wasn't just the positivity that oozed from the woman that irked Jess; there was something off about her. Whether it was the smile that never reached her eyes or the sour, gone-off odour that emanated from her clothes when she walked by, something must have happened to the woman; maybe a break-up or an illness in the family. Either way, Rosemary Eve didn't seem the same.

"And this week's *'Weight Loss Wonder'* is… drumroll, please…" The cavernous school hall filled with the muffled sound of hands drumming on the back of red plastic chairs. There were only twenty people in the room, and the drumroll echoed off the white metal roof.

The lady at the front of the room was short, just over five-foot-tall, and her pale skin sagged down her bulbous neck and under her eyes. Her hair, a vivid orange like flame, stuck up at all angles. Jess wondered how much hairspray she used every morning. Rosemary wore a striking floral dress that did nothing for her figure. She'd lost over six stone, and Jess hated to think what she must have looked like before.

"Congratulations…" Rosemary let the excitement build like she was presenting an Oscar. "… Lydia, well done," she looked across the crowd and found Lydia sitting quietly in the second row. She grinned a toothless grin and beckoned. "Come up here to collect your award."

Lydia stood, the black metal legs of her chair squeaked across the floor. She was still very overweight. Moving with a sideways slump that reminded Jess of being full-term pregnant, she squeezed past the people in the middle row, not looking up once during the walk to the front of the hall. Lydia looked like she'd just been found guilty of manslaughter.

Jess understood why. The weight-loss consultant was so enthusiastic that it hurt—the sort of positivity that doesn't motivate others so much as sap them into submission. Something about Rosemarie's lipstick-stained smile made Jess think of tin-foil shark teeth. Jess had avoided one-to-one conversation with the woman over the past couple of visits; she had as much fake positivity as she could handle at work on a day-to-day basis as well as having to deal with it here.

Lydia finally reached the front and now stood next to Rosemary. She looked like a lamb next to a wolf with blood dripping from its mouth. Rosemary reached for Lydia's hand with her own weighted down bear paws, and when they met, Lydia jolted as if an electric current pumped through her.

Jess looked around the brightly lit room. The rest of the group sat in silence, applauding politely. She heard the strip-lights buzzing above, just under the applause. Jess turned back to the front and watched a terrified Lydia receive the award. She took it hesitantly, as if it would bite her, and waddled back to her chair as the clapping died down.

Jess leaned forward, looked down the row past the other women, and watched Lydia sit. Jess settled back in her chair, glancing over at Lydia every so often, not taking in what Rosemary was saying at the front.

As Jess watched, she noticed Lydia's skin had taken on an ashy hue, her usual bloodshot cheeks pale. Her foot was tapping against the faded wooden floor of the sports hall. Jess heard Rosemary say, "… See you all next week," and before she could stand and make her way to Lydia, Lydia was gone.

It amazed Jess, that a woman of Lydia's size, could move so quickly. She stood and looked around. The mostly all-female group divided into groups of fives and sixes and were all gossiping together in hushed tones. She contemplated mingling with some other women but thought better of it; she loved gossip as much as the next person, much to Mike's chagrin, but she was more interested in Lydia.

They'd been best friends ten years ago. Just out of university, ready to take on the world. They would drink bottles of wine on work nights, go on double dates and have movie nights-in gorging on pizza and white wine. Then Jess met Mike, started a career, and had kids. Lydia hadn't had it so easy.

She walked out of the artificial light of the sports hall and into the early evening sunshine just in time to see Lydia's beaten-up, dark green 53-plate Mondeo pulling out of the school car park. The sky was a swirling watercolour of reds, pinks, and purples. She kicked at the gravel as the car drove off, grey smoke coming from the exhaust. By the time she got home and helped put the kids back to bed, she'd forgotten the whole thing.

Lydia hit the steering wheel as the smoke coming from the exhaust enveloped her rear-view mirror. "Fuck, fuck, fuck." She was feeling strange from the touch of Rosemary. It was a muted, dull, anxious sensation in the back of her mind.

The engine light came on, and the power waned from the car. She hammered the warning light button once, and the monotonous sound of the lights ticking filled the vehicle. The radio had broken months ago. She pulled over to the grass verge, got out her phone and flicked through her contacts. The smell of the exhaust came inside the car with her.

Nick wouldn't come out to help, that was a given. Maybe her Dad, but she didn't want to interrupt him if she didn't have to. She kept on searching through her phone, scrolling through the names of so many people she no longer talked too.

While she was scrolling, she didn't see the black BMW pull up behind her or the dark figure that got out and approached her car from behind.

4

Jess rubbed her eyes as the morning sunshine blasted in like an atomic explosion. One of the kids must have left a gap in the curtains last night when they were playing before bed. Having a south-facing garden was terrific for long days in the garden, but not so great for trying to lay in. Mike grunted next to her, but did not attempt to move, even though he was closer to the window.

"I'll get it then, shall I?" she said, climbing out of bed, carefully avoiding the coathangers, toys, and clothes on the floor. Once she'd blocked out the light, she climbed back into bed, but sleep evaded her. The train-like sound of Mike's snoring irritated her enough to get up and go downstairs.

The house was silent; the monsters not yet awake. She settled on the cream sofa and pulled a fluffy blanket with cats printed on it up to her shoulders. Something stuck to her pyjamas bottoms. She picked at it and pulled away something sticky, red, and warm. The battle for sleep carried on downstairs, and when she lost again, she turned on her phone and started scrolling through Facebook.

She got lost among the scarily accurate adverts and news stories until she saw Lydia's face staring at her from the screen. The picture was posted by a family member and shared by a mutual friend. She sat up, totally awake. Jess threw the blanket off her and shifted her body, so her feet were on the soft carpeted floor. She leaned over with her nose almost touching the screen as she read the article.

Have you seen our daughter?

Lydia Roundtree, our wonderful daughter, and 35-year old mother-of-one went missing last night after attending her local "Weight Loss Wonder Group" at the Green coat school on Blue Lane, Westford. She was last seen leaving the group at 7.45 pm; however, she never made it home. Her car, a 53-plate, dark Green Ford Mondeo, is also missing. Her three-year-old daughter is currently being looked after by a family member. If you have any information about her whereabouts, please contact us via messenger or call the local Police on

01779 810810.

Jess sat back in the chair. She looked around her home and thanked God for everything she had and everything she took for granted–for her healthy little boys asleep upstairs–even for her snoring husband. She didn't know Lydia any more, didn't know anything about her life. Whether she was a good mother to her daughter, whether she cuddled her little girl while they watched films together, or kissed her and held her when she was poorly? Jess didn't know where Lydia lived or what her life was like now, but because of their past, she felt responsible for her. She stood and went to the dresser in the dining room. She opened the mahogany cupboards at the bottom and sat cross-legged on the floor while she searched for an old shoebox. Jess found it at the back of the closet behind the boy's forgotten toys they really should have thrown away, but which she couldn't bring herself too.

It was covered in a layer of dust and fluff. The box was a cream colour with black letters written across the top that said Converse. She couldn't remember why she had kept it; why when they last moved, she hadn't put it in storage in the garage or just thrown it away. Inside the box were pictures and letters between her and Lydia.

Maybe, just maybe, if she had caught her last night after group, she could have spoken to her, and she wouldn't be missing right now?

She wanted to wake up Mike and ask him what he thought, but she knew what he would say, "It's not your problem." That's what he always said when she gossiped, or when someone else's behaviour wound her up. "It's not your problem." Only this time, it felt like it was. She opened the living room curtains to let in the morning sunlight and stared out at the bright blue sky, wondering if she was the last person who'd seen Lydia? As she stared up at the sky, she saw a bird circling; a kite, she thought. She remembered how scared Lydia had looked at group last night. She frowned as the unnerving feeling that something terrible had happened, settled into her bones. Jess played it back over in her head–how Lydia was acting at the group after her interaction with Rosemary, followed by her swift exit and disappearance. She knew it wasn't right. Jess picked up her phone and looked at the picture of Lydia again. She tapped on the number at the bottom and rang the Police.

The phone call was short, abrupt even. She flushed hot when she put the phone down, and her hands were shaking. They didn't take her seriously; they thought she was just a local busy-body. Jess threw her phone down on the sofa and paced the living room. Walking around the low oak coffee table, she picked up one of Mike's football magazines and sat back down and attempted to read it–she had zero interest in football–she threw the magazine down on the sofa and went to the kitchen to make coffee.

She stared into the back garden while she waited for the kettle to boil; she watched as one of their cats prowled across the green-yellow lawn. The unusually hot summer had taken its toll, and the hosepipe ban was still in effect. Jess ran back to the sofa and picked up her phone. She Googled the contact number for her local 'Weight Loss Wonders' and rang the number. She picked at her pyjama bottoms as she waited for someone to answer–it went to voicemail, and she hit her forehead with her palm as she remembered the time. No one was going to answer at 6.30am on a Wednesday. Idiot. She remembered the smoke coming from Lydia's car as she watched her driving off, which way was she going? Not towards town–she was heading out of town.

She did some Facebook stalking. Lydia's profile wasn't private–although looking at some photos' it should have been. She swiped through the pictures hoping to see one with Lydia's house in it from the outside. It had been so long, the guilt of not even knowing where she lived made her heart sink. She found one picture of interest; it was winter as there was snow on the ground. She saw Lydia and a little girl with blonde hair about the same age as her youngest. The little girl was smiling at Lydia as she stood next to a snowman in a front garden. Across the road, Jess saw a park she recognized. It had blue climbing frames and a faded, dangerous-looking metal fence surrounding it.

"Gotya," she said to herself, feeling smug at her detective skills.

It was still early, and she was the only one awake in the house. She found a pen and paper and wrote Mike a note saying she'd gone for some milk. She went upstairs and got dressed silently in the bedroom, listening to his snoring. She left the letter on his bedside table, poked her head around the boy's bedroom door, and went downstairs and out the front door, closing it carefully so as not to wake them.

5

The sun was warm on her skin, even though it was still early, and a cool morning breeze washed over her, sending her strawberry-blonde hair flowing into her face. She could hear the non-stop noise of the cars on the motorway. Jess considered walking to the blue park from the photo, but then thought better of it. The vehicle was unlocked, as it always was on the drive. She got in and found the keys at the bottom of her handbag.

The roads were quiet; it was the middle of the school holidays and just past seven am. She drove past the Shell garage and the empty fields, sticking to the speed limit even though the road was empty. She ignored the no-through-traffic sign and turned into Maverley Gardens; a winding road of bungalows with gnomes in the front gardens, and stopped at the end of the road. She waited for a white van to pass before pulling out and taking the next right. She followed the road past the closed chip shop and the chinese takeaway. Jess didn't sense the grimace that had taken over her face as she drove further into the estate, or the way her jaw clenched.

Jess pulled over 150 yards past the shops and put the handbrake on. Her pristine white Nissan Qashqai looked out of place amongst the dusty cars and vans on the road. The park was a short walk away, just the next left turn, and she planned on walking the rest of the way.

Before she got out of the car, she had a moment of clarity, what was she doing here? Lydia and her hadn't been friends for years'. What could she possibly do, and why did she feel it was her problem to solve? Jess sat behind the steering wheel, staring out onto the depressing-looking estate. Even under the blue sky and bright sun, it looked grey and dismal. What did she expect to find at Lydia's house? For all she knew, Lydia had moved since the snowy photo. But she felt guided as if an invisible fishing line was pulling her here–it was a déjà vu feeling she hadn't experienced since she was a child.

When she was younger, her parents used to joke about it. If they ever lost their keys or her little brother lost a toy, they would say, "Jess, do your thing," and she would find it by concentrating on it. As she grew older, it happened less, and until today, she had forgotten about it. She'd left her parents behind like she left most people behind in the end. She concentrated on the image she held of Lydia with the feeling there, in the back of her mind. She knew she was in the right place.

Jess got out of the car and closed the door, locking it this time. When she was younger, before she met Mike, she had lived in this area. Her parents weren't poor, but they weren't rich, and two streets over was where they'd bought their first house—the house she'd been raised inside.

Jess started walking, a faint tang of food grease on the breeze came from the bins behind the chinese takeaway and the chip shop. She rounded the corner and saw the park from the picture.

The climbing frames were now more blood-red from rust than bright blue, and grass and weeds had invaded the black tarmac. Where there had once been woodland behind, there was now a new housing estate full of red-brick houses crowded onto a small plot of land.

The houses overlooked the older, greyer homes and the park. A crisscrossing metal fence surrounded the grass and tarmac area while jagged, sharp metal stuck out from where the gate was torn, which made Jess think of a prison yard. She crossed the road so she was on the same side as the park and not the houses. As she walked, she inspected the front of each house, but her instinct already told her which one she was looking for.

Jess peered over the hedge as she passed. She saw shapes moving in the front room, but nothing or no-one specific. She walked on. A puzzled look crossed over her face. Why was she here? And then she saw it.

A dark shape in the driver's seat of a black BMW parked across the road moved. She hadn't noticed it earlier, whoever it had been, had been statue-still, watching her and the house. The car started. A puff of smoke came from the exhaust, and the car pulled out and did a U-turn in the road. Jess ran towards it, but it was already too far gone, the sunshine glimmering off its roof before she could get close. She recognized that car.

Jess ran back to her car. Her keys already in her hand. She climbed in and sat in silence, her hands at ten and two on the steering wheel. Nothing made sense. She knew who that car belonged to, but the person in it could have been there for the same reason as her. Rosemary could be looking out for a missing member of her group like she was. Why was she being pulled to follow the car, a feeling akin to the one that had brought her here?

"Fuck." She hit the wheel with both hands and started the engine. Jess didn't know where she was going, she didn't know where Rosemary lived, but she trusted her instincts even if all she wanted to do was go home and snuggle her boys. As she drove, she saw a few more people out on the streets, mostly dog-walkers. She was heading towards the town centre past the tree-lined streets of the Recreation ground. Jess didn't believe Lydia had gone missing just for the evening. The tingle in her mind spoke of dark things. And it was linked to her Weight Loss Wonder group consultant, somehow.

96

Jess had been going to the group for nearly a year. During that time, she hadn't taken much notice of the surrounding people. It wasn't a social group for her; she just wanted to lose some mummy-weight she'd been holding onto. Yeah, she'd recognized a few of the people, old friends like Lydia and a few others, but it was strictly business.

Had other people gone missing from the group? She couldn't remember all the faces, and people dropped in and out all the time. If there were other missing people, there would have been posts on Facebook, and it would have been on the news, wouldn't it?

A bright white light invaded her vision, blinding her. She moved her hand to shield her eyes, and the car swerved on the road. She braked hard before hitting a parked blue VW Golf. She rubbed at her temples with both hands, as the blinding light faded. Faraway, she heard a car horn blaring. A new image filled her mind. It was like an imprint after staring at a pattern for too long. Lydia. She'd been here, in one of these houses. Jess was sure of it.

Curtains twitched in bedrooms in the houses running along the road she'd crashed on. They were red-brick Victorian-style properties with little courtyard gardens to the front with beautiful stone walls and wrought-iron fences and old stonework. She reversed the car, hoping she hadn't caused too much damage. One of the front doors opened, and a man with dark hair, glasses, and a dark red dressing gown ran out the door and into the courtyard.

"You. Hey, you! Stop!" he shouted, as he ran to his gate and looked between his car and hers. "What have you done to my car?"

Jess wound the window down. "I'm sorry. I am so sorry. It was an accident. I have insurance."

The man's eyebrows furrowed. He slid the bolt of his gate across and walked out onto the path. He slowed as he approached.

"Jess, is that you?"

She looked closely at him. Another blast from the past! She hadn't seen him for over five years, but it was him.

"Jason. Jason, hi, I am so sorry."

"Jess, what's going on? What happened? Are you okay?"

"It was an accident, Jason; I will sort it, I promise. But I can't stop right now."

"What do you mean? We need to sort this out?" He looked at his watch.

"I know, but I can't. I'm in the middle of something Jason." She put her foot down and pulled off, leaving Jason standing in the middle of the road behind her in her mirror; his dressing gown blowing open, showing his black boxer shorts.

As soon as she started driving, her instinct kicked in again. Jess stopped the car. She put her head on the steering wheel. "Shit." Jess reversed back up the road. She was sinking into her seat as she saw Jason getting larger in her mirrors. He was inspecting the damage to his car. He didn't see her coming as she pulled over next to him and undid her window.

"Jason, do you remember Lydia?"

"Lydia? You crash into my car, and now ask about a school reunion. Seriously Jess, what's going on?"

"Lydia Roundtree, Jason? I don't have time to explain, but do you still see her?"

He kneeled and inspected the state of his car; he ran a finger over the jagged dent. "I haven't seen her for years', I tried to keep in touch, but it's hard, isn't it?"

Jess nodded. "It is. She's missing, Jason, she went missing last night."

Jason shrugged. "She's done that before; she'll turn up later. Why do you care Jess? I didn't think you cared about us dregs anymore?" He stood up, leaning on his car.

The word 'dregs' hit her like a fist to the gut. That's what she'd called them all when she went away; when she left them. "I'm sorry Jason, I wish I could take that back, but Lydia, she has gone missing, I saw her last night, and she didn't look right." Seeing Jason brought back a flood of memories and she thought, relationships, like sparklers, sparkled brightly for a moment, but they always fizzled out.

"In what way?"

"She looked scared. Jason, I think someone took her."

"What? Who? That's crazy, Jess."

"Before the crash, did you see or hear another car?"

"Nothing, Jess. I was asleep until I heard the crash."

A crowd had formed behind them, neighbours wanting to see what was going on. They all stood in various stages of dress. Jess looked at them and then poked her head out of the window. "Morning," she addressed the crowd. "I'm looking for someone, did anyone hear or see a car go down here before I crashed, please, it's important."

An older man shook his head, and a woman in business dress looked at the ground. From behind them, Jess heard a little voice, "I did." A young boy in a blue hoodie with a logo of a monster truck pushed through the man and woman. Jess got out the car and crossed the road. She lowered herself as she approached, and when she was in front of the boy, she kneeled.

"Hiya, what's your name?" she asked, in that voice parents save for their children.

"Toby." He looked into her eyes. "I saw something."

"That's a nice name, Toby. I believe you, what did you see?"

"It was a black car. I've seen it before. It's one of those sporty looking ones with a blue and white badge. The sort my dad calls bad names."

Jess couldn't help a small chuckle. "That's it, Toby, where did it go?"

"Nowhere..."

"What do you mean, Toby?"

"It didn't go anywhere; it never does—one minute it's there, and the next, poof, it's gone." Toby made a 'poof' action with his hands as if he was releasing an invisible bird to the sky.

"Have you ever seen anyone get out of it, Toby?" She reached out and held his shoulder.

Toby didn't answer. His eyes teared up, and he crossed his legs.

"Toby, I know you're scared, but did you ever see anyone in that car?"

His wet, blue eyes looked into hers, and he nodded. Jess squeezed his shoulder. "Was it a woman, Toby? Did she have funny hair?"

Toby started to sob. He nodded his head. He looked towards the businesswoman, she moved forward and held his hand. "She stopped outside our house; I was looking out the window. I thought she looked funny, you know, like haha funny, and then she turned to look at me." Jess felt his body shudder. "Her eyes weren't eyes like yours or mine. They looked like the pictures of dinosaurs from my books, does that make sense? And then she poked her tongue out, but it wasn't a tongue, it was forked like a lizard but fat like a rope and then, and then... maggots and worms fell out of her mouth and down her face."

His tears fell fast now, and he was trembling. Jess pulled him close and cuddled him. The old man walked from the crowd and put his hand on his shoulder, "Come on, Toby, let's get you a nice glass of milk, what do you say?" Toby looked up at the man and turned to go, but before he did, he turned back to Jess one last time, "You know, I saw that car one more time after that."

"Where, Toby, where did you see it?"

"It was parked outside the Priory, you know, the one near Morrisons, just off the roundabout. We went there on a school walk, and I saw it parked up on the grass verge."

6

Jess looked at the clock on her dashboard. It was only 8.30am. This wasn't how she expected to spend a Thursday morning during the school holidays. No phone call from Mike yet, she guessed they were still in bed. What she couldn't understand was why her weight loss consultant had been at Lydia's house this morning and what Toby had seen? She waved out the window at Toby as she carried on into town. He was calmer when she left, as was Jason; after she gave him her insurance details.

At last night's group, she'd had a feeling, but it was only a sensation, like a flicker of your eyelid that stops after a moment. This was ridiculous. But then when had her instinct ever been wrong when she was a child? Her instinct had taken her to Lydia's house, then to Toby, and now she could feel the draw to the Priory. She might find Lydia, and this would all be over, but how did Rosemary Eve fit?

Rosemary had been the 'Weight Loss Wonder' consultant for years.' Her clients loved her; she got great results. But, thinking now, Jess didn't know a thing about the woman. In a small town like Westford, that was strange. Jess didn't know where she lived: if she had kids, if she was married. For a woman Rosemary's age that wasn't just strange, that was downright freaky. She'd always seemed kind though, a natural empath. It wasn't until a few weeks, or maybe even months ago, Jess noticed the changes, only ever-so-slight ones. Like the smell that came from her. Or how her smile no longer touched her eyes. Or, how she looked at her members hungrily, like a juicy steak after being stuck on a desert island.

Jess picked up her phone from the empty passenger seat and searched on Facebook–nothing. She searched Instagram and Twitter–again, nothing. The pull to get to the Priory was intense; she felt it pressing on the back of her mind, tapping away like a woodpecker until she followed.

"Okay, I'm going," she said, looking in the rearview mirror into the empty back seat.

Everyone in Westford knew the Priory. Its full name was St. Wilfrid's Priory, and it stood opposite the posh retirement home just off the Morrison's roundabout. It was set back from the road, shrouded in dark shrubbery and ancient Beech trees. A wrought-iron gate, with a thick black and rusted chain wrapped around like a snake, denied access to the overgrown land, which led down to the river. Jess went around the roundabout and turned onto the tree-lined street. The shadows crisscrossed the road like cracks in shattered glass.

She drove past the care-home on her right and followed the moss-covered stone wall until she saw the Priory on her left. In the sunshine, five tall arches like gaping mouths, looked at her, shrouded in their cold shade. Beyond, she watched yellowing fields and tall trees swaying in the breeze as far as she could see. She had never taken much notice of the building, but as she parked up, she took it all in. She remembered a school trip, but couldn't remember the history of the place. Jess thought she might have smoked a joint down here at some point before she met Mike, but the memory was hazy.

It was a single building standing abandoned yet protected. Jess wound down the car window and listened. She heard traffic from the roundabout, but underneath the canopies of the trees, there was no other sound; not even a bird chirping in the warm summer morning. There were no other cars parked on the road. She peered out the back window but saw nothing out of the ordinary

There was a scent on the breeze that wafted in through her window. A mossy, earthy smell that reminded her of worms and bugs and gardening with Hugo and Billy. The bright light that had made her crash earlier invaded her mind again, and she raised her hands to her head and pushed to stop it from splitting open. She sank in her seat as she waited for the pain to pass, closing her eyes tight against the light. Another blast of light and sound this time shot through her mind. And, then it went quiet.

She saw the black BMW approaching from behind. She turned her ignition on, flicked on her indicator, and pulled back onto the road, sliding down into the seat as she passed.

The BMW had blacked-out windows so she couldn't see inside as it passed, but she followed it in her mirrors and saw it indicate and pull into the care-home carpark. Jess followed the road she was on and took the first right onto a residential street of large houses with double garages. She pulled over and stepped out of the car, checking to see if anyone was watching.

She jogged to the end of the road and then power-walked the last 100 yards till she saw the Priory again. Once it was in her sight, she slowed down to a gentle stroll. She wondered if she should call Mike, but he'd only worry.

There was a modern art-déco style house on her left, and she lingered close to the wall leading to the driveway. After a moment, she saw a figure cross the road from the care-home and hop the gate to the Priory. There was no mistaking the bright orange shock of hair in the dazzling sunlight.

Jess stayed in the shadows as she approached the Priory from the side using the stone wall for cover. She heard muttering and a low whine from the Priory grounds. She found a gap in the shrubs that were growing over the stone wall, and found a foothold from a dusty, chipped stone sticking out. Jess put one hand on the top of the wall, feeling the soft damp moss, before pulling herself over and landing in the field on the other side. Her ankle nearly twisted in the long grass, but she righted herself.

The only thing between her and the Priory was fifty-yards of dry grass, old trees, and a rickety fence with some panels missing. She crouched and moved forward, stopping under a large tree next to the wall. From here, she could see the front of the Priory.

It had a large sharp oval in the centre, under the pointed roof, with two smaller ovals inside, that made it look like a crudely drawn picture of a vagina that a teenager would make. Beneath this were seven low arches cut into the stone, with three dark windows beyond that cast no reflection from the sun. Underneath were three more arches; the large one in the middle housed five-diamond shape cut-outs in the wall that formed the shape of a cross. Jess shivered in the sunlight.

The muffled whines and muttering had stopped. Rosemary was nowhere to be seen.

Jess guessed she was inside the Priory, somehow. She kept low and snuck up to the building, avoiding any dry branches on the ground. She reached the Priory and ducked under the arches to the front. Jess placed her hand on the stone. It was cold. Jess moved along the building with her back against it.

From the diamond cut-outs in the walls, inside the Priory, the whimpering came again. Jess cocked her head to the side, her ear towards the window to make out what the voice was saying. She thought she heard the words "…please," and "…don't." Jess stood on her tiptoes and peered into the dark.

It was pitch black. A damp breeze that smelled of decaying leaves and earth came from inside. She looked through the hole while feeling for her mobile in her back jeans pocket. She wanted her torch. Jess got hold of her phone and unlocked it. She was looking for the torch app Mike had made her download for when she was out after dark, when a high-pitched shriek came through the building, starting at the far end in the black and flowing out of the hole and into Jess's face.

She turned to run, but stopped as gnarled and twisted dry fingers, like tree roots, emerged from each of the five holes. She stood staring stupidly as the bare, leathery fingers writhed and strained, and when she turned, she turned straight into orange fire–Rosemary. Her legs gave way under her, and she heard a snap and felt a sharp pain in her ankle. Rosemary grinned, and as Jess looked into her face, she saw it melt away.

7

Jess woke in the dark and cuddled herself against the cold. She could see the bright blue sky outside through the holes in the wall, like a light at the end of a cave. The floor was damp. She moved and her ankle screamed out in pain. Her hands dug into the soft ground, her fingernails scraped against the cold stone underneath the moss and twigs, smooth and whole. Jess could hear someone in here with her breathing harsh and shallow breaths.

"Who's there?" she whispered. Her voice echoed around the cavernous darkness. Her skin flushed hot as her heartbeat increased in her chest. She felt her throat close as she struggled for breath and saw stars in the dark.

A whimper came from the black, Jess couldn't tell from how far away. "We need to get out of here…"

"Lydia, is that you? It's Jess."

Jess heard the woman gasp. "Jess, what are you doing here?"

"After last night, I couldn't stop thinking about you. I'm so sorry for the past, Lydia. I will get you out of here."

"It's Rosemary, she did this to me."

"Did what, Lydia, what did she do?"

"How long have I been gone, it feels like days?"

"Group was only last night, today is Thursday."

"That can't be. I've been here for weeks, she's picked me apart for days, weeks."

"I saw you just last night. Don't worry. It's dark in here and confusing." Their voices echoed in the black and it was hard to keep track of the conversation. "What do you mean picked you apart?" Jess asked.

Lydia muffled a whimper. "Like you'd pick apart a bread roll; rip off a bit here, rip off a bit there, dip it in some Olive Oil, haha…" The laugh echoed in the dark. Jess' skin crawled. She should have stayed in bed.

"Lydia, you've only been gone for one night."

There was silence for a moment. "No, that's not possible, it's been days."

"Can you move? Where are you? My ankle, I think it's broken."

"There is no way out—once she enters the door disappears and when she leaves, it disappears. The only light comes from those holes." Jess heard movement and guessed Lydia was pointing.

"That's crazy, a door can't just disappear?"

"Shhh… she's coming back, I can hear her… or it could be him…"

Jess pressed her back up against the cold wall, her legs straight out–in the dark, every movement caused spots to sparkle in her eyes. What the fuck was going on? She could hear Lydia in the black, her breathing fast and shallow. What had happened to her in the few hours she'd been missing?

A vision of her boys, fast asleep at home in their beds, swam through the dark. I will not sit here trapped like a rat. No-one has ever trapped me, I am strong. She reached into her jeans; her left and back pockets were empty, her phone missing, but in the right pocket she felt metal–her keys. They were attached to a polished metal keyring Mike had gotten her for Mothers' Day. She could feel the inscription on the metal, it said, 'Momma Bear' and he had engraved them with a big bear holding a smaller bear's hand. The edges were smooth and round. Her fingers surrounded the keys, making sure they didn't jangle as she pulled them from her pocket. Her ankle howled with pain. She bit her lip, drawing blood.

Jess heard soft footsteps approaching, dampened on the grass, but close. Jess picked through the moss until she found a rough part of the stone floor. She dragged the keyring over it, in quick sharp movements. Not feeling guilty about ruining a nice gift.

The footsteps changed, gravel crunched under foot outside. She moved the keyring across the stone faster, like a chef sharpening a paring knife. Testing the corners with her thumb, she smiled when she felt a sharp pain followed by warm liquid spilling down her hand. In the dark, she could hear Lydia crying. Soft whimpers, like a dog afraid of its owner. Light flooded through the priory as a doorway opened in the wall opposite.

Jess' eyes adjusted to the bright sunlight, and the room was more cavernous than she'd imagined. The old stone walls dripped with a black liquid that twinkled in the sunlight. Upside down crosses hung from the walls, with the carcasses of rodents, cats and animals hanging from them. Their rib cages ripped open. She saw other fleshy things hanging from the roof above, past the exposed rotting beams. An arm still wearing a silver watch. A hollowed out leg with tendrils of flesh hanging like snot from a child.

She looked around for Lydia and saw her in the corner. Jess choked back a sob as she saw her old friend; now a mess of mangled cloth and maroon stained hair; a shape heaving in time with the sobs that came from her. Where her leg should be, there was a stump covered in writhing maggots. How had she been talking?

Jess looked at Rosemary as she entered through the door, her face and body silhouetted against the bright light spilling into the room.

"What do you want?" Jess screamed, part in anger and part in the hope that someone would hear her.

Rosemary didn't say anything.

"What are you?"

No answer. Jess could see her face finally. The door behind her was already closing. Rosemary turned, her whole body flowing in the light as if she wasn't solid. A forked tongue flicked from her mouth, tasting the air in front of her. She took four steps to Lydia and stood over her. She turned to Jess, before her body melted and reformed.

The creature that emerged from the melted Rosemary had black, smooth skin, that, like the liquid on the walls, shimmered in the now fading light. Jess stared open-mouthed at the creature—the pain in her ankle forgotten. It looked like a salamander, but it was the size of a St. Bernard. It stalked the figure lying on the floor, its forked tongue flicking over Lydia's body as she sobbed.

Two milky white eyes stood out from its reptilian face, one on either side. Something like a smile crossed the stupid-looking face of the creature. It was happy with itself. Jess watched as its webbed and spiked legs floated on top of the dark bed of moss on the floor; spinning like flat tyres, making swooshing noises that farted on the damp moss. A new smell came with the creature, one that reminded Jess of sewage and rats and filth.

I was saving this one, but now you're here, let's eat! Jess heard Rosemary's voice in her mind.

Her hands scrambled against the wall as she watched the creature open its gullet and take Lydia's remaining leg into its still smiling mouth. It belched, and Jess retched from the smell before it gulped. Deep bubbling sounds echoed around the darkening room. Jess looked past the creature and towards the light; Lydia had been right, the doorway was disappearing. It was being eaten up by the darkness from all sides.

She watched until it was the size of a hobbit door. She pushed from the wall, launching herself forward, rolling onto her side over the mossy floor. Pain flashed in her mind from her her ankle—she kept on rolling, with the keys clutched in her hand, as the light got smaller. The creature blended into the darkness, but she could see its bulging white eyes. Jess saw Lydia's ragged body, up to its hips, in the creature's mouth. The thin yellow slit in its milky eyes never left her, as she rolled clumsily towards the light.

Jess closed her eyes and said a silent prayer before she made one last push towards the hole. She moved the keyring, so it was between her index and middle finger. She was five feet away from the feast in the room's corner. Her momentum stopped ten feet from the ever shrinking light. Jess couldn't put any weight on her ankle. she crawled, using her elbows to move forward. She pushed with her one good foot and ignored the pain coming from the other.

Concentrating on the light, she moved slower than she'd ever thought possible. Certain that any second the thing would finish Lydia with one final gulp and move onto her, bad ankle first, she kept on moving. Her eyes were wide and her heart jack-hammered in her chest against the damp floor as she reached a hand out through the hole and into the light.

She felt the soft caress of the sun's heat on her skin. The doorway was the size of a boat porthole now; she reached outwards, both hands on each size of the hole and pulled herself forward. She got her head through, and then her shoulders squeezed through, followed by her chest. She sucked in the fresh air as she wiggled the rest of her body out the hole, landing heavily on her side and hitting her shattered ankle, again. Stars swam in her vision, and she had to bite down on her tongue to stop from passing out. Jess rolled onto her back, using her elbows to push herself away from the hole. For the first time, she noticed the white piece of bone jutting from her ankle, but before she could take it in, a smiling reptilian face with large white eyes, looked out at her from inside. The hole closed.

Jess lay on the dry grass and stared up at the blue sky, her chest heaving. She heard the traffic from the roundabout. The whispering of the breeze through the trees. The door opened again and Rosemary's head poked through the hole, only it wasn't Rosemary, not yet. Her eyes were on the side of her head and her forked tongue flicked out hissing. Jess launched herself at the face and stabbed at the creamy eyes with her keyring. Black, warm liquid oozed between her fingers and the monster screamed as Jess attacked its face and eyes again and again and again. The face slid back into the dark, insidiously becoming part of the shadows once again.

Jess crawled through the dry grass, her broken ankle screaming behind her leaving a trail of glistening red on the yellow and green..

As she approached the road, she heard cars driving past; full of people on their way to work, just a normal day. Jess reached the gate and leaned against it. She sobbed in the sunlight, her tears sparkled like diamonds cutting clean lines through her mucky face, as she thought of Lydia digesting in that thing's stomach. She'd failed to protect her, just like she'd failed to look after anyone but herself throughout her life so far.

All she wanted to do was go home to her family and hold them tight. But, the thing knew who she was.

8 LUCAS

After she finishes, I tell her my story, unashamed of how crazy it sounds—she told me about being attacked by a monster after all. (If I've learned anything over the past fifty days, it is to appreciate that everyone has their own story to tell, if you just let them tell it). We're still alone on the top floor in the Burghley Baron. She flinches as I tell her about being inside her last week. Something that sounds like it should be naughty, but in these circumstances just comes out weird. I tell her what I've found out about Theo Whyte and his real name and address.

I ask her about the Priory, interested in a new place. It isn't somewhere that's popped up in my search so far. She tells me about the history of the site: about St Wilfrid, the monastery, William the Conqueror, and the secrets that supposedly lie beneath. It makes no sense to me, but the Priory is a definite place of interest.

"Were you really inside of me?"

I nod. "I met Mike, Billy, and Hugo. They seemed like great kids. Do you remember anything? Were you still in there somewhere?"

"They really are," she replies, looking past me out the window. "I thought I was going crazy. No, I remember nothing, I woke up the next day and that was it."

I reach out and touch her hand. "I know it's a lot to ask, but will you take me to the Priory?"

The colour drains from her face. "I haven't been back since they found me, but I dream about it." She pulls her hand away from mine.

"I need to see it," I lean towards her across the table.

She turns away from the window towards me. "We'll need a car," she says and looks down at her leg. "I can't keep on walking everywhere."

"Definitely, I'm not from around here though, do you have one?"

"Mike has it today."

"Mike, your husband?"

"Yeah."

"Bugger."

"What about the guy whose body you're in, do you think he has a car?"

"Good call. How do I check, I don't want to walk all that way if he doesn't?"

"Call his wife, ask?"

"What, like, 'Hi honey, how's your day? By the way, I forgot, do I drive and if so where's my car?'"

"Point taken, but you've been doing this long enough, you must have had some random conversations?" Jess raises her eyebrows at me.

"Screw it, give me a sec." I pull the man's phone out of my pocket. No signal. "Wait here." I get up and head towards the landing. Ignoring the memory of the last time I was here. Still, when I get to the landing, I check left and right before I go down the stairs.

Five very confusing minutes later, I walk back into the Baron Burghley and make my way up the stairs. Jess is where I left her, staring at the oil painting on the wall. "Well?" she asks.

"I hope she doesn't send him to therapy after that phone call. But, yes, he has a car, and it's parked right outside the house."

"That's great news," she says, but her face looks troubled. "I've been thinking, Lucas. If it is all connected, then there must be the main source where it's all coming from. Whether that's the Priory, the willow tree, or somewhere else, I'm not sure. That symbol, that's just creepy. Whatever is going on, Lucas, will you promise me you'll help me finish it? No more people will go missing: No children, no grown-ups, no-one."

I walk over to her and kneel in front of her. "I'm in it for the long run; I need to figure this out as much as you, okay?" I feel the softness of her touch as she places a hand on my face.

"It feels so good to tell someone that believes me finally."

"I know the feeling." I get up off the floor. "Now, Miss Daisy, would you like to wait here while I fetch our automobile?" I doff an imaginary flat cap at her, and she laughs, a pleasant sound that makes the room seem alive as it echoes off the tall ceilings.

"Go," she says and pushes me away.

It takes twenty, sweaty minutes to get back to the house and a further ten minutes to get in and find the car keys. The car on the driveway is a light blue 2012 plate Ford Fiesta. I open her up, and I'm pleasantly surprised to find she smells of bananas and coconuts from a plastic moulded cocktail glass that hangs from the mirror. I'm surprised. My car at home smells of decaying food and feet because I've never driven it, and it just sits behind the flat I share with a colleague. I only use it for smoking in when the nights are too cold in the winter. I've never passed my driving test. However, I've had many lessons, and the man whose body I'm in has a valid driving license. I pull away from the driveway and onto the estate.

The back roads of Westford are as familiar as the back of my hand (wink-wink). Now I'm driving and not walking everywhere, I understand why people are crazy about the roads in this small town. The cars don't pull over and wait for me to finish coming; they just keep on coming; squeezing by with the width of an ant's arsehole in between my car and theirs. They pull out at junctions without looking. It's damn scary. And don't get me started on the pedestrians who don't wait for the lights at zebra crossings. Everyone in this town had a god-damn death wish!

I make it back in one piece; the traffic as I get into the town centre moves at a crawl, which feels safer than the back roads. A white Range Rover driven by a yummy-mummy type pulls out of a space just as I turn onto the road leading to the Baron Burghley. I swing the car into the area before anyone else has the chance. I don't straighten it, leaving it with one shiny wheel sticking out. I run into the pub and up the stairs. She's still here. I see she has another drink, probably for courage, and I think I could do with one too. But then I realize I'm now the designated driver. I'm not cut out to be a designated driver; I feel too grown up.

We make our way down the stairs and out the front door into the afternoon heat. I don't tell Jess I don't have a driving license. I feel my driving skills are adequate, and wise words from my flatmate come back to me. *Fake it till you make it—no one in the big old world knows anything about you, so just act like you know what you're doing, and they'll believe it.*

"Smells nice," Jess says, getting into the dark leather passenger seat next to me. "Where to first?"

I've been thinking about this on the drive. "The Priory, I haven't been there yet. You can stay in the car, and then onto Whyte's house?" I still call the artist Whyte, even though I now know his real name.

"Okay," she says, reluctantly "Sounds like a plan–a shit plan, but a plan. Do you know the way? It's a couple of minutes' in the car."

I shake my head. "Lead the way."

The car hums a pleasant sound as I drive to the first set of traffic lights and turn right when the lights turn green. We follow the road to the bottom of the hill and take the first exit at the roundabout.

"Keep going straight," says Jess. "And it's on the right."

As I drive past identical houses, Jess's hand reaches up, and she takes a sharp intake of breath. "Stop!" I pull over, and we bounce as I mount the curb.

"What?"

"That van, the one pulling out." She's leaning forward in her seat, glaring out the window.

I look up the road, and I see a white van with tinted windows pull out from a hidden dirt road past what I assume is the Priory. Black smoke spews from its exhaust. On the side, I read the words, *'Duncan Fuller: Painter & Decorator,'* in bold, black italic lettering.

"That's the van from my dream."

I watch as Jess moves closer to the windscreen and peers at the dirty, white van. I see an odd thing as it pulls out; one of the dusty back doors opens an inch, and then it closes itself. The van drives up the road and out of sight. Thirty-seconds later, from the same dirt road, three teenagers appear. Two boys and a girl. The pretty, red-haired girl is holding the taller of the two boy's hand, while the other one, who's wearing glasses and holding a dusty-looking hessian sack, looks on. They walk towards us, but stop at the opening to the Priory. Their voices carry on the warm and heavy breeze through the car windows. They're shouting a name, 'Lisa.'

We get out of the car and walk up the road. The kids had given up shouting a few minutes earlier. and are now sitting on the grass. They look pale, an unreal, ethereal glow on the green and yellow grass. As we approach, the boy who was holding the girl's hand stands up in front of his friends.

"Who are you?" he asks, his fists clenched.

"Woah there cowboy," I say, raising my hands. "This is Jess, and my name's Lucas."

At the mention of my name, the kid's faces drop almost comically. They study me as if I'm the walking, talking ghost of Elvis. "We overheard you shouting. Can we help?"

I might as well have spoken to myself. They just stare at me—a big 'O' on each of their faces where their mouths should be. I shrug at Jess and then whisper, "What's wrong with them?"

Jess shrugs. "I don't know."

"Hey, kid. You in there?" I ask and go to knock on his skull like a door. He bats my hand away and says something I can't pick up. "Speak up, kid. I can't hear you."

"Bug...," he says.

I grab him by his shoulders and put my face into his. "Where'd you hear that name?"

"It's you," he says, and turns to his friends who are still sitting on the grass. "Lucas..."

"Bug. Where did you hear that name?" I ask again. The girl and boy stand up behind him.

"In the bag." He points to the sack in the bespectacled boy's hand. "Messages for you... From Bug."

"What? That makes no sense..." I brush past him and grab the bag off his friend, who mutters something that sounds like, "Don't touch the rock."

The bag's heavy in my hands, and I tip its contents onto the grass. "Don't touch the rock," the boy mutters again, and the other kids nod their heads. I look at the rock they're talking about; it's the size of a small fist and is a dull, matte black-dark colour. Next to it lays a large see-through baggy and a dictaphone.

"Listen to the dictaphone first," says the boy, who I've worked out is in charge. He puts his hand back, and the girl takes it. She has said nothing yet. Jess is observing us all, using the moss-covered wall for balance.

I put the dictaphone next to my ear and press play. Bug's voice comes through clear as day. The hairs on the back of my neck stand up as he speaks about the willow tree, and when he mentions Theo's name, my mind melts. He sounds scared, and that makes my stomach churn and turn. When the message finishes, I pass it to Jess to listen while I kneel and open up the baggy with the envelope inside.

I read the short letter, and my eyes wander over the rock when it becomes clear how important it is to Bug. What does he mean about the willow tree not being evil? My brain feels like it's swimming through a thick swamp. I can't pull a linear thought together from what I'm seeing and reading. He wanted me to come here, and he wanted me to find Theo; is the Priory ground zero? Is Theo the main piece of the puzzle. The King from a game of chess?

I look up at the kids. "So, you've been following these clues? Where did you find the bag?"

They are standing in a row, like a line-up for interrogation. "It was in a field near my house," the kid with spiked black hair says again.

"A field?"

"Yeah, just sat there, we figured it was dog shit at first." The others nod in agreement. "Ruby and Lisa found it." I see the boy's eyes glaze over when he mentions Lisa's name. "Lisa is my sister—she's gone, we can't find her. Ever since that thing came in that van and pulled out that body..." I see the girl, who I take to be Ruby, put her hand on his shoulder and he turns into an embrace with her. The other boy moves in, and they stand hugging.

"Lisa, was she here at the Priory with you?" Jess asks.

"Yes," he replies. "We got separated, Me, Petey, and Ruby were behind the Priory, and she was at the front."

"Is she a brave girl?" The kids peer at me, their eyes narrowing. "Would she, for example, climb into the van to follow someone or something?" They all nod. "I think I know where your sister is... what's your name, kid?"

"Luke, my name's Luke."

"Good name. I'm Lucas."

I reach out, my hand steady than it has been recently, and the kid takes it. He has a good firm grip considering he's as skinny as a bird.

9 THE TEENAGERS

The man let go of Luke's hand and asked, "Your sister, Lisa, does she have a mobile?"

Luke looked up at the man; how was it possible that this man was Lucas? Jake was Lucas, or Lucas was Jake, according to the bar girl in the Red Lion. But Luke had known about Bug, and he couldn't fake that reaction when he heard Bug's voice on the dictaphone. He glanced over at the pretty woman with her leg in a cast. She looked familiar. Lisa was in the back of the van, he was sure of it, and they would need help if they wanted to get her back. He flipped a coin in his head, and it came up heads.

"Yes, are you thinking what I'm thinking?" asked Luke.

"Track it?" Lucas said.

"My parents' downloaded an app so they could track the phone while she was out and about, 'you can't be too careful,' was what my dad said when they gave her the phone."

"They sound like likewise parents," Jess replied.

Luke shrugged his skinny shoulders. "They're okay, I guess." He remembered how mad his dad had been last night. He turned and looked back towards the Priory. "It's not human, you know?"

"What's not?" asked Jess. Luke noticed the woman looked pale.

"Whatever's driving the van. I saw it. It pulled who we thought was you..." Luke poked Lucas in the chest. "... out from inside the Priory. There was no way in, and then there was."

"Jake! Was he alive?"

"Yes, I saw him moving. One of his legs... it was covered in... maggots."

The woman pushed forward past Lucas. "Was it a woman–the driver of the van–was it a woman with bright red hair?" Luke saw her eyes; wide and wild.

Luke shook his head. "No, it was the painter-decorator, Duncan Fuller."

"Who is he?" asked Jess.

"No-one, just a guy. I looked him up on Google, and all he had was good reviews. People said he was friendly and helpful–he painted our house last weekend." Luke reached to his back pocket and removed the piece of cloth containing the fingernail and the portion of flesh. "I found something in the paint."

His scruffy hair came up to Lucas's chest; Lucas hunkered down a little, so he was at eye level with him. He reached out for the piece of cloth. "What did you find, Luke?"

He opened the cloth to Jess and Lucas. Ruby peered over his shoulder too. "What's that?" she asked. "You never told us about those things." She pointed at the fingernail and piece of flesh. Ruby looked at Petey. "Did you know about these?" Petey shrugged, and his face flushed red. She turned back to Luke and shoved him hard in the chest. "You knew... you knew, and we came anyway. What about Lisa, did she know?"

"No, I was going to tel–" Luke started.

"Actually, Luke, I told her. But, only when the guy turned up in his van." Petey said.

"Look, I'm sorry," Luke said to Ruby, and stepped forward to hold her. Ruby took a step backward. "Not now, Luke, stop. Let's get Lisa back, and then we'll talk."

Luke's face reddened. He felt like someone had kicked him in the balls. Shortest relationship ever. He guessed his mum and dad were right when they said there should be no secrets in a relationship. He hadn't made it half a day. Ruby walked off and sat near the gate leading to the Priory's grounds. Lucas put a hand on his shoulder. "Don't worry, kiddo, she'll calm down soon enough. They always do."

Jess let out a snort. "Yeah, Luke, we always do..." She raised an eyebrow at Lucas. "So, how do we go about tracking your sister's phone?"

"There's an app you need to download, then you input her number, and that's it."

"What no code or password?" asked Lucas.

"My dad disabled the password as Lisa kept on changing it–she didn't like them snooping on her."

"She sounds like a smart girl. Luke, you didn't finish about the fingernail, and that thing, what's going on?"

"I found them in my walls after he'd decorated. You'll think I'm crazy, but I think the painter decorator is grinding people up into paint and then using them to paint houses." He glanced at the floor and kicked his shoes together. "Getting rid of the bodies and doing something else; I'm not sure what, though."

"That's sick."

"It's just a guess," said Petey. "Luke doesn't know for sure."

"But I've been right so far, haven't I?" Luke turned to Lucas, "Unlock your phone, I'll install the app, and we can get going."

Lucas did what the kid said and handed it over; with a few quick taps on the screen and a 30-second wait for it to download, Luke passed it back. A satnav style map filled the screen, and a red circle moved through the estates of Westford. They stood around the screen, watching the blinking red dot. Ruby stood up and came over. "But she didn't have any data?" she said, avoiding contact with Luke, standing next to Jess.

"The app doesn't need data for us to track her." Luke smiled.

"If he's turning the bodies into paint, he'd need a large warehouse or industrial building. The dispersion tanks used to make paint are huge and noisy. And, he'd need to store the other ingredients: the resin, the pigment, you know?" Jess said.

They all looked at her, question mark wrinkles standing out on their faces.

Jess blushed. "What? I saw a kid's program last week that showed how they make paint." She shrugged.

"What was the address for the painting business?" Lucas asked.

"It was a home address; no big buildings or warehouses near it."

"Look," Ruby said, pointing at the screen. "It's going away from town, out towards Lisa's house." Luke frowned, it was no longer his house or his and Lisa's house—just Lisa's again. They watched the red dot blink up the long road towards Luke and Lisa's estate. It didn't turn left onto the estate; it went right onto a no-entrance road. It sat blinking in the middle of a field.

"I know where they are," Luke said

The three kids crammed into the back of the Fiesta, while Jess fixed the phone onto the dashboard. Lucas started the engine. Jess turned around in her seat. "Seat Belts," she said and looked at Lucas too. They rolled their eyes and then clicked themselves in. They sat in silence as Lucas drove around the roundabout and towards the centre of town.

"What will we do when we get there?" Luke asked.

"I think we should scout the place out, then go from there, plan?" Jess said.

"Plan," they all agreed.

They drove through a seemingly never-ending supply of traffic lights and along roads with queues of cars parked along the side. Twice, Lucas had to hammer on the brakes, to stop them crashing into cars that had pulled out without warning. They drove past the Red Lion on their left and the Shell garage on their right; Lucas breathed a sigh of relief to be out of the chaotic town centre.

He followed the road, and Luke, Petey, and Ruby sat huddled together in the back, their knees touching. Luke looked at Ruby. She glared back but said nothing. They reached the top of the road, where a left turn would have taken them onto Luke's estate, and followed the road which would have taken them into the village of Great Beckton. Lucas flicked on his indicator and pulled into the garage and warehouses on their right. He stopped the car behind the first building and turned to the kids.

"This the right place?" he asked, looking around at the industrial warehouses with red-rust stained white corrugated walls. A crumbling brick wall separated them from the fields that led to the quarry.

They nodded. "Just past the used car lot and over that hedge. That's where the warehouses are," said Petey.

Lucas reached for his door handle.

"Where are you going?" Ruby asked.

"I'm going to scout it out."

"Not alone, you're not," Luke said.

"Listen, we still don't know what's going on. let me scout out the area, and then I'll come right back."

"I'm coming," Ruby said, and crossed her arms over her chest. You go, girl, Jess thought from the front seat. She hadn't mentioned that her own (as yet undisclosed) tracking sense had already confirmed to her they were in the right place.

"Me too," said Luke.

Jess shrugged at Lucas. "She's their friend, and they know the area better than you. I'd come too if it weren't for my leg."

"I'll stay with you if that's okay?" Petey asked Jess; she could see his sad eyes in the mirror.

"Yeah, of course, it is. Jump in the front. We'll do some research while they're gone."

Petey and Jess watched as Lucas, Ruby, and Luke walked across the cracked concrete towards the tall warehouses, past cars with little whiteboards with handwritten prices in the front windows. To their right was a line of sharp-looking light-grey metal fencing and beyond that, yellow fields of dry grass that had died in the sun. Two large white warehouses stood tall, glinting in the bright sunshine. Behind them was open farmland, and the warehouse they were looking for. Workers sat on green, plastic patio chairs smoking rolled up cigarettes in the sunshine outside the closest warehouse. Jess and Petey watched their friends sneak around the back, leaning against the corrugated metal of the building like detectives.

Lucas peered around the edge of the longest side of the warehouse, and when he saw it was clear, he moved forward into the yellow field, followed by Luke and Ruby. Crouching down, they made their way towards the concrete yard of the warehouse they had glimpsed from the forecourt of the garage.

The roof of the warehouse was a perfect dome. It was a pitch-black that contrasted against the blood-red of the rust on the white metal of the building.

Their view was partially cut off by tall ferns and blackberry bushes, and they could only see the roof and one side of the warehouse. The smell of diesel and cigarettes lingered in the air.

They pushed through out of the dry straw field and into spiky undergrowth. Lucas led the way, holding low-hanging branches with thorns out of his face until he came to an old, rickety wooden fence bound to the next with rusted barbed wire. Ruby and Luke caught up and kneeled next to him, peering through the bushes to look inside the compound.

The painter had parked his white van outside the warehouse in front of a large up-and-over blue metal door that stood open. They couldn't see beyond the black inside and stood in silence, waiting for the man to appear. After a moment, Lucas turned to get Luke and Ruby ready to move, but they were gone. "Fuck," he muttered to himself, and hunched down and looked around the perimeter of the yard. In the bracken—one hundred yards away—he saw two dark shapes moving through the trees. They were close to the van, just beyond a large, red metal skip. When they emerged, they would only be ten steps away.

Luke entered the dusty yard first, followed by Ruby. He turned to check she was over the barbed wire fence and then put his arm around her shoulders as they crouched and ran towards the van; her red hair flowing in the warm breeze. When they were five steps away, a loud mechanical growl like the crunching of machinery, came from inside the warehouse. They sprinted to the cover of the van and stood with their backs against it. They were out of the line of sight from anyone peering out of the warehouse and were past the closed double doors at the end of the van, blocking the writing on the side.

Luke looked towards where Lucas stood in the trees. He saw him crouched, invisible unless you were looking for him. Luke gave him a thumbs up. Lucas put up one finger, signalling for them to wait. From behind the van, they heard shuffling footsteps in the dust. Someone was approaching from the open doorway of the warehouse. Ruby's hand groped for Lukes. He took it, squeezed, and then turned to look at her. He raised an index finger to his lips. She nodded back, tears wetting her hazel eyes.

A hacking cough made Ruby's grip tighten on Luke's hand, and then the hacking cough was replaced with the phlegmy sound of someone spitting up something onto the floor. It landed with a sickening squelch.

The footsteps approached the side of the van closest to the warehouse. Luke thought about running but knew it would hear them. The steps moved along the opposite side of the van. They stood still like statues, holding each other's hand. Luke felt Ruby shaking, sending tremors through his arm. He looked towards Lucas, who was gone. They were alone.

The doors of the van swung open—one of the doors swinging back and stopping an inch away from Luke's nose. A shadow of a man loomed long and disjointed on the dusty floor. If the man who owned the shadow looked down, he would see the red and white converse trainers Luke wore. Another hacking cough came from the man, followed by another gloopy spitting session. They heard muffled grunting, and the van started to rock as someone inside struggled.

Luke and Ruby heard someone get dragged out of the van and land with a thud on the floor. A muffled scream, followed by pained grunts, filled the empty courtyard as they heard the dull sound of kicks. The shadow moved, and Luke watched as decayed grey fingers grabbed the side of the door before slamming it shut. They held their breath as they listened to the body being dragged into the warehouse.

The trees rustled to Luke's right from where they had come from, and he saw Lucas waving to them. Luke glanced towards Ruby and raised three fingers, counting them down from three, two, one. On one, they ran across the empty yard and into the bushes.

"Was it Lisa?" Luke asked.

Lucas shook his head. "It was Jake, I think. He looked in bad shape."

"Did you see Lisa?"

"No." Lucas looked past Luke and Ruby to the warehouse. "You two, go back to the car. I'll find Lisa."

Ruby nodded and started to move, but Luke pulled her back. "My sister is there, I'm not going anywhere." Ruby looked up the field and towards the car park, before turning back to Luke. "I'm staying too," she said.

"Okay, I don't have time to argue. Stay here, though. I'm going to that van. She must still be in the back."

There was no argument from Luke or Ruby. They stayed hunched amongst the thorns and brambles as Lucas snuck over to the van using the red skip for cover. The clanging of machinery rang through the air, followed by a whirring sound, not smooth and greased, but clunking and stubborn. They held still as Lucas approached the van from the rear, and then moved towards the side where they had been moments before.

Lucas knocked on the side of the van three times. "Lisa? Lisa, I'm with Luke and Ruby, knock if you can hear me."

He tilted his head to the side. Silence except for the industrial sound from the warehouse. "Lisa, this isn't a trick, my name's Lucas, you've been looking for me, please, knock if you hear me."

Lucas thought he heard a gentle tap, but he couldn't be sure over the clunking of the machinery. He took three deep breaths, steadied his hammering heart, and swung around to the rear of the van, and opened the double doors. The stench hit him like hot air when you get off a plane. He gagged, and had to stop himself from retching against the truck. It was a hot metal, decaying flesh, maggoty smell, tinged with something sour. The inside of the van was dark and wet. A trail of writhing and wriggling yellow maggots littered the floor of the van. The walls were sweating with putrid pieces of flesh and gore.

"Lisa," he said into the gloom.

A rank, dirty piece of once-white cloth splattered with paint, moved at the back of the van. He saw the full whites of her eyes, followed by the rest of her as she wriggled free from beneath it.

"Lisa, I'm Lucas. Luke and Ruby are in the bushes." He pointed. She raised a hand to block the sun from her eyes. "You'll be able to see them if you get out of the van."

Lisa looked at him. "You don't look like the picture?"

"That was Jake… it's a long story, but Bug, he was my friend."

"You could be one of them."

"I could, but I'm not. Petey is here as well; he's in the car with my friend." He opened his arms wide.

"What's your friend's name?"

"Jess, she's nice, you'll like her." He moved to climb into the van.

"Don't." Lisa moved towards him, she smiled shyly. "You don't want any of that shit on your shoes. I'm going to stink for days."

"You believe me?" he asked, as she carried on towards him, careful to avoid touching the sides of the inside of the van.

"Well, it's believe you, or stay here–so I'll take my chances."

"Okay." She was right about the smell, Lucas thought, as he helped her down from the van and pointed towards the tree line. "See them? Run! Now!" She ran through the puddles the creature had hacked up and sprinted across the yard, leaving shiny black footprints in the dust. He watched her go, and when he saw them together, hugging, he shooed them off with the back of his hand. Lucas mouthed to them, "I'll be right behind you." He closed the van doors and leaned back against the vehicle as he watched them go through the bushes, and when he was confident they wouldn't come back, he crouched down and sprinted to the side of the entrance of the warehouse.

The shade of the building was cooler than the day, but the noise coming from inside was monstrously loud. Lucas didn't know if the man was alone or not, and didn't fancy his chances either way, but he couldn't leave Jake alone to his fate when that fate was meant for him. He'd let go of Bug; he wouldn't let go of Jake.

He saw a breadcrumb trail of dying maggots leading inside the warehouse. Some were still wriggling, while others were squashed into a sticky goo. He tucked himself against the dark of the shade and slunk inside.

To his left, a black metal staircase led up to a barrier and a crisscrossed stainless steel floor that circled the inside of the warehouse as far as he could see. Straight ahead, was the trail of maggots. He climbed the staircase, crawling along on his stomach. The cold metal pressed against his exposed flesh where his shirt pulled up.

Hidden among the shadows, he waited and peered through the darkness into the centre of the cavernous room. The warehouse was empty besides five large white vats the size of a Fiesta turned on its side. The centre of the warehouse was the only part of the building lit up. Large strip-lights hung from thick metal coils sending a fluorescent white glow to the floor below. A white metal ladder led up to the lip of each vat, and running down the sides, creating a semi-rectangular open workspace, were metal industrial tables and storage shelves that reflected the fluorescent white light. Large semi-transparent plastic containers with white plain labels were stacked on the shelves. On the table, were substantial black iron weighing scales, like those used for weighing meat at a butchers.

Jake lay on his back on one of the metal tables. His hands were bound like a prisoner in hospital, with leather cuffs. He was tossing and scrambling to get free. Lucas saw the remains of his leg and the shower of maggots that fell to the grey painted floor when he moved. He wanted to run to him, to untie him, and help him out of this place.

He looked around the room. Besides the vats and the tables, it was dark, the corners deep in shadow. The man could be watching.

Lucas heard a scuff from behind and below him at the entrance. He lay his head against the crisscrossed metal floor and fought to control his breathing, which was coming in quick sharp rasps that burned his throat. Footsteps approached. He watched the entrance and prayed that the kids hadn't come back. A shadowed figure silhouetted against the brightness of outside entered the warehouse.

The profile was wrong. It was human in shape, but the arms were elongated, and the hair was tall and spiked in all directions, an image of Medusa from the old movies he'd enjoyed with his grandad played through his mind. He watched the figure enter the room, then it was lost in the dark, before appearing again under the fluorescent lights. It was a woman with shocking red hair that looked like fire under the lights. The woman Jess had asked about. Were the painter decorator and the woman working together?

He heard a hacking cough followed by the wet sound of something landing on the floor. Then the man appeared under the lights next to the woman. They stood in silence, studying Jake silently as he squirmed on the metal table. A gentle breeze blew through the open doors, and a leaf danced and moved on the floor.

Lucas didn't see them change. There was no metamorphosis; they just turned. Gnarled and twisted mandibles extended from the man's mouth, and above those, ten shiny eyes popped up where his forehead had been. One after another after another dome-like eyes, with slits that opened and closed sideways, flicked around the room. The woman looked reptilian, with a spiked, black forked-tongue which flicked over Jake's body. Two milky white eyes protruded from her scaled face. Webbed hands held onto the metal table; Jake had one to each side of his squirming body. Lucas watched them sniff and lick and taste Jake's flesh. He saw the woman's forked-tongue covered in maggots making it look alive and wriggling under the white lights.

Lucas turned away at the first wet sounds of ripping flesh and sinew. He heard a crack that reverberated around the warehouse; a bone snapped, and Jake's muffled cries filled the air and then went silent. All that was left was the wet sounds of dogs feeding. Lucas lost track of time as he listened. He turned his head towards where Lucas lay and saw the painter decorator licking out the contents of what looked like a leg bone–maybe the thigh bone–still covered in red flesh, like it was an almost-empty can of drink. Maggots and strips of flesh and black blood and gore were dripping from the creature's faces. A dark puddle formed below the table in which he saw a forearm and a hand with three fingers sticking up from the pile of gore–still twitching. The man and the woman leaned over the bloody mess, gorging themselves on Jake's intestine, and Lucas bit his lip to stop from screaming.

He turned away, not wanting to see the creatures as they licked up the remains of the body he had once lived in. He froze, a chill running through him, thinking about the other people he had been, and Jess. Is this what awaited them? The slapping of lips consumed him; he wanted to raise his hands to cover his ears but thought, if he moved, they might hear him. He couldn't escape the squelching and crunching.

Lucas pictured Ben's helpless four-year-old body being picked apart by them. His big brown eyes looking up at him out of the dark, crying out for help. Lucas shivered, his skin came out in gooseflesh, and he turned back around and looked as Jake's insides got lapped up by the creatures. Tears ran down his face, but he had to watch. He had to see what else happened. His eyes met Jakes, and he prayed for forgiveness.

The creatures stopped feeding and, in a blur, were back in their human forms. They looked at each other and nodded. The woman moved towards the table with the weighing scales, and started to measure out a white powder that looked like washing powder into them from a large container. She lifted it like it was only a bag of sugar. Once she'd weighed out the amount she required, she moved on and opened another container and poured that onto the scales too, creating a mound of white powder.

Meanwhile, the man worked silently behind her; he carried three containers to the side of one vat. He climbed the metal ladder; his steps echoed in the room. The man Ruby had called Fly-Face, poured the wet liquid into the tank from one container, and then repeated the process with the two further containers.

The woman waddled to the table with Lucas's remains and nonchalantly, using a tool like a window squeegee, scraped off the bloody remains into an empty transparent container. She licked at the blood and gore on her fingers after. Once the table was clean, she had two full containers of red liquid with floating flesh that sloshed around the bucket. A scum formed on the top and pink bubbles bubbled to the top, leaving frothy white ring marks amongst the pieces of scalp and entrails. Carefully, like an old lady baking a cake, she carried the two buckets over to the man standing halfway up the ladder waiting. He took them from her and poured the contents into the vat. Like the woman, he licked his fingers clean afterward.

With the contents in the vat, the man and the woman held a silent conversation between themselves, communicating on a frequency that Lucas could not hear. Lucas watched the woman turn her back on the man and disappear into the dark, before reappearing at the entrance. She passed within five feet of him, directly under where he lay. His body tensed as she looked back into the warehouse and seemingly up at him on the metal staircase. She hacked and coughed and spat something wet onto the floor and left. He looked down at where she at spat and saw a toe with the nail still attached sticking out of a dark red puddle of gore.

As she left, Lucas heard the mechanical sound again. While she had been inside, he'd thought it was silent, however, now he reckoned she'd either done something to the acoustics of the building, or it had faded into background noise. The man flipped a switch on a bank of glowing buttons that hung from the vat, and the large metal arms started to spin slowly. He'd seen enough. Backing down the staircase, going down on his knees, Lucas kept low and moved into the shadows below; he peered around the corrugated warehouse wall to check the woman had gone.

The courtyard stood empty beside the dirty white van that sat looking at him. He looked back once into the lights in the centre of the building and saw the man still working. He readied himself and ran to the white van using it as cover before sprinting straight left, past the red skip and through the wooden fence, ignoring the scrapes and sharp cuts on his legs from the thorns and the barbed wire. He ran as if hellhounds were on his trail. A blur of white and blue and the pale yellow fields against the vivid blue of the sky flashed by as he ran with no thought of form. His hands fluttered uselessly at his sides, and he took quick glances over his shoulder. He blazed through the opening that led to the other warehouses not caring about the workers smoking their cigarettes outside. Lucas reached the car, jumped in, and slammed the door.

He sat in the front seat, breathless, his chest heaving, and his white shirt dark with sweat. The kids were crammed in the back seat; he'd interrupted their reunion. Jess sat next to him, her smile from seeing the kids together changing to a frown.

"We've got… to go… now!" he said, his words coming between pauses in breath.

"Why what happe–" Jess started.

"Not now, let's go."

He started the car with shaking hands and put the accelerator to the floor, pulling a 360 in the garage forecourt that made the kids moan as they squashed together in the back. He heard a thud as one of their heads hit the window hard. At the exit of the garage, Lucas checked his mirrors for the man and woman. He saw normal-looking people putting petrol in their cars. And a few smoking workers in overalls watching the commotion. They all looked at him.

"Which way?" he asked, turning his head.

Petey leaned forward and pointed right. "Go down there; I know a safe place."

They pulled out in front of a powder blue Nissan, leaving dark skid marks behind them as they sped down the road towards Great Beckton. The kids in the back seats looked at each other. Petey held the side of his head, tears welling in his eyes. They were squashed in, and as Lucas looked in the rear-view mirror, he realized he needed to get off the road before they were pulled over or reported.

"Next right," Petey shouted as if he'd heard Lucas' thoughts. "Go down a bit and then pull over on the right."

"What? We're nowhere near far enough away!" Ruby said.

"Pull over!" Petey said again. "Everyone out as soon as we pull over."

Lucas turned right onto a country lane, eyeing Petey in his mirror. Petey nodded at him, and he pulled the Fiesta over onto a grass verge overlooked by a large newly built house with a massive paved driveway where a black Porsche Cayenne stood. They scrambled out of the car. The kids climbed through the front and emerged like clowns from a much too small car.

"This way, quickly, follow me." Petey ran back up to where Lucas had turned, leaving him and Jess standing at the side of the road. The car had been full of the stench of the warehouse, and it seemed to have got Petey's flight response primed to full gear. He was fast for a small kid, Lucas thought, as he helped Jess up to the junction.

Petey stopped at the side of the busy road, waiting for a slow-moving Ford Mondeo to go past. As Lucas looked up the way they came, he could just make out the roof of the warehouse. They hadn't gone far. Once it was clear, Petey ran across the road and disappeared into the bushes. The others followed. They scrambled down a dry, muddy path, ignoring the stinging nettles and branches. Lucas heard running water. The kids, knowing where Petey was taking them, overtook him, sure of the way.

Dappled sunlight on the fast-running stream reflected off the stained bricks of the bridge. Two large semi-circular openings led to darkness, where the sound of water flowing over the natural dam of washed-up twigs and rocks echoed off the walls. The ceiling shimmered as light bounced off the flowing water. A rotten log lay in the middle–two ends poking out like a serpent from a Greek myth. A decaying tree, half-in–half-out of the water, sat to the side, its long-dead trunk lying lazily on its side. White butterflies floated over the water, and the only sounds they could hear was running water and the twittering of birds.

A frayed blue rope hung from an overhanging branch from an old oak tree and swayed in the gentle breeze. Ivy curled down the old bridge, and a dirt path ran across the top. A faded fence, with one part missing, blocked the edge. They reached an opening, and below it was a fifty-foot drop. As the kids ran, Jess and Lucas took a steadier pace, careful not to lose their footing. On the other side of the bridge, a steep, dusty slope led down to the river bank. The kids were leaning against an old tree catching their breath when Lucas and Jess caught up.

"Where are we?" Jess asked.

"We're just down from my house," Luke answered. "The fields opposite the garage."

Jess shook her head. "It feels like we're miles away from anywhere."

"That's the point," said Petey.

"Are you okay?" Luke asked Lisa, who nodded. "That was stupid, don't you ever do that again."

"Buttface," Lisa replied, and pulled him close for a cuddle. The rest of the kids joined in, while Jess and Lucas looked around the secluded riverbank.

"This'll do," Lucas said, as he lowered himself to the ground.

Jess sat next to him; her cast stretched out towards the water. "What happened?" she asked. The kids broke free from the hug and came and sat down in the shade under the trees, creating a circle.

"I saw him, Jake. I couldn't help him." He pulled a hand through his hair. "Those things… they ate him, I saw it and then… Luke, you were right. They put his leftovers into a container and then into a big machine. I think they were turning him into the paint."

"Lucas ,was she there?" Jess asked.

"Yes, she was there, big red hair," he said, mimicking the hair with his hands above his head. "They were human, and then they weren't." He put his head in his hands. "Oh my god, what did I just see?" He laid back on the riverbank, small rocks digging into his back. "What the fuck is going on? What are those things?"

Jess looked at the teenagers sitting opposite. The two girls were pretty, Lisa and Ruby; cute names too. Lisa had wavy brown hair with natural curls and was Luke's brother. Jess believed Luke to be in a relationship with Ruby, the fair-skinned, red-headed, freckled girl. Petey looked like a nerd straight from TV; shaggy brown hair and wide-rimmed glasses–but he'd kept control and had a plan when no-one else did. She felt protective of these kids already, especially Petey. What had they seen?

"So you listened to and read the messages for Lucas, huh?"

They nodded in sync.

"Tell us your story, and Lucas and I will tell ours, and we'll see if we can find anything that makes sense."

Like scouts at summer camp, the four teenagers, Jess and Lucas swapped stories sat in a circle under the shade of the trees at the riverbank. The shadows grew longer as they told their story, and when Lucas finished, they sat in silence; the only sound, the gentle lapping of the river as it flowed on like it always did. They stared out over the river, watching the water flow, and the butterflies fly above.

"So I guess we're all looking for T R Whyte?" Lisa said to break the silence, she sat next to Ruby, holding hands. Jess noticed Luke glancing at them now and again.

"Looks that way, only… shit… I forgot a part, didn't I?" Lucas said.

"What part?" asked Lisa.

"Wait a sec, I've got it here somewhere." Lucas searched through his pockets. "I couldn't remember the name off the top of my head, but there, on the top of this piece of paper," he said, pointing as he unfolded it and passed the page he stole from the gallery to Lisa. "That's Whyte's real name–T. R Whyte was a fake name."

Lisa's eyebrows raised, and she passed the piece of paper to Luke. He shook his head once as if shaking away the cobwebs. They both looked at Lucas.

"This can't be," Luke said.

"Why? Do you know that name… that address?"

Luke and Lisa looked at each other. "That's our grandad."

PART THREE

1 HENRY CURTHOSE

Henry Curthose sat in his favorite, battered, red-leather chesterfield wingback with his feet on an equally aged red-leather stool with a glass of Brandy at his side on the antique mahogany coffee table. He looked out across the countryside from his front window; the fields were turning yellow in the scorching hot summer, and things were ending.

The house was clean, if not tidy. Stacked magazines and books lay on the welsh dresser, the coffee table, and anywhere something could be laid. A faded, red Persian rug with a triangle pattern covered the exposed stone tile floor.

A tatty, blue leather-bound journal with gilt-edged pages lay on his lap. The pages were frayed and mustard yellow. The time is nearly here, he thought. He wondered which of them it would be? *Time healed all hurts,* wasn't that what they used to say? *As you get older, you realize that the people you love the most, don't love you back, and you don't even know what you did*—except Henry knew what he'd done—he'd had no choice though. He hoped time would heal the hurt he'd done to the people he cherished the most. But, you did it for duty, another voice told him. It had to be done this way; they had done it this way for generations.

His old bones ached and screamed, as if filled with shattered glass, as he stood up and made his way to the welsh dresser and his vast collection of books, and more importantly, the bottle of brandy. He filled his glass and ran his fingers over the covers of the books; titles such *The History of Monasteries and Churches in England,* and, *The Normans: Myths and Legends,* looked at him from the shelves, daring him to reread them. Once was more than enough, thank you. Everything he needed to know was in the leather-bound journal he'd left on his chair.

He'd been twelve when it had happened to him. Events led him to his estranged grandfather's house, where the secrets of their family were passed down to him, ready for him to pass down to his grandchild. It always missed a generation, and he thought they were the lucky ones.

Would it be Lisa, or would it be Luke? The Pull didn't discriminate between sexes, so the odds were fifty/fifty. How long had it been since he'd seen them last? Five, six years? A photo of them stared down at him from the top shelf of the dresser. She'd been a little shy thing with masses of curly brown hair, while he was skinny as a rake with scruffy blonde hair and mud under his fingernails. Standing side-by-side, the similarities between the two were striking. Both had thin noses, wide eyes, and high cheekbones. They were beautiful things. He remembered how they used to play games and colour pictures on the floor in the very sitting-room he was now drinking in, alone. That was when Juliette was still alive.

Henry walked back over to his chair and sloshed brandy onto his jeans when he slumped down. It had awoken. He didn't know how many of the things it had let loose on the town, but the recent disappearances worried him. With the time he'd had, he'd been able to put together a rough timeline of events—which he hoped would convince his grandchild how vital their mission was and the part in the story they would play. They needed to understand; he was too old and haggard now.

He prayed he would be around to help, though. It wasn't fair for it all to fall on their young shoulders. The brandy tasted sour. It was a strange, long and twisting story which he'd practiced telling many times when he sat alone in the dark of the empty house. As with anything in life, there was no choice but to meet the threat head-on. He looked past the empty chair opposite and towards the locked room beyond. It would be open soon, and that meant the end for them or it.

He was exhausted from the momentary memories of the past, and the promise of death in the future. So he took a glug of the amber liquid and closed his eyes. When he opened them again, with a new sense of purpose, he picked up the journal from the table.

The leather journal felt alive in his hands, a secret history he'd kept safe since the age of twelve. Dark secret schools wouldn't teach if they even knew it existed, and that governments would bury deeper than they hid the truth about the Kennedy assassination. He examined the cover and then the piece of once maroon cloth, now faded, that tied around the front of the book to keep it together. Faded, but still there,if you knew where to look, was a symbol older than time. Henry thought about what that symbol meant and how mass-misinformation and conspiracy had skewed its meaning over the years'. If only everyone knew the truth. When his ancestors created it, it was a symbol of a secret vow they shared—a secret he alone now carried. But, not for long.

The sun was getting low in the sky when he heard a car pull onto his gravel drive. Though he had been waiting for this moment for years', now it was here, his hands shook holding the journal. Passing on this knowledge, meant the end of a normal life for one of his grandchildren. Which had turned up on his doorstep? Lisa or Luke? He stood to look out through his window, expecting to discover a taxi, when he saw a dusty blue Fiesta. Two adults, a woman, and a man sat in the front, and behind them, he could see the outline of four others. He pulled back from the window, and ambling, because of old age, went to unlock the door that had been locked for decades.

A car door opened, and scuffed footsteps on the gravel drive made their way to his front door. He fiddled with the old brass key in the lock until he heard it click, and entered the room. Henry shut the door and locked it behind him. Then he waited. His hips and back ached while he crouched in the corner of the dim room. The blinds were drawn and didn't allow any light in through the two sash windows that overlooked the side garden and fields.

Muffled whispers seeped under the door to him. They were outside the house, at the front. He heard the deep voice of a man and then a woman's voice, followed by two further voices, one higher pitched than the other. It sounded like an argument. Three knocks on the door made his back twitch, and his hands clenched into fists.

"Grandad," he heard a boy's voice shout. "Grandad, are you in? It's Luke."

The voice was deep and new, close to being the voice of a man—could it be Luke? Who else was with him, and as if in answer, the voice spoke again, "Grandad, Lisa's here too. We need to speak to you."

Muted voices again, and then Luke said, "It's about T. R Whyte."

If that was Luke, and they knew the name T. R Whyte, it was time. He stood, holding onto the wall for balance, unlocked the door, and shouted through the gap, "If that's really you when was the last time we spoke?"

Silence came from the other side of his front door. He moved to the room at the back. Specks of dust quilled in the air, like faeries. A gap in the door allowed a beam of light into the usually locked room. He reached inside for the Remington 700 hunting rifle he'd left there so many years ago. His fingers touched the cold stainless steel bar and made their way down its walnut stock. He prayed it was loaded and still worked. He listened. He heard whispers. He went back to the front door.

"I'm armed. If you try to break in, I will shoot you—all of you." He cocked the gun.

"It was six years ago, on my eighth birthday," the voice replied.

"And what did I say?" Henry asked.

"You said something about not seeing us for a while, but it was for the best," a girls' voice answered. "Grandad, it's Lisa. I don't know what happened back then, but we need your help."

They were both here, alongside four strangers. "Who's with you?"

"Two grown-ups, my friend and Lisa's friend—grandad, we need your help,"

Henry looked at the gun; it's polished walnut barrel heavy in his hands. He'd been alone so long waiting, was he going to turn them away now?

"Okay, back away from the door."

He tucked the journal onto a shelf on the dresser and leaned the shotgun against its side. Henry unlocked the door and opened it a few inches, keeping the chain on. Sunshine burned in, in a long rectangle of light that made his stone floor sparkle. There were six of them. Lisa and Luke, two adults (the woman he noticed had a cast on her leg, and he knew who she was) and two other children; a pale and a freckled girl and a short boy with thick glasses. "I guess you best come on in then, don't you?"

As he opened the door to let them in, he peered out over the countryside; before locking the door once they were inside. His two estranged grandchildren ran over to him and put their arms around his waist. Flustered, he gently stroked their hair before wrapping his arms around them. He started to cry, and the kids cried too. "God, I've missed you both." He kissed them both on their foreheads. They were filthy, covered in dust and dirt, and the tears created white paths of skin down their cheeks.

"Come in, come in," he said, motioning to Jess, Lucas, Petey, and Ruby, who were still lingering on the doorstep. All thoughts of a trap diminished now he'd held Lisa and Luke.

"We've been looking for you forever," the man said to him, and offered his hand as he made his way from the mud-encrusted, shoe-lined porch into the house. "Lucas."

"Henry, Henry Curthose. It's a pleasure to meet you all."

130

2

After offering everyone drinks (Lucas and Jess both readily accepted brandy while the kids had cans of Coke), Henry requested each of them to tell their stories and how they came to be together at his front door. They sat in the cosy sitting room, with views of the fields across, surrounded by Henry's assortment of peculiar antiquities and books. Jess and Lucas took the two-seater sofa that matched Henry's wingback chair, while the kids sat side-by-side on the patterned Persian rug, taking glugs from their cans of Coke. The room smelled of old paperbacks and dry mud.

He nodded as he listened to each of their stories, Luke being a narrator for the kids. Henry didn't interrupt; he just sat in his wingback chair, taking the occasional sip of brandy. His eyebrows raised once when Lucas mentioned about jumping from body to body. When Lucas finished, and they had told the stories, the sun had set.

Henry looked at the teenagers sitting on the floor with their legs crossed like they were at a school assembly and said, "It's late, you best all call your parents'. Petey can you tell yours you're staying at Luke's and likewise for you Ruby?" Petey and Ruby nodded their heads. "The phone's in the kitchen, hanging on the wall–my mobile's somewhere around, but I don't have Facebook like you hip kids." He winked at Luke, as Ruby and Petey went to the kitchen. "You two," he said, looking at Lisa and Luke. He placed a forefinger lengthways across his lips and left it there, thinking. "Tell your parents' the truth; it may surprise you, but I've been talking to them, and it won't come as a surprise that you're having a sleepover at your granddad's. Ste… sorry, your dad will be pissed, but if he is, just pass him over to me."

"That's great! What are we going to do after? Roast marshmallows over a fire?" Lucas stood up. Jess slid towards him on the sofa and tried to pull him back down. He looked at her. "No, Jess." Then towards Henry, and pointed. "We have told him everything we know, and we have heard nothing yet, no explanation, no nothing."

Henry leaned forward in his chair, his brandy glass in his left hand resting on his knee. "I understand Lucas, I do, but I needed to hear your stories first—it may have changed things. I will tell you everything, and I mean everything, once we know we won't have a search party looking for four more missing children!"

Lucas sat and folded back into the sofa as if reeling from a slap to the face. "Ben…" he said.

"Lucas, look at me. There is still time, he may be alive, and if he is, I will help you find him, okay?" Lucas nodded once and then emptied his glass of brandy. "Help yourself to another; it may well be a long night."

All four kids were in the kitchen waiting to use the phone as the grown-ups sat in silence. Henry heard Petey promise his mum he would be good, and that he loved her, while Ruby did likewise. Jess and Lucas sat together, sneaking glances at Henry, who didn't mind.

It was the first time he'd had visitors for a long time, and the house felt good being full again. He smiled. He'd been expecting one grandchild on their own, scared and alone, and instead, both had shown up in a team, a family even. There was a bond between them that was clear straight away. They glanced at each other before speaking and shared little smiles; if you couldn't smile in the face of adversity, then adversity had already won.

"He's crazy," Lucas said, getting to his feet, pacing around the small sitting room, his arms flailing in the air. "Listen to it; it's crazy!"

"Crazier than waking up in a new body every day?" Jess countered from the sofa.

"We're talking about religion and history here, it's crazy," Lucas said. "Let me get this right–An ancient French king from an evil bloodline buried something under the monastery here in Westford; an egg of an ancient monster, no less." Henry nodded. "And you are an ancestor of William the Conqueror–the William the Conqueror of the Battle of Hastings?"

"That's correct."

"And to make up for his own great, great, great grandfather's pillaging of England, he rebuilt the destroyed monastery and turned it into the Priory which is still standing? And, he did this because while on the crusades–the sodding crusades–everyone are you listening to this? He heard about an ancient evil buried in little old Westford and formed the Knights Templar–the Knights Templar…" Lucas shook his head.

"Correct again."

"And, now you, Henry… wait, does that make you a member of the Knights Templar?" Henry nodded again. "So, every other generation, you pass this down to your grandchildren who sit and wait for the evil to wake?"

Lucas looked at the kids sitting cross-legged on the floor. "You don't believe this, do you?" They shrugged their shoulders. He turned back to Henry. "What about the willow tree then, Henry? And, why now, why has it suddenly awoken, and what are those creatures?"

Henry rubbed his hands together. "Finally, some good questions," he said. "Did you know that willow trees only live for 75-years maximum?" Everyone, except Lucas, shook their heads. "It's true, look it up. However, do you know how long that tree has been standing?" They stared at him. "Me neither, no-one does. From every generation to the next, everyone you ask will tell you they remember it; it's in old sketches and oil paintings dating back centuries. Why? Pagans associated the willow tree with the serpent. They believed it would drive them away." He opened up the journal that had been sat at his side until now, he thumbed through it and showed them a sketch of the Leviathan. "That is the Leviathan; it is a serpent; some say it's Satan himself. That is what Dagobert II buried." He looked at Lucas. "Your French King." He turned back to his enthralled audience. "Willow trees are trees of dreams and inspiration; they also believed they retained the soul of the dead person buried under it. And, when the time is right, and the person is right, it can show that person the future and the past and the present."

Luke took the journal from his granddad, and the others gathered around him to look at the drawing. It was a black and white sketch on aged, yellow paper. Luke thought it looked like a sea monster you'd find in Middle Earth. All spikes and pointed teeth set against a moody sky and a stormy sea.

Lucas blew out his cheeks and looked at Jess; she tapped the empty seat next to her, and he sat down. His reddened cheeks fading, he turned to Henry and asked, "So Bug was right, he said that tree wasn't evil. But why did it take him?"

"I don't know, but maybe it was to lead you all to me, not just one of you, or two of you, but all of you, together. And maybe Bug still has a part to play."

"Do you think he's okay?" Lucas asked.

"As you said, it's not evil." Henry glanced up, his eyes wide. He looked from face to face and then to their hands. "The stone? Do you have it?"

Lisa, Ruby, Luke, and Petey sat in front of the sofa in a row. Petey's cheeks flushed, and he reached behind him and brought out the hessian sack.

"Did any of you touch it?" he asked.

They turned to look at Ruby, who lowered her head as if she'd been scolded. Luke turned to his granddad. "What happens if you touch it?"

"It's a moonstone—it's connected to the willow tree, if you use one, but not the other, they don't work in harmony…" He saw the puzzled looks from their faces. Henry looked to the ceiling. "Let's say you have a jigsaw puzzle, but with only two pieces—now say where it was manufactured, made a mistake with one shape, and it doesn't fit. You end up with a picture which isn't right; it's like that. You can see the picture, but not as it's supposed to be, does that make sense?"

Luke nodded, and the others followed. "So, she'll be okay?" he asked. Her fingers reached for his as she waited for an answer. He took them in his hands and squeezed and hoped she understood he was sorry.

"She's linked to it now," Henry continued. Ruby's face dropped. "No dear, that's not a bad thing, it may even be good. If I may explain." He opened his arms. They nodded. "The moonstone works with the willow tree. The moonstone is supposed to show the holder the future; combined with the willow tree, it is a powerful weapon against the Leviathan. We could see the future and the past; we could see how to destroy it."

"How does it work?" Jess asked.

"Well," Henry scratched at the back of his neck, "the story goes that two lovers must kiss under the willow tree while holding a piece of moonstone in their mouths."

Ruby and Luke looked at each other. A look not lost on Henry. "And, I believe we have our pair of star-crossed lovers in this very room." After a moment, Petey and Lisa fell onto each other laughing. Lucas and Jess joined in from the sofa. Ruby moved a piece of red hair from her face and smiled at Luke. The room filled with laughter, and Henry sat smiling to himself. They needed some joy before the darkness before them.

"Now, you must kiss and make up, literally," Lisa laughed. Petey leaned around the back of Ruby and Luke, who were still holding hands. As the laughter continued, both turned a bright shade of red. "High five," Petey said, and Lisa slapped his hand.

"You appear to be a chip off the old block, hey, Luke?" Henry said.

At that, they all laughed, the warm sound reverberated off the floral wallpapered walls. Once the laughter died down to an occasional giggle, they sat in silence, which Lisa broke, "So grandad, how do we kill it?"

Henry took the journal from Luke and closed it on his lap. "First, we need to find it. Those creatures you mentioned sound like the Taniwha, which takes the form of a woman, and a Metshin, an insectoid creature from Mongolian mythology. They will prepare the Leviathan's feeding ground—which explains the guise of a weight loss coach and a painter decorator." The others looked at him stumped. "The woman, to put it bluntly, finds the fattest people, while the man marks their houses with the scent of their victims."

"What about Ben?" Lucas interrupted.

"Ben—the little boy—now he is a bit of a mystery. You said he went missing at Westford Water, right?"

"That's right; I met his grandad yesterday."

"Interestingly, Westford Water has popped up before." He cupped his chin in one hand. "It is the largest body of water for miles. So if that egg made it to the river, it would be the perfect place for it to gestate. It had been one explanation I had."

"But, how would it have gotten there from under the Monastery?" Petey asked.

"I've thought about that. My guess is that when the monastery was destroyed, (before William rebuilt it) that the egg was no longer buried. All it would take would be a large flood, and it could have got swept away into the Bennane river." He started to nod to himself. "Yes, and from there, it could float to Westford Water before finding a spot to gestate." He picked up the journal and flicked through the pages. "Only a hundred yards from the willow tree, under St Martin's bridge, is one of the largest pumping stations to Westford Water. Yes, it all links, doesn't it?"

"Was there ever a flood that large?" asked Lucas?

"I'm not entir–"

"July 15th, 1880," Petey interrupted, and when Luke, Lisa, and Ruby stared at him, he replied, "Am I the only one who went on that historic trip around town?"

"Well done, yes, and then they flooded Westford Water in the 1970s–something that big would need time to gestate, grow, which all fits. I wonder though; we haven't seen it yet, maybe, just maybe it hasn't hatched!" Henry said.

"So, we could stop it?" Lisa asked, leaning forward.

"Potentially, yes." Henry looked past Jess and Lucas on the sofa and out into the dark, clear night. "We can't do anything tonight, get some sleep, all of you. Let me read through my journal and books again," the room erupted in a tangle of voices, Henry raised two fingers. "Rest! Let me research; we can't fight this thing if you're dead on your feet," they quietened as one. "Let me get some blankets–Jess, you look like you could use a bed? Take mine, I'll be up most of the night, and if I need some rest, I can rest in this old thing." Jess went to say something, and he shushed her again with a finger. "Take Ruby and Lisa with you; us boys will stay out here, and, tomorrow morning, we will have a plan. That's if you all want to kill this thing?"

They nodded like a losing football team after a half-time team talk. "Good. We can, I promise you. I will find a way."

"Sounds good," Lucas started. "But if I go to sleep, you will wake up with a very confused stranger in your living room," he looked at the mobile phone he'd felt vibrate several times this evening, "and, if his wife doesn't hear from him soon, she'll send the police out looking for him. With his car on your drive, it won't take them long to track it."

"So…" Henry looked at Lucas like a school science project. "Is that how it happens? You fall asleep, and you wake up in someone else's body–as simple as that."

"That's about it, have you come across anything like that before?"

"No," Henry answered too quickly for Lucas's liking. "So, what do you suggest then, Lucas?"

Lucas thought for a moment, "I could take the car back, act like I got stuck late at work, and once I wake up in someone else's body. I'll come straight back. It's the only way. One person I have been is dead because of me; I won't have this man's death on my conscience, especially when he has a wife and kids at home."

"So, the body of someone without kids is worth less than a man with kids?" Lisa said, turning to look at him from the doorway of the bedroom. Her hands-on her child hips.

Lucas shook his head. "That's not what I meant, I don't want anyone to die, but if I have to fight, I'd rather… you know… oh, never mind, you won't understand."

"Why, because I'm just a kid?" Lisa pressed.

"I didn't say that. You're twisting my words."

Luke stood up and stepped between his sister and Lucas. "We can't fight guys, not between ourselves. There is no other way," he turned to Lucas. "Go home, settle the man's wife, and come back as soon as you can. When you come back, knock three times and use a password." Henry watched Luke taking control. Luke's chest was puffed out, and he didn't look like a boy anymore. Henry silently clapped to himself. "Use the password, the Knight's of Westford."

Everyone in the room looked at each other, at first with their eyebrows raised, and then they smiled. Lucas got up and ruffled Luke's hair on the way past. "You're all right, kid, you know that?" He pulled on his boots and stood. "Right, I'll see you all tomorrow morning, fresh and early." He opened and walked out the front door, glancing back at them just once. They heard the car start and pull off the gravel driveway.

3

In the dead of night, when the soft snores of children filled the house, the sound of a wounded animal, jeered solemnly through the cottage. The moans of Jess, having a nightmare. Henry heard her tossing in the bedroom while he poured over the journal and scraps of paper he'd retrieved from his desk.

He sat in his wingback chair, a lamp to his side, illuminating the room in an orange glow. Lucas troubled him. He had an idea why the body switches were happening but hoped it wasn't so–if it was, they were further gone than he'd expected, and tomorrow one or more of the group would die.

He stood and walked to the unlocked room. He closed the door behind as he entered and flicked on the lights. On the walls, dull and tainted swords and axes and other weapons hung from protruding iron nails, standing out against the off-white wallpaper with faded flowers. Gilt-edged, oversized books stood open on wooden stands, their pages showing swirling calligraphy and colourful images. Dull landscape paintings hung on the walls, and In the middle of the room was a large, wooden circular table; a round table he thought and chuckled to himself, remembering what Luke said about Knight's of Westford. His face tightened. His grandson would be at the front of the fight, and he had little time to train him, he was just a kid.

A black, cast-iron fireplace on a stone hearth nestled into the exposed brick wall at the far end of the room. Above it was a solid-oak mantelpiece. Aged, deep lines ran across its surface. On the mantelpiece, in a dark-wood box not much bigger than a matchbox, was a white stone that shimmered in the moonlight that cascaded through the side window when he opened it. He held back a sneeze from the charcoal dust from the fireplace. He picked up the box and closed its lid and placed it in the middle of the empty table.

Turning back to the fireplace, he looked up at the heavy axe and the massive broadsword that criss crossed each other on the wall. Each was well over a thousand years old. The metal was a dull grey; the edges notched and blunt, but he knew it would buff and shine again.

On the ax blade, were two intricate engravings of lions. Henry knew the same lions were on the reverse of the blade as well, having hung them himself.

On the sword's hilt, the worn grip was a red-wine colour with silver wire which ran around from the bottom to the top. Above, the steel pommel housed the shape of an eye the size of a baseball, with an even cross with four dots engraved into the space. This same pattern appeared three times at the top of the blade close to the cross-guard. Latin was etched onto the blade, Jam Accepisse Regnum.

It was William the Conqueror's sword, his great ancestor. He had royal blood in his veins, and so did Luke and Lisa. Henry knew the tale of the sword and the axe from the journal by memory.

William's son, Robert, had been the black sheep of the family. His father, William, had grown tired of his antics. When William died, Robert, hearing he was about to be disinherited, stole the axe of William's grandfather Rollo, and William's sword. Hiding them somewhere only he knew.

However, he wasn't disinherited, and was instead granted the Duchy of Normandy. Around 1096, after arguments against his brother William Rufus, aka William II, Robert formed an army and left to fight in the first crusades. It was while in Jerusalem he found out about the terror under the monastery in Westford through a priest and a knight, who would later become a founding member of the Knights Templar.

His brother William II died while he was still traveling, and in his rush to get back to claim the throne, he left the sword and the axe in the knight's care; he also asked the knight to care for a son he had sired while on the road. His son grew up, and upon learning of his father's death in 1134, he took the sword and the axe as his own.

Now with the elderly priest (the knight had since died of malaria), they traveled to Westford to watch over the Priory. The priest became a part of the Priory and watched while Robert's son made a home in Westford, ready for his ancestors after him. He married and had two children before his death. Since then, a Curthose has always lived in Westford. The priest's name was Theodoros. And, set one rule: The Curthose family must live a quiet, humble existence. In business and enterprise, they must complete everything under a pseudonym.

It was a crazy story—Henry knew it—which is why he had never repeated it to anyone until now. He took the sword and the axe from the wall, both nearly toppling him over backward with their weight and placed them on the table next to the little box. He opened the box with the glowing stone and re-positioned it, then left the room.

Luke was asleep on the floor; he'd given Petey the sofa. Henry woke him, shaking his shoulder. "Luke, you must come with me now," he said. Luke pushed himself up from the floor, rubbing his eyes with the backs of his hands.

"What time is it?" he asked. "Is Lucas back?"

"Sssshhh… you'll wake Petey," Henry replied. "Get up, Luke, Lucas isn't back yet."

Henry led Luke to the closed door of the unlocked room and turned. "Wait here," he said and entered the bedroom where they could hear the soft snores of Jess, Lisa, and Ruby in the dark. Luke heard whispered voices and then glanced at Ruby in the doorway, pulling a shirt over her naked, pink stomach. Her red hair was in disarray like she'd been sleeping amongst hay-bails, and she sleepily went to fix it when she saw Luke. She gave him a shy smile and yawned.

He raised his eyebrows, waved, then blushed, realizing how stupid he must have looked.

"Come with me," Henry said to them, putting a finger over his mouth. He opened the door and led them into the room. He closed the door and turned on the lights. Luke and Ruby looked around the room, their mouths open and their eyes wide. They turned on the spot—back to-back—taking in the ancient wonders on the walls. Ruby saw a hideous painting of a serpent lying on top of a mound of human bodies, surrounded by entrails and skulls and blood. She reached behind and took Luke's hand.

"Quite a collection, I know," Henry started. "My family—your family, Luke, has been collecting these since we first settled here over one thousand years ago. We've been preparing for this battle for a long time." His eyes beamed over the room. He'd been in charge of keeping secure for his time on earth before coming to rest on the sword, the axe, and the stone. Luke and Ruby followed his gaze to the table.

"What are they?" Ruby asked.

"They are history and our best weapon against the Leviathan. The sword belonged to William the Conqueror and the axe to his great, great, great grandfather, Rollo, a Viking and the first ruler of Normandy."

"And the stone?" Ruby said.

Henry moved to the corner and pulled out the hessian sack they had found only two days ago. "I hope you don't mind, but I wanted to keep it somewhere safe," He poured the contents onto the end of the table, the stone landed with a dull thud. It was bigger than the white stone that sat comfy in the box in the centre of the table. He picked up a black chisel that was to the side of the mantel.

"Don't…" Ruby moved forward; one arm extended out towards Henry.

"Luke, hold her, please. Nothing will happen, Ruby, watch."

Luke put his arms around Ruby; he was behind her, and once she felt his arms, she pulled them tight around her chest. Her nails dug into his hands, leaving crescents of white in his skin as they stood together. The warm smell of the coconut of her hair and the heat of her skin was intoxicating. Luke was so sure he fell in love all over again. He felt her heart beating beneath her chest; it was racing; he whispered in her ear, "It will be okay, I promise."

At the words, she calmed, and Luke felt her heartbeat slow. Her fingers no longer dug into his skin, and she let him hold her. They were one as they watched Luke's grandad break open the black rock with his chisel. Stone chippings came off in little chunks. Luke saw the glint of something glowing inside. Holding Ruby, he knew why he was here. He was meant to protect, to calm, to love, to fight.

"It's its partner," Henry explained. "Separate, they aren't complete; together, they are whole–powerful." Luke watched the last of the black dirt crack off the white stone hidden beneath. Ruby moved forward and dragged Luke with her; she wasn't ready to let him go.

"It's beautiful," she whispered.

It was, Luke thought. The surface moved like grey, glowing clouds in the night sky when it was a full moon. Luke looked at the other one; its surface too moved, floated across the hard surface. It was darker and had an imperfection running through it, a blue-black line like a vein. 'That's mine,' he thought.

"Are you two ready? It's a full moon outside," Henry lent on the table. "I can't force you, but will you come to the willow tree with me, now?"

"The willow tree?" Ruby asked. She pulled Luke's arms tighter across her chest.

"What's at the willow tree?" Luke asked, sensing Ruby's growing fear.

"You remember the story–the story about the willow tree and the lovers?"

They nodded and then stopped, realization crossing their faces. Luke tightened his grip on Ruby.

"Something unexpected has happened, something wonderful. I was just expecting Luke or Lisa, but you've all come to me. There is a reason for it. Something beyond our understanding is working for us, just like something is working for it, but I believe we are stronger. Together." He held his hand out to Ruby. "It's a lot to ask, but will you come with me to the willow tree?"

Ruby took Henry's hand and felt his cold, dry skin, so different from the warmth and softness of Lukes.

"I can't guarantee we will all survive, if any of us, I want to tell you both this now. I don't know what will happen, but I won't force you to do anything. Do you understand?"

Ruby looked into Henry's kind face. His blue eyes danced in the glow of the stones. "That thing, what will happen if we don't stop it?"

"The end times, the end of days, the apocalypse; it has many names," He took a deep breath. "That thing out there, it is the enemy of everything;

anything you have ever loved, or that makes you happy, it will destroy, that is what it does. It's not fair to ask this of you, but remember, always remember everything you love: Remember the sounds of children laughing, running streams, of birds, tweeting. Remember the warmth of a loved one when you hug, remember the smiles of your parents, remember the feeling of the warm sun on your skin. All of those things are what that thing will take away." Henry's eyes were wet, and Ruby squeezed his hand. Luke let go of Ruby and approached his granddad. He took his other hand in his and then Rubys, completing the circle. He looked to the ground for a moment, before looking up, a determined look in his eye. Ruby pursed her lips and smiled.

"We'll do it," Luke said.

They snuck out of the house, leaving the others still sleeping. There was no need for all of them to go, and they'd be back before they woke, Henry said. Luke looked at Petey asleep on the sofa. His glasses had fallen from his face, and his hair was messy.

It was a five-minute drive to Bath Row and the Meadows. Henry drove his black Renault Clio under the speed limit while Ruby and Luke held hands in the back. Luke stared out of the window, watching Westford flash past in the dark. They drove down the hill towards the town bridge, past closed shops, pubs, and hotels. This end of town had kept hold of its Georgian charm. The streetlights gave the tall buildings an orange glow. Long shadow fingers stretched over and through the car via the sunroof.

At this time of night, Luke was in a contemplative mood, he thought, *This too shall end; all the pain and anxiety. The dark clouds that storm your mind at every moment of silence will clear, and light will appear, and at the end of the light, there will be peace. Friends and family will be there. Life goes on; darkness isn't impenetrable. Patience, belief, and positivity; these things will help you through. Like a hangover or an illness, keep the end in sight, knowing that your peace is coming and today will soon be over.'* He didn't know where the thought came from, it arrived fully formed and that scared him.

At the bottom of the hill, they saw the hangman's gallows that hung over the road and the dark green sign for the Monk Hotel. The old hotel where King Charles I and Sir Walter Scott, amongst others, had stayed, was an ever-present in the town, and they watched the pretty planters that hung on the old windowsills. At the same time, they waited for the traffic lights to change.

They could have gone left at the traffic lights and parked at the Cattle Market car park, but Henry drove over the bridge and towards Bath Row. Luke and Ruby looked to the left when they crossed the bridge and saw the top of the willow in the moonlight. The streets were dead; it was the darkest depths of the night. No traffic either.

They passed the town hall on their left, and at the top of the hill stood a tall church, St Mary's church. The spire was jagged in the night light, like the serrated teeth of a shark. It was three times as tall as any other building on this road. They followed around to the left, past shops with expensive suits and fancy-looking estate agents with pictures of huge houses in their windows. And, then they passed the tall monolith and took the turning down to Bath Row. It was empty, not a single car, unlike during the daytime when it was always full.

None of them said a word on the drive, and now Henry pulled into a parking spot and turned off the engine; still, no-one spoke. The silence was all-consuming as they stared out across the meadows towards the willow tree. The moon and stars sparkled on the moving water, and the silhouette of the tree's overhanging branches was all they could see of the tree. Luke turned to Ruby and smiled, "Shall we go?" Ruby nodded back and opened her car door and stepped out into the night.

Luke wondered if Ruby had ever kissed anyone before? Would he be her first kiss, like she would be his? He watched as she came round the front of the car towards him. The sound of their doors closing was loud in the night, and they heard something splash into the water.

Was this what love felt like? He couldn't see anything but her. In the moonlight, her skin glowed, and her hair looked darker than it was. Her pupils were large, which gave her a helpless look that made him want to run away with her. Henry motioned for them to come towards the little white bridge that led onto the meadows. Luke waited for Ruby, and she took his hand, and together they crossed the bridge onto the meadows.

"I'm scared," she whispered to him.

"Me too," he replied. "But, I trust my granddad, and I believe him. We can't let this happen."

"I know, but why us?"

"Because we're… you're special." As if an afterthought, he added, "I've liked you for ages." Ruby, didn't miss a step.

"I know," she replied. "It was kinda obvious," she teased, and playfully bumped her hip into his.

"Come on, we can do this." Luke put his arm around her slender shoulders.

Together they rushed and caught up with Henry, who was past the first bench and on his way to the willow tree. The only light came from the black streetlamps on the path that separated each side of the meadows. As they approached the willow tree, it got darker.

In Luke's right hand hung the hessian sack, which now contained a wooden box with two moonstones inside. Up in the black-blue sky, the moon hung large suspended from the unseen pull of gravity. As big as it was, Luke and Ruby could see every line and crater on its surface. The cold glow turned the green grass a dull shade of grey. It was beautiful, especially the watercolour ripples created in the river from its reflection.

The grass turned to dust under their feet as they got within five feet of the willow tree. The hanging branches hung just above their heads. At the edge of the water, Luke spotted a shanty-looking little pier made of wood.

"So, what now?" Luke asked Henry.

"We follow the legend."

"Then what?" Ruby asked.

"I'm sorry this is my first time too. I don't know what is about to happen."

"That fills me with confidence," Luke replied. "So, the legend; two moonstones, one each and then we put them in our mouths and… you know…"

"We kiss," Ruby finished for him, kicking her ankles, looking at the floor.

"Right, yeah, we kiss."

Henry pulled out the matchbox-sized wooden box from the hessian bag and opened it. The contents glowed in the darkness. He held the box out to them so they could pick their moonstones. Luke let Ruby go first, a warm look crossed her face as she did. Luke pulled the last moonstone out the box, and Henry took a step back far enough away to give them some privacy, but close enough to help if something went wrong.

Luke and Ruby stood under the willow tree, its black spiderweb branches allowing white lines of white light through. The surrounding dusty floor danced with white spotlights, like a school dance. Far off, Luke thought he could hear bird song. She looked so beautiful under the starlight with the soft, blue glow from the moonstones giving her face a porcelain look. Luke moved closer, reaching for her elbow with his right hand. She came to him and stood in his arms. She rested her head on his shoulder, and he whispered into her ear, "I love you."

Ruby looked into Luke's earnest face, and she placed the moonstone into her mouth. Luke did the same. Her wide eyes looked at him, "I mov sho too…" she mumbled and then laughed and spat the moonstone into her hand. "I love you too, Luke."

They shared their first kiss under the willow tree with the moonlight shining down. Henry tried not to watch but found himself unable to. He smiled and silently clapped his hands together once.

The kiss was soft and gentle and full of love and respect. Luke's hands ran around the edges of Ruby's waist, and she wrapped her arms around his neck. When their lips parted, they opened their eyes and looked at each other. A soft glow came from within their partly open mouths.

A root emerged from the earth between them, not twisted and gnarled but smooth with little leaves and shoots emerging from its body. It tied itself around Luke's ankle, followed by Ruby's. Ruby moved closer, pushing her head down into Luke's chest while he held her secure and tight and protected. The root wound up Luke's back and then tied the two together around their waists. They were lifted weightlessly off the ground as white light, not dissimilar from the light of the moon, opened in the tree trunks side.

Luke turned to look at Henry before the tree took them, and as he did, he saw a shadow move behind him.

The painter decorator approached silently from behind. Luke could see the dark overalls and the paint splatters. He went to shout, but it was too late. The figure melted into itself, and Luke saw the moonlight shimmering off its eyes. He was already vanishing into the tree, and the last thing he saw was Henry's eyes bulging as his smile turned into a grimace as the creature completed its transformation and tore off a chunk of flesh from his grandad's shoulder. The autumnal smell of mud and trees and leaves was all that remained, as he disappeared into the light.

4

Petey was awake, his leg tapped against the exposed wooden floorboards as he sat on the leather sofa in the sitting room. Lucas hadn't returned, and now Henry and Luke were missing.

The early morning sunshine shining in through the window had woken him, and as he rubbed his eyes and sat up on the sofa. He saw the space and a pile of blankets where Luke had gone to sleep. He looked around the room and saw Henry's empty chair. Petey walked through to the kitchen and opened the door to the unlocked room. Nothing.

From the bedroom, he heard Lisa ask, "Where's Ruby?" Then he saw Lisa and Jess, both still dressed from the previous day, emerge from the bedroom.

"Where's Ruby?" Lisa asked him.

"I don't know," Petey said. "Henry and Luke are gone too."

"What do you mean, gone?" Jess asked, scratching at her hair.

"Gone…" Petey opened his arms. "Did you hear anything last night?"

"They can't be gone, did you look for them?" asked Jess.

"Inside the house, yes, I haven't been outside yet, though."

Lisa and Jess moved forward, out of the shadow of the bedroom doorway. "I heard nothing, did you?" Lisa asked Jess. Jess shook her head. "Nothing."

"I told you, they're gone," Petey said. He sat on the sofa and held his head in his hands; his elbows rested on his skinny knees. Jess approached him and sat next to him.

"What about Lucas?"

"He's not back either; it's early, though."

Jess arched her neck and looked out the window, past the pictures on the sill, and over the yellow fields. The sun was still low in the early morning sky. Where are you?

Henry's beat-up Clio, that they'd seen when they first arrived, had gone. The gravel driveway was empty. Why did you leave in the middle of the night?

Luke's blankets littered the floor in a pile that hadn't been tidied as if they'd left quick. What are you up to? She heard sobs coming from Petey next to her. Jess didn't like to see this young boy cry. He was a nerd through and through, and as a mum, she felt the need to protect him. He was smart, that was clear, and he'd been quick on his feet. They needed him; they all needed each other.

Lisa sat on the other side of Petey, while Jess stood and hobbled around the house, her crutch clicking on the wooden floor as she searched the house for their missing friend's. Upon the realization they were gone, Jess flicked on the kettle to make a cup of coffee. With a coffee in a white mug with a character duck on it in hand, she sat in Henry's wingback chair. She was resting her head against the back.

"Did Henry say anything to you after we went to bed?" Jess asked Petey.

"Nothing."

She put her cast up on the stool and puffed out her cheeks. "Do we go searching for them, or do we wait for them? Should we wait for Lucas first?"

A crunching of gravel from the driveway made them turn to the front door.

"Is it them?" Petey asked.

"Shhh…" Jess said, putting a finger against her lips. "It's coming from the other side, around the house, not from the front drive."

They sat in silence, listening to the crunch of gravel and the footsteps from outside. There were two sets, Jess was sure of it. Two people are circling the house.

"Down," she whispered. "On the floor, now."

They crouched on the floor and crawled to the wall under the window. They huddled together with their backs against the wall. A shadow moved past the window in the kitchen opposite. Jess looked at her white, doodled-on cast sticking out uselessly. Another shadow from above stretched into the room towards Henry's chair.

"It's them, isn't it?" Petey whispered, his eyes still wet.

Lisa and Jess looked at each other. "You need to move; you need to make a run for it," Jess said. Petey shook his head. "I can't."

"Yes, you can, Petey, remember the Priory? You said you couldn't then, but you did. You can do it." Lisa squeezed his hand. "You can do this."

Petey and Lisa crawled towards the front door. Jess stayed at the wall, watching. Once clear, she slithered along the floor on her belly, her cast dragging behind her. She moved through to the kitchen, where she quietly opened the drawers and found three, hopefully sharp, kitchen knives. They were from a matching set with conker-brown handles and dull blades. A Chef's knife, a Santoku knife, and a Cleaver. She crawled to Petey and Lisa, who crouched in the porch. Jess passed the Santoku knife to Lisa, the Chef's knife to Petey, who took it and looked at it as an alien object, while she kept hold of the massive knife.

"On three, run towards the road… don't stop. Nod if you understand?" Jess said.

They nodded. Lisa took Petey's hand in hers. Petey was shaking and holding back more tears while Lisa bit her bottom lip, drawing blood. Jess reached across and hugged both of them. "It'll be alright," she whispered. She reached up with her right hand and touched the cold metal of the doorknob. Beneath it, she felt the warm end of the key sticking from the lock. Jess turned it, and they sucked in a breath as the lock clicked like a gunshot in the empty house. She grabbed the doorknob again and turned it towards her. With her other hand, she counted down three, two, one with her fingers.

Petey and Lisa ran. They ran down the yellow gravel drive along with tall green fern bushes towered over them on either side. Jess brandished her knife in front of her on the doorstep as she watched them go. She heard guttural cries from the side of the house, and she shouted, "Run. Faster."

The house was down a country lane, surrounded by fields. The closest house was a ten-minute walk. She saw them shoot out of the driveway in a flurry of colour and onto the empty grey road. Then they were gone. Please God; she prayed, let them getaway.

She left the door open as she made her way back to Henry's wingback chair. She thought about Hugo and Billy back home. This was the longest she'd ever been away from them. She remembered their smiles and their voices when she called them last night. She'd told them not to worry; Mummy would be home in the morning. Mike asked what was going on, and she told him one of her girlfriends had broken up with her partner. Would Mike cope without her? How would he explain her not being here to the boys? Jess shook the thoughts away; she looked at the cleaver knife in her hand. She was doing this for her boys.

"Come and get me, you sonofabitch." Jess fell back behind the leather wingback chair. Her boy's faces swam through her mind one last time as she closed her eyes and cleared her mind. She smiled as she waited with the cleaver by her side. Rosemary ducked through the doorway, her bright red hair touching the ceiling.

"Where are they?" Rosemary hissed.

"Long gone, you bitch."

She watched as Rosemary melted, her skin turned inside out and split like an overstuffed doll. A festering, decaying smell filled the room. The creature beneath emerged, it's flicking, black forked tongue whipped in front of Jess's face. The remaining pink skin turned in on itself and became one with the oozing black underbelly of the creature. Two milky-white salamander eyes closed sideways, then came to rest upon her—the pupils' long black slits.

"Come on, then!" Jess pushed herself forward. She held her cast an inch from the ground. The creature looked at her and moved forward, its body close to the ground on all fours. Its tongue flicked the air, tasting the scent of the others.

"If you want them, you must come through me first." She swung the knife in front of her. "COME ON!"

The creature lingered, pacing side-to-side. A fire burned inside Jess, anger rising to the surface like lava. "I SPIT ON YOU, YOU PIECE OF SHIT… FUCK YOU, YOU CU–"

The creature lunged. Its sharp, sparkling talons sliced forward through the air, aimed at her face. It leaped like a big cat, not a reptile. Jess swung the cleaver down from above her head and sliced through flesh and tendons on its arm. Its thick and stinking blood erupted across the room, onto the curtains, and over Jess. The creature pulled back, hissing and spitting. She cursed her cast, which stopped her from finishing the creature.

It readied to launch again, its long tail swishing across the room, knocking off books and picture frames from the sides. It licked its wounds, tasting its own thick, metallic blood. This time it leaped headfirst, sharp jaws open like an alligator as it bounded into her and knocked her flying. She sensed its hot breath on her neck as it snapped its jaws shut, trying to puncture her flesh. The creature was on top of her, and she felt talons tear into her sides. The warmth of her blood created a hot, sticky puddle underneath her. She used the slick blood to slide out underneath the monster, hacking away with the cleaver at the beast's chest as she did. Its chest opened up in a series of hacked, jagged wounds and rank; boiling liquid flowed into her mouth and down her neck. Still, it didn't stop coming. Once free, she kicked at its rear with her good leg from the floor and heard the thing scream. It turned its long head, and she saw its pin-prick black slit-eye staring back at her. It was pissed. She looked beyond it to the open door and the darkroom. If she could get past it, she could block the door and take a moment. She couldn't crawl, it would rip her to pieces from behind. She had to run. Jess looked at her leg in the cast and grimaced.

She pushed herself up and used the dresser to stand. Her side hurt and bled slowly. The creature eyed her, waiting for her to move. Knowing if she made a wrong move, it could rip into her. Jess feigned to go to the right, and the creature snapped its jaws at empty air. She launched herself forward and unsteadily ran past the wingback chair. Her cast slid on the wet floor and then cracked under her weight. A sharp pain shot through her leg like electricity. She swallowed the pain. The creature turned on the spot, its tail knocking over the side table next to the chair. She was two metres from the door when the beast lunged, shredding the back of her ankle with a sharp talon, just missing her achilles. She fell forward, with two useless legs under her. She reached for the doorway, and her fingers brushed against the wood. Her legs wouldn't move. Blood pooled under her ankle and from her sides, but she reached again. The tips of her fingers found the corner of the doorframe, and she pulled herself towards the door. The creature was scrambling behind her, sliding in the blood on the floor. She pulled herself into the room and slammed the door behind her. She leaned back against it as the creature slammed itself against it, again and again, and again.

The room was dark, and she reached up with a sticky, bloody hand and felt for a light switch. She felt her sides rip as she reached and clenched her teeth together against the pain. The room lit up, and she saw the antique weapons on the walls. There were two spaces above the fireplace. The creature stopped slamming against the door. The pain in her body had been numb during the fight, but now she felt the sting of the cuts on her skin as sweat dripped down like vinegar. She felt lightheaded and leaned her head back against the door to stop from passing out. Her heart pumped against her chest, she could feel it in her ears. As she listened, it slowed. She could smell a tint of metallic in the air. Keep moving. A voice in her mind said. Don't stop.

Jess opened her eyes. She listened for any sound from the other side of the door. It was still. She heard its shallow breaths and snorts. It was waiting. She couldn't stand. It had broken her body. Her ankle bled as did her sides. The leg with the broken cast throbbed. Jess pulled herself towards the circular table in the middle of the room. She raised herself with her arms and holding herself there, she saw an old, blunt-looking axe sitting alone in the middle of the table. Reaching for it, she heard the creature from the other side of the door as it started to pace–getting ready to attack. She couldn't reach the weapon. If it launched itself now, without her back against the door, it would come crashing through and finish her.

As the thought passed through her mind, she heard a high, gargled scream and the creature came crashing through the door covered in fragments of wood–

Petey and Lisa ran. Their feet slipped on the gravel at the end of the drive. Petey took a glance behind him and saw Jess standing in the doorway for the last time. They turned left and ran down the middle of the narrow road. Bushes, taller than them, stood as if like maze walls on both sides. He was faster than Lisa, so he ran at three-quarters speed to let her stay with him. They heard shouts from behind, back at the house. Lisa took over him, finding an extra ten percent, and he raced to catch up.

There was no path, just a steep green grass bank on either side, so they had to stick to the road when they rounded a corner. Petey closed his eyes and prayed an oncoming car wouldn't take them out. He opened his eyes. The way ran downhill, and he could see fields of yellow as far as his eyes could see. To the bottom left of his vision, he could see the start of Westford; from up here, it looked like a toy town in the middle of the English countryside. As they ran, they picked up speed. His legs were moving faster than his body could keep up with. He glanced at Lisa, and her legs were a blur of motion, the knife glinted in the early morning sunshine, and he saw the concentration and the gleam of sweat on her face. They needed to get off this road.

Up ahead, to their left, he saw a wooden gate with four horizontal beams. It led across the fields. "Lisa," he shouted and pointed with the hand that held the knife. The act of pointing upset the rhythm of his running, and he almost toppled over. He watched Lisa divert her course and head towards the gate. He followed, trying to slow his forward momentum as he approached.

They put their hands out as they ran into the gate to stop themselves. Petey felt the impact reverberate through his bones, and he dropped the knife. From behind, he heard an engine, and as he looked up the road, above the hedges, he saw grey swirling smoke.

"He's coming," he said.

Lisa looked towards the smoke. "Quick, Petey, over the gate."

He started to climb, just as the dirty, white van rounded the corner and without slowing plowed into the gate, which he was halfway over. He went flying, before landing on his back on the grass verge.

Lisa had dived out of the way as it hit and now stood opposite the smoking van. She held the knife in her hand in a fighter pose, moving on her toes ready to brawl. She looked at Petey; he wasn't moving. The door of the van opened, and she ran at the man climbing out, the knife extended and glinting in the bright light. He side-stepped her at the last moment and caught her extended arm, which he pulled behind her back as he smashed her face into the metal side of the van with a dull thud. Lisa crumpled to the floor. The man looked at the two knocked-out children and smiled.

—Its jaws snapped at her as it flew through the room. Sharp splinters of wood arced through the air. It was a black blur, and behind it, she could see the trashed sitting room. A mixture of its blood and hers dripped from every surface, pooling on the exposed wooden floor. Time slowed, as reaching above her, onto the table, her fingers touched warm leather and cold metal. She pulled the axe up and off the table and brought it crashing down through the creature's skull. Its head split in two, between its salamander eyes. The forked tongue flicked out once, as an electric current ran through it, and then lay limp. Its massive body landed on top of her. A sharp pain spread from her back, and stars danced in front of her eyes. Using the last of her strength, she pushed the body of the creature off her and passed out. The last thing that went through her mind was the imprinted images of Hugo and Billy.

5

The tree didn't spit them out; it placed them gently onto the dusty floor surrounding the willow tree. The sun was low in the sky and their breath left vapour clouds floating in the air. They shivered together; their skin breaking out in goosebumps.

"Grandad? Did you see it? Did it get him?" Luke asked Ruby.

"I don't know, oh God, the others. Do you think it knows where they are?"

"He's clever, my grandad, he'll fight it off – won't he?"

"Luke, what about the others? It must have followed us. It knows where they are."

"Shit, shit, shit. There's nothing we can do," Luke said, and looked around where the tree had sent them. Ruby turned in a circle next to him, checking out their surroundings. It looked like the meadows, but the river was higher and the older buildings looked newer.

"Where are we?" Ruby asked.

"We're at the tree," Luke answered, then looked around. "But, I don't think we're in 2019 anymore."

The white metal fence that ran along the path and separated the other side of the river from the car park and the road was gone. So were the more recent buildings. There were no cars. They walked out from under the tree and spotted a man sat in an old-style deckchair with a blue and white striped pattern just ten yards from them; watching them. He wore a white cotton shirt with suspenders and rolled-up, brown wool trousers. He smiled, and shouted, "Took you long enough."

Holding hands, Ruby and Luke walked over to the man. He didn't look much older than them; late-teens, early twenties. He had an angled face with a strong jawline and short brown hair. His eyes sparkled just like Luke's granddad's.

"Grandad, Henry, is that you?" Luke asked.

The man chuckled; it was a kind laugh. "Henry? Not me I'm afraid–it's a nice name though."

"But, you have the same eyes." Luke continued.

"Listen kid, I'm not Henry. I'm Fairfax, Fairfax Curthose at your service."

"Fairfax Curthose," Luke said to himself. "You're my great, great grandfather."

"Is that right?" the man chuckled again. "Come with me–dressed like that you stick out like a sore thumb!"

They traipsed through farmland and fields that were housing estates in 2019. Muddy paths had formed where the grass had been trodden down. Horse shit was everywhere. Fairfax looked over his shoulder at Luke and Ruby as they shivered and huddled together.

"Not much farther now," he said.

"Where are we going?" Luke asked.

"If you're here now, it's because I sent you back via my grandson or granddaughter, I suppose. And, it's because of what I found yesterday."

Luke tried to do the calculations in his head. He counted on his fingers as he walked. They passed fields full of corn surrounded by hedgerows that glistened with early morning dew in the low sun. Tall trees reached to the cloud-filled sky. Everything smelled fresh and clean.

"What did you find?" asked Ruby.

"You'll see, sweet girl, you'll see."

They kept on walking. A cold wind blew. The mud floor was solid under their feet, Luke stopped and turned full circle checking out the landscape.

"I know where we are, Ruby."

"Where?"

"We're standing where the big new build houses have been built; just over that hill is the A1, the Great North Road."

"Clever young man," Fairfax said, not stopping. "Although, I do not understand about new houses or what this A1 you mention is, but yes the Great North Road is over there." He pointed a pale, skinny hand over the fields. "That's where we're going. We're meeting someone on the road. He has a very interesting story he told me yesterday that you ought to hear. And, then you can be on your merry way back down the rabbit hole."

"Who?"

"A young explorer. About the same age as myself. A bit of a personal hero of mine actually. He's just got back from an expedition in the Antarctic, if you believe that? Brackenford's his name. And, boy are you going to want to hear what he has to say."

"Ernest Brackenford?" both Ruby and Luke said.

"Yes, that's the one. He must have done well for himself if you know about him 120-years from now." Fairfax scratched at the scraggly black stubble on his chin.

"You could say that," Ruby looked at Luke. This was crazy. They'd time travelled on a willow tree using magical moonstones and were fighting monsters. This was crazy. Henry had told her she'd be okay. Henry. She hoped he was okay, but Luke was right; there was nothing they could do from here. They needed to keep on moving, to keep going–that's what Henry would want them to do. Maybe there was a way to warn Henry from this time, so he would know in the future? Was this really time travel? Or was it something else?

She looked at Fairfax. They had gone so willingly along with him thanks to Luke's belief, but, but what? She thought. And, now, Brackenford. A world-famous hero from the Antarctic explorations. Her head was a fuzzy mess, and she found it easier to just go with the flow, trusting herself to Luke; otherwise she'd turn herself inside out. Shouldn't this be in one of Henry's journals though? Henry would have told them about this, surely. What's so special about this moment, and why doesn't Henry already know about this meeting. Or did he? Did Fairfax not write it down? And, if not, why not?

"Luke," she whispered. "Are you sure about him? I mean if this is so important, why isn't it in Henry's journal?" Luke frowned at her, then looked up towards his great, great grandfather ten paces ahead.

"I don't know, I hadn't thought about it," he said, leaning in to her as they walked. "I think we should be careful while we're here," Luke agreed.

"We're here," Fairfax called from ahead.

6

A small, one-man blue tent swayed in the breeze. A little fire burnt next to it. The sound of crackling and little pops came to Luke's ears. Flames danced in the air, their shadows flickering against the light-blue fabric. The smell of burning wood followed. In front of the tent, sat on a brown fur, was a young man with a neat centre parting and furrowed eyebrows. His face was severe and serious. He didn't look up as Fairfax, Luke and Ruby approached.

Fields of crops gave way to a huge expanse of level land which stretched for miles forwards and behind the man. Luke could feel the warmth coming from the fire from five-yards away and ached to sit next to it.

"Sit. Warm up," the man said in a gruff voice that sounded older than he was. "You're the boy Fairfax was telling me about. He said he was expecting you." He turned to Ruby. "He said nothing about you though?"

"I... uhm... ahhh." Ruby flustered. She'd seen pictures of this man on the internet. In the photos he had always been older, but she could tell this young man was him.

"She," Fairfax started. "is a pleasant surprise, wouldn't you say, old chap?"

"Indeed it is, sit down and I'll begin–I know time is of the essence."

"Thank you," Ruby said, and took a seat next to Luke just in front of the fire.

7

"We were young men. Looking for adventure. There were four of us who went on the expedition, setting off from Southampton on the 21st of September 1898. As with all young men, there was a competitive nature to our business..." Brackenford started.

He spoke for a significant time, creating vivid images of the mountains and the snow and of being above the clouds. It had been an adventure that had lasted a great many years. Ruby sat entranced by his words. The sun rose in the sky, never warming the surrounding countryside.

After the great explorer had finished, Fairfax, Ruby, and Luke sat in silence. The only sounds the flicker of the fire.

"You saw inside the mountain?" Luke asked.

"That's right," he said. "The immense darkness as I looked into it was overwhelming, and then a light, like a pinprick in a piece of paper that you hold to the sun, swam up from the bottom," Brackenford looked to the sky. "It never got bigger; it was always the same size; it made me feel as though I was falling."

"What was it?" Fairfax asked.

"Not what, when," Brackenford answered.

"It flew into me that light, right down my damn throat. I tried to cough it up, I hacked, and I even put my fingers down the back, but it wouldn't come. Then I felt a warmth inside of me, a buzzing. And, I closed my eyes," He stopped talking and took a sip from a metal cup next to him. "I saw everything, I saw the first Beast crawl out of the ocean, I saw the first men in the desert, I saw it, and I saw something else. I saw a man standing in front of that Beast. He was like an ant next to a bear. The Beast writhed and wailed, and the man stood like he was carved from ice. The Beast was black, its scales shining and reflecting off a hot sun, much hotter than today. They were in the desert, surrounded by flat-top mountains and long shadows. The Beast's long talons were razored sharp, and a forked tongue flicked out and licked at the air. The man raised his sword to the sky, and lightning flashed down from the clear blue sky. I watched as the beast attacked, again and again. The man deflected its talons and its tongue until too tired and unable to stand any longer. The man collapsed to his knees. I expected the death blow to come, but the Beast toyed with the man, knocking him from side-to-side before standing him back up again," Something howled in the countryside, stopping Brackenford's story. Luke looked at Fairfax, who was grinning like an excited child.

Brackenford started again, "The sword lay useless on the floor next to him. The Beast pulled back its long neck and snapped forward. The man jerked to the side, the sharp fangs of the Beast missing him by the smallest margin, and he picked up his glowing sword from the ground and hacked through the Beast's neck. Time and time again, the man brought his sword down, but the last thick pieces of sinew held tight. The Beast lay on the ground, its head half decapitated, but even from where I watched, I could see it still had life in its body. The man left it lying in the hot desert, hoping that buzzards and other foul beasts would finish the job. But, he was wrong. A crack opened in the earth, and the Beast was swallowed down to the hell below, where it shrunk down to its birth size and using the last of its power, it rewound itself in time to a foetus in its shell."

Fairfax pushed Luke playfully on the arm, "Some story, huh?"

"Fairfax, that was the Leviathan, wasn't it?"

"I believe so, Luke, I believe so." Fairfax replied.

"And, the man, do you know who he was?"

"The time that our friend here saw was before the Knights Templar were created. It was before history began. He is our forefather, the first warrior against the Leviathan. But, there is no way to know who he was."

"What about the sword?"

"You already know the answer to that."

"It's William the Conqueror's, isn't it?"

"It was, yes. I believe it has been called to a new owner now."

"But, why show us this?" Luke asked. "We already have the sword, there's nothing of use here." Ruby grabbed his hand and held it between hers. "There's nothing here," he said to her, before shaking his head.

"I don't guide where the tree brings you, Luke, but this is something it wanted you to see?"

"But, why?"

"Maybe," started Ruby. "So we know what we're up against, and now we know chopping the things head off won't kill it."

"I like her," Brackenford told Fairfax. Ruby shot him a glance.

"How do we kill it then?" Luke asked. The crackling fire was the only sound in the cold countryside. Brackenford took another sip from his metal cup, and Ruby nuzzled into Luke. Fairfax stood over them, his arms crossed, watching the flames dance.

The Priory

8

Fairfax thanked Brackenford for sharing his story again. Luke and Ruby shook Brackenford's weather hands and thanked him too. Then they set off on the walk back to the willow tree. They walked in silence, one in front of another with Fairfax leading the way. Ruby was behind him, and Luke was behind her through the weathered path.

There must be more, Luke thought. That can't be everything. If that was all the willow tree wanted to show them what a waste of time. They could have stayed at his grandads. He wanted Fairfax to walk faster; he tried to get back to his own time and help his grandad.

Ruby thought about the story the great explorer told them. He had seen nothing first-hand; it was all dreams and visions. She needed something concrete, something she could touch. Her hand fiddled with the moonstone in her pocket. She needed to see something with her own eyes. Why didn't the willow tree just send them back to watch that first fight themselves?

Fairfax stopped ahead of them and turned around.

"There's something else, something important. If you don't know it already, it means I didn't get the chance to write it down." He was frowning as Luke got closer. "The sword isn't enough alone. After I heard Brackenford's story, I did more research."

Luke and Ruby stood and listened to what Fairfax had to say. Even though he was just wearing a vest, they hadn't seen him show any sign of being cold.

"It's not just a serpent; it's not a mindless beast; it's devious and cunning. It wanted that man to think it was dead." Fairfax paused and raised a hand to his chin. "It's evil; we know that. There are always two sides; the light and the dark. If we could have found the egg, we could have destroyed it, but my grandfather couldn't get under the monastery. We'd had enough of sitting and waiting and watching. I believe, as my grandfather did before me, that we can kill it, but only when it's gestating in the egg. Before he could try to get it, twenty-three years ago, in 1880, the flood swept it away. I'm sure of it. I've tried to find it, but the river must have taken it away."

Luke watched his great, great grandad as he got more animated as he talked. He was like a college professor. Luke felt like he was on a school trip out in nature with an excited biology teacher.

"How do we kill an egg?"

"Good question. Are there any other creatures in your time? There's one here for sure."

"Yes, two," Ruby answered, and shivered as she remembered Fly-Face.

"If there's two, then it's getting stronger, which means it's been gestating for at least twenty years, if not longer. A creature that largely takes a long time to become ready to hatch. But, in the meantime, have you studied biology?"

Luke and Ruby both nodded.

"Okay, so 'Budding' is when an outgrowth of a cell separates and becomes its organism. That's what those creatures are. Does that make sense?" Budding hadn't been covered at school yet, but Luke understood the idea. "If there are two of them, then they are working together with two main objectives. Number one, keep the egg safe and hidden. Two, prepare for its birth."

"Right, so they're like ants looking after their queen?" Ruby asked.

"Exactly, gosh, you are quite quick, aren't you. Luke, are you keeping up?"

"Yes, still here," Luke replied, rolling his eyes.

"Great, so have you seen these creatures up close, do you know where their lair is?"

"We've had a couple of close encounters, so have the other guys," Luke said.

"So, it's not just you two in your own time, fascinating." Luke noticed Fairfax smiling at Fairfax as if he was a friendly uncle. "I knew it, I told my granddad, I told him, I said, *The rules of your generation don't configure the rules of another,*' he never believed me though."

"So, what, the myths passed down aren't always correct?" asked Ruby.

"Exactly, the myths of one's own time are set by the standards of the time; with new advances in technology and evolution, you would be a fool to think that the rules of myths and legends don't change over time too."

"But what does it all mean?" Luke asked.

"It means, just because something mystical, say an ancient sword, had to be used to kill something years ago, that something from your time might work just as well in your time! Think about magic, hundreds of things thousands of years ago were considered magic, gosh, even in the past couple of decades people thought the lightbulb was magic. But, it was simply good science."

Ruby nodded. "Fire, mobile telephones, wireless internet, Fairfax, you're a genius."

"Why thank you, I don't understand what a few of those things are, but thank you dear." He was pacing now, off the dirt track, into the long grass and back again.

"How do you kill an egg?"

"You crack it," Luke said.

"Wrong! What if what's inside is already alive? You'll just unleash it."

Ruby took a sharp intake of breath. "Oh my god, Fairfax, you are a genius." She turned to Luke. "We need to stop waiting for that egg to open and find it first. If it hatches, then it's too late."

Fairfax did a shimmy on the spot and smiled. "Which brings us back to the creatures; they're the only way to find the egg."

"Maybe not," Luke said, thankful that he finally had something to contribute. "Lucas," he said. "The little boy, Ben, and the story his grandfather told…" Fairfax looked confused. "Ben, a missing little boy from our time, found shed reptile skin, and what looked like the shell of a large–and enormous egg."

"That's it–it must be it," Fairfax said. "The creatures would have shed their skin before they took a host."

Ruby stared out across the fields. "But, what about Ben, how is he involved? Why did they take him?"

"Ben's the little boy?" Fairfax asked, and Luke nodded. "The Leviathan needs an innocent host for its first time; after that, it can move into whoever it wants. But, the body must be alive yet empty."

"What happens to the person inside?"

"No-one knows–they're just gone," Fairfax replied. Maybe not, thought Luke. If Lucas were swapping bodies, then Ben might be out there too.

"We need to go, Fairfax, now!" Luke said.

"Follow me, there's a quicker way." Fairfax cut through the long grass away from the muddy path, and Luke and Ruby followed. "I hope what you have planned works."

They were closer to the river now, keeping it on their left-hand side as they ran through the brambles and the long grass. The river flowed slowly, the cold weather causing parts close to the banks to freeze in white, patterned cobwebs. The sky above was heavy with bloated white and grey clouds that strolled across the sky.

A harsh cry from behind scared a flock of birds into the air, leaving the branches swaying. They ran, looking back over their shoulders towards the noise. Luke saw it. First, fifty-yards behind them running on short, sturdy legs. The long grass folded in front of it. A scene from Jurassic Park entered his mind. A scaled tail stuck up above the long grass, reminding him of a shark's fin. Another harsh bark broke the silence of the afternoon. Wet, white flakes started to fall from the sky. Luke saw white spots in Ruby and Fairfax's hair. The snow came down faster in a flurry of grey that blocked his vision like looking into mist or fog. He heard the squelching of wet mud behind him as the creature gained ground. Luke turned, ready to hold it off while Ruby escaped. He stood like a knight, his feet firmly planted into the ground. A flash of black in the snow ran past him towards the creature. Fairfax shouted, "Keep going, Luke, run…" Luke took one glance back, as he lost the dark shape of Fairfax into the flurry, and sprinted to catch up with Ruby. His family members weren't fairing too well in this fight so far, he thought.

Piercing wet screams and the shocking snap of bones filled the air. Luke caught up to Ruby and reached for her hand and pulled her along faster.

In the falling snow, it was hard to guess distances. Luke thought he could still see the dark, flowing shape of the river on his left, so he kept following. He heard Ruby's rasping shallow breaths beside him. It was sharp and fast. Fairfax was dead, he knew it.

They dodged a tree that appeared from nowhere, followed by another. He was glad for the trees; they provided cover, and it meant they were getting closer to the meadows, and the willow tree. He ran straight into the wooden fence that separated the second meadows from the first. It felt as if he'd taken a baseball bat to his chest. Blood splayed out his mouth, adding colour to the white. He lay on the floor, winded and unable to breathe. Ruby knelt next to him.

"Go… Ruby… get to the tree," he whispered through the metallic taste of blood.

"I won't leave you, Luke."

He tried to push her away but struggled to lift his upper body.

"Go, please… Ruby, you must leave me… go," Luke's eyes closed.

"No, shut up. You're coming too," She grabbed him under his arms from behind and dragged him through the settling snow, leaving a crimson trail behind. Ruby heard the sounds of ripping flesh and sinew on the wind. There were no more screams. Ruby dragged him along the fence, looking for the gate. They were close to where they'd read the letter from Bug, what felt like so long ago. She turned, holding Luke with her left arm as she pulled herself along the gate with her right feeling for the gate.

She touched a piece of fence which moved, but it was just a loose panel. Tears doubled her vision; the struggle had drained her of energy. She felt like sitting down and leaning against the fence with Luke lying over her legs, as they waited for the end. A shadowy figure appeared from the other side of the fence. Ruby could make out long dreadlocks and a tanned face that looked orange against the white of the storm.

"Pass him over to me," the man called out to her.

She grabbed Luke in a bearhug around his waist and heaved him up the fence one step at a time. The man took hold of him around the waist, and she let go. Ruby dropped to the floor, spent. In the hazy snowfall, she saw a dark shadow approaching. A black tower stuck high into the white sky. It looked like a church steeple; she thought before she blacked out.

The intense cold on her face woke her up. She was sitting next to an unconscious Luke under the willow tree. The man in front of her had a wrinkled, kind face and greying dreadlocks that swung close to the floor. He poured snow onto Luke's face, and Ruby saw him stir.

Luke looked at the man and tried to speak. His hands flayed in the air, and the man took hold of them and set them back in Luke's lap. "Don't speak, just do your thing, quick. It's coming," The man held out a moonstone to each of them, "Sorry, I went through your pockets," he said.

Luke took him and put it in his mouth while Ruby did the same. They reached out to their saviour, and each took hold of one of his hands. They took hold of each other and kissed under the willow tree in the snow just as the creature stampeded through and launched itself at them.

Roots wrapped themselves around the three of them; one shot out like a snapped guitar string, and the head of the creature left its body in a splatter of black against white. A warm orange glow came from the tree as it engulfed them.

9

The door stood open as Lucas arrived back at Henry's house. He was in the body of a middle-aged man in a flannel shirt and a pair of expensive jeans. He had floppy brown-blonde hair swept into a side parting and a glorious beer gut. A shiny, white Range Rover Evoque sat with one door open on the driveway behind him.

He looked on in horror at the tacky blood on the floor, the chunks of flesh and the broken furniture. What had happened here? Lucas passed through the front door and into the smashed up sitting room, it looked like the aftermath of a Mötley Crüe hotel stay. The metallic taste of blood hung in the air as did a faint decaying smell, that made phlegm rise to the back of his throat.

He saw the shattered door at the back of the sitting room and he stepped over the pools of blood towards it. The decay smell was stronger back there. He peered around the side of the door and saw a monstrous, broken reptilian body laying on the ground. Its head split in two. To the side he saw Jess. She was covered in blood and her cast was hanging half off her leg. In her hand was an ancient-looking axe.

Lucas rushed to Jess and slid onto his knees into the puddle of blood next to her body. She was a mess. Her clothes were tacky with blood. Her face was pale. He reached out and touched under her chin. He felt a gentle pulse, but he wasn't sure, first aid wasn't his speciality. Lucas went to bend her fingers back to release the axe so he could check her pulse on her wrist. As he bent back the first finger, her eyelids twitched, and she muttered.

"Jess, it's me, it's Lucas."

She mumbled again, her eyes flickering. She pulled him closer with the hand he was holding. He could feel her warm breath on his ear, "Lisa, Petey."

"I didn't see them," he said.

"I'll find them."

"How?"

She closed her eyes and Lucas thought she'd passed out again. Her eyes shot open. "Westford Water, not Lisa and Petey, I can't find them, but it is there."

"How are you so sure?" Lucas swept a piece of her hair out of her face.

"I just know, trust me." Those were the last words she said. Her head fell back; Lucas caught it and laid it to the floor. He bent over her and kissed her forehead.

"Hold on," he whispered.

Lucas kicked the creature and pulled out the mobile phone in his pocket. He dialled 999 and waited for the right person. Once they confirmed an ambulance was on its way, he searched the rest of the house. From the kitchen he filled a glass with water and took it back to Jess. He raised her head and made her take a sip.

"I'll find them," he said through tears. He took the axe from her hand and stood. Lucas walked out of Henry's house, threw the weapon into the back seat of the car and got into the front seat. He looked back at the house once, before starting the engine and reversing off the drive.

Five hundred yards down the road, he rounded a blind corner and saw two knives reflecting the sun on the grass verge and a splintered wooden fence. He pulled the car over and walked back to the scene.

The grass had been trampled and the bush behind held a scrap of bloodied tee shirt, flowing in the breeze stuck to a sharp thorn. He picked up the two knives and examined them, turning them over in his hands. One of them had still wet blood on the tip of its blade. He stepped back and heard a crack under his shoe. Lucas bent down and found Petey's glasses. He'd snapped the temples and shattered both lenses; cobweb lines flowed through them. "Petey," he said.

He sank to his knees. First Jess, and now Petey and Lisa. He couldn't protect anyone. It had ambushed them. Separated them. Would it have happened if he'd stayed with them and stayed awake? Where was Henry, Luke and Ruby? He was alone. He couldn't think. Their faces flashed through his mind, like an old-school PowerPoint presentation. Not just Jess, Henry and the kids, but Ben and his grandad's too. He couldn't finish it himself; he had failed them. Then he thought of Jess back at the house, covered in her own blood. She'd fought one of them and won. He looked out over the fields into the distance. He could try. He owed it to them to fight, not be like the old Lucas, the Cambridge Lucas, who would have given up, that wasn't him anymore. He would try. He wouldn't let anyone else down.

He wiped the tears from his eyes, stood and threw the knives into the backseat alongside the axe. They clinked against the axe-head. He climbed into the front seat and stared at the shattered gate. Lucas pressed the button to start the engine and typed his destination into the onboard SatNav.

10

At the same time Lucas was finding Jess; Petey and Lisa were being blindfolded and transported in the dark; and Luke, Ruby and the man with dreadlocks were emerging from the willow tree; the thing growing inside the egg under the beach at Westford Water opened its eyes for the first time in thousands of years'.

It pressed a tiny talon against the membrane of the shell. It was still hard. It wasn't time. The two had done their job well.

For so long it had slept in the black, no notion of time, or place, but now it was awake. Its senses were getting sharper. It could sense the two bodies nearby, one innocent and the other powerful, both wonderfully empty. It would soon be time.

11

As soon as the roots released him Luke ran to the spot Henry had been attacked. Henry was gone, but there was a dark stain on the dry mud. The blood had been sucked down into the ground. There were two sets of footprints in the dust. There wasn't as much blood as Luke had expected. The blood stained the floor in two places, in two distinct shades.

Had Henry fought off the painter-decorator? Ruby and the dreadlocked man looked at Luke, their eyes wide and mouths open.

"You were on death's door not a minute ago?" The man said.

Luke marvelled at his healed body, holding his arms out one at a time to the warm morning sun.

"Your chest was caved in, you should be dead," he said again.

Ruby ran to Luke and kissed him firmly. Luke felt electricity run through his body. She wrapped her arms around him. He picked her up in his arms and span her around. When they broke free of the kiss, she looked down at his chest. "You should be dead," she whispered. "I do love you, Luke." Her hands ran up the front of his shirt up to his collar. She gently undid the top button and the next. She ran her fingers over the soft unbroken skin. "It's a miracle."

Luke smiled and then turned his attention to the man. "Thank you, without you we wouldn't have made it," He studied the man, from his dreadlocks that touched the floor to his wrinkled, tanned face. "I know who you are," he said.

"Is that right?"

"You're Bug. You're Lucas's friend," Luke said.

Bug's eyes narrowed. "Who are you?" He stayed close to the willow tree, not coming out from under its overhanging branches.

"We found the bag and your letter. We're friends with Lucas."

"What year is it?" Bug asked.

"It's 2019, Lucas is with us," Luke said.

Ruby stepped forward. "I'm Ruby, this is Luke. There's seven of us in total. Lucas will be ecstatic, he's been searching for you."

Bug's bottom lip quivered. "Is it really 2019?" Ruby and Luke nodded. Bug put a hand to his face, when he took it away Luke and Ruby expected to see tears, but he was grinning.

"How did you end up there; at that time?" Luke asked.

Bug looked at the willow tree behind him. "The tree. It sends me where it needs me to be. How many days since I went missing, do you know?"

"Yes, just under a week, I think," Luke answered.

"Is that all? It feels like years'."

"You were in the paper, it was just under a week ago. Before that obviously, it was a little longer."

"Ah, yes. And, Lucas, is he okay? Did he get back into his own body?"

"Not yet, but we're working on it."

A panicked look came over Bug's face. "How much do you know?"

"Most of it, I think," Luke said.

"Did you find Theo?" Bug stepped forward, not out from under the tree, but close.

Luke and Ruby looked at each other. "Theo isn't his real name, his real name is Henry Curthose. He's my grandad," Luke said. "Before we left," he nodded at the tree, "we saw one of those creatures attack him. We don't know where he is."

"Was he injured?" Bug asked.

"I think so," Luke pointed to the stain on the ground. "That's blood."

"He's not dead."

"What do you mean?" Ruby asked.

"Time is disjointed in the tree. Something I did today, may not have happened yesterday, and what I did yesterday may not have happened yet. I jumped between different times. One time the tree brought me out on a night so bright, it seemed like day. I watched a man with a sword fighting a beast, under the largest moon I'd ever seen. The man had his back to me, so I didn't know it was Theo." Luke and Ruby listened intently as Bug recounted what he'd seen. "The man was injured, blood poured down his back. But, he pierced the creature through its stomach. I watched the creature turn and run. The man fell to his knees, but he didn't die. Before the tree sucked me back in again," he took a breath, remembering the moment. "I saw her running towards the man. She saved him, I think."

"Who was she?"

"She was my fiancee, Eve."

"Your fiancee? The one who went missing? Where would she take him?" Ruby asked. Luke looked shocked.

Bug stood for a minute in silence, then spoke, "It was the first time I'd seen her since… since it took us. It was her though. She was beautiful."

Luke approached Bug and stopped a metre away. He was taller than Luke by six inches. Luke reached up and put his hand on his shoulder. "Where is he? Let's finish it. I know how."

"There's a place, a secret place me and Eve liked to kid only we knew about. We didn't of course, everyone knew about it. It's close. Just over the fence in the second meadows. Under a low hanging tree canopy. It feels like the rest of the world can't see you."

Ruby looked at Luke. "It can't be?"

He smiled back at her. "Nothing surprises me anymore," he said. "Everything's connected. Now let's go find my grandad." He looked over at Bug. "And, your fiancee."

12

Lisa woke in the middle of a huge cavernous warehouse. A circle of neon light spread out around her for twenty feet and then it was black. The room was as Lucas had described it. Five, large, white vats sat in the centre of the room surrounded by gleaming metal tables and storage. Across from her was Petey. He was still unconscious. Dried blood ran from his nose, and his right eye had turned a yellowy-green colour. His glasses were gone, and without them he looked kinda cute. She saw his chest rise in shallow breaths and his fingers flinched as if dreaming. They were tied to cold metal chairs with a frayed blue rope, similar to the one from the swing by the river.

She thought about Jess, the sacrifice she'd made so they'd survive. Only it hadn't worked. She prayed in the dark that Jess was alive, and Luke, and Ruby, and Henry, and Lucas. If you're there God, please save us.

A quiet laugh broke the silence. She turned in the seat, but couldn't see anyone.

"No point praying little girl, it'll be over soon. And, your friend's aren't coming, not this time." The man stepped into the light to the left of her. His face was covered in blood, and pieces of torn flesh were stuck between his teeth. She saw a deep stain on his overalls and what looked like a puncture wound. "What, this?" he said pointing to the hole. "It's nothing, it'll heal soon, or I'll take another body." He looked over at Petey and winked. "Very incognito, I'd make that little shit look cool. What do you think?" He walked towards Petey.

"Leave him alone," Lisa said, struggling under the rope.

"Or what? Your grandpops can't save you now, or that crippled cunt."

Lisa felt like someone had slapped her.

"That's right, girly-girl. Dead, dead, DEAD." He licked his lips, and pulled a piece of flesh from his teeth, which he then popped back into his mouth and chewed like a piece of gum. "As for your body-swapping friend, he's a million miles away by now, or hiding in whatever body he's in. Don't worry though. His own body looks like it'll be a perfect fit for my master."

"I'll kill you, I swear to god. I. Will. Kill. You," She shook her seat. Banged the metal legs against the floor. The echoes flew around the room and then died down.

"Shut up," He surged forward and with one kick from his big, mud-encrusted boot, sent her flying backwards. She landed on her back, the chair sticking into her kidneys, staring up into the dark. The painter-decorator leaned over her, grinning. A tiny drop of blood-filled saliva dropped and landed on her cheek.

"See ya later," he said. "It's shooowtiiimmmmeeee!!!"

She heard the man's footsteps fade into the distance.

"Petey," she called. "Petey, can you hear me?"

The warehouse was silent, the last of the echoes of the man's footfalls reverberated around the building, then died. Her body ached in the awkward sitting position. She couldn't move the chair, only wiggle her back. She felt something in her pocket and she let go of a little pee. It was vibrating. It was her mobile. That dumb fuck hadn't taken her mobile. She wiggled her body, trying to get it to slide out of her jeans pocket. She saw the top of it. The screen lit up. She kept up her sideways wiggle until it fell onto the floor next to her.

She cried out when she saw the name of the caller—'Grandad.'

"Answer," she said.

The screen turned green, and she heard Luke's voice.

"Luke, it's Lisa. The painter got me and Petey. I think he killed Jess. Where are you?"

She couldn't activate the speakerphone, but in the large open room she could hear him clearly.

"No time to explain. Lisa, I know how to kill it! Grandad's injured, but me and Ruby are okay. Where are you?"

"In the warehouse; the one near the garage. Luke, it's Petey, I'm not sure he will be okay."

"Listen to me, can you escape?"

"I'm tied to a chair... he kicked me over, I'm lying on my back. Help us Luke."

"I will, I've got a plan. Is the painter still there?"

"He's gone. He said it was showtime."

"Perfect," Luke said down the phone. "Hold on Lisa, friends are on their way."

13

Lucas arrived in the car park. The gift shop was shut, as was the ice-cream kiosk. The reservoir was calm. The water looked like a mirror. He opened his car door and grabbed the axe and the two knives. He slid them into his belt on both sides. The axe he carried in front of him. The car park was empty except for a white van. A white van he'd seen drive past when he was pulled over on the side of the road.

It was time. No more messing, no more mysteries, no more questions and riddles. Down by the sand, he spotted the owner of the van. He was bent over on the sand, like a child digging sandcastles–like Ben must have looked. As Lucas approached, he saw two bodies lying on the ground. They looked peaceful, arms tucked into their sides and their chins jutting up.

One was a young boy, Ben. The other was a good-looking man with close cropped black hair and stubble, it was him. The sensation of seeing his own body from this perspective made his stomach lurch.

The man in blue paint-stained overalls was preoccupied with the deep six-foot across hole he was standing digging in. He had his back turned to the well-to-do middle-aged man who was approaching carrying an ancient-looking axe. Lucas heard the grunts of the man as he continued to dig, bringing up wet sand and mud and leaving it in a pile next to the hole.

Lucas raised the axe above his head when he got within five metres of the man. He increased his pace, not running, but jogging. When he was within three feet, he swung the heavy axe from above his head.

A glint of sunshine reflected off something behind the man onto the wet pile of sand and mud above him to his right. He ducked as the axe swung down, feeling the breeze as it missed his head by an inch.

The axe buried itself into the sand between Lucas' feet. The momentum of the arc made Lucas stumble. He lingered on the edge of the hole, but caught his balance and pulled the axe free. The man in overalls jumped out of the hole from a standing position, landing on both feet like a superhero. His skin melted and Lucas looked at the man in his true form.

Wet, shiny black mandibles clicked together and at least ten, bulbous jaundiced eyes reflected Lucas' form. They stood a metre apart, Lucas brandishing his axe and Fly-face hissing. He'd gotten himself between his and Ben's bodies and Fly-face. Protecting them. The hole was to his left. He glanced into it and saw an off-white membrane running along the bottom of the hole. A shadow moved beneath it.

"This axe killed your girlfriend, you fucker. And, now it will kill you too."

Fly-face dropped to all fours. It rocked from side-to-side, as if having a fit, and translucent, membranous wings broke through its flesh, covered with thick black stubble-like-whiskers. The wings started to vibrate, and it took off into the sky, hovering just out of reach of Lucas and his axe. It buzzed in front of the sun and Lucas brought up one arm to shade his eyes. Fly-face spat a sticky substance at Lucas, and dive bombed forcing Lucas to the edge of the hole. The shadow beneath the membrane moved again. Fly-face dived at Lucas, and he let go of the axe as he jumped to the other side of the hole to avoid falling in. He was in a plank position, his stomach exposed. Fly-face screamed and Lucas saw his silhouette dive bomb one last time.

Behind him, Lucas heard a car skid into the car park, he turned his head and Henry's blue Clio arrived in a fog of dust. It bumped over potholes on the gravel and dirt road and didn't slow as it approached the edge of the road that led to the beach. It came to a screeching stop five-metres behind where Lucas lay over the hole.

Fly-face hissed and spat and pulled out of the dive bomb as all four doors of the Clio opened. Out of the driver's side. Lucas watched as Bug got out the car. His dreadlocks dragged along the floor. Lucas smiled, despite the burning in his arms and legs. From the passenger side a short, skinny woman got out of the car and smiled. Last, stepping out together, Luke and Ruby emerged from the blue car and walked around the bonnet where they took each other's hand and made their way towards him. Luke held a long broadsword in his hand and Ruby a crossbow that had been hung on the same wall as the axe.

Lucas felt tears well up inside of him. Bug and his fiancee arrived next to him and helped him to his feet. Bug patted his shoulder like an old friend. They stood with him on his left, while Luke and Ruby took their place next to him on his right. Bug and his fiancee stood empty-handed. But, they weren't here to fight. They were the getaway drivers.

"Lucas, we need it to hatch," Luke whispered.

Lucas gave him a look. "Are you serious?"

"Deadly. Keep him busy," Luke looked at Fly-face. "Kill the fucker."

Ruby loosened an arrow from the crossbow and Fly-face glided to the left dodging the metal arrow which landed with a plop in the water behind. As he dodged, Lucas swung the axe upward catching the creature's foot. It sliced the flesh, but didn't sever it. Between them, Ruby and Lucas moved Fly-face away from the hole and towards the shoreline.

"Right kid, you're up. How do we wake this fucking thing?" Bug said to Luke.

"It's already awake. We just need to release it." Luke stabbed at the outer membrane of the shell. It was tougher than it looked. A shadow moved inside it.

"Will that sword cut through it?"

"I hope so." Luke climbed into the hole and hoisted the sword above his head. He brought it down, and it rebounded off the shell with a soft bonk. "Shit."

"The axe?" Bug said.

"Go get it." He passed the sword up to Bug. "Give this to Lucas."

Bug ran to the shoreline towards where Lucas and Ruby were fighting the hovering beast. The water behind them was still and reflected the bright blue sky perfectly, as if it was a mirror. Fly-face saw Bug running towards them and dive bombed. Lucas jumped and swung with the heavy axe but missed by a hair. He turned to see Bug get slashed across his chest by a razor-sharp wing when Fly-face twisted at the last moment.

"BUG!" A woman's scream cut through the clear sky.

The short, skinny woman ran towards Bug's twitching body. Blood poured from his chest staining the sand and soaking down into the earth. The sword lay by his side. Lucas ran to his fallen friend, leaving Ruby alone on the shore taking aim at Fly-face. He hovered above Bug, fifteen-feet off the ground, and didn't see the thick arrow until it was too late. It pierced one of its eyes. Yellow puss bubbled out and its wings stopped buzzing. It fell to the ground between Bug and Lucas and Ruby by the shore. Lucas stepped towards it, he could still see the mandibles clicking. With one motion, he heaved the axe above his head and swung it down. Fly-face's head rolled towards the shore. The mandibles clicked once and fell still.

Lucas knelt down next to his dread-locked friend. The slash ran deep through his chest and he saw torn muscle and the white of the rib cage. He put his hand on Bug's shoulder, shaking his head. The woman sobbed on the other side as the light left Bug's eyes for the last time. Ruby stood behind them, the crossbow hanging limp.

"The axe, I need the axe," Luke shouted to them from the hole. "NOW."

"I'm finishing this," Lucas said, he raised himself to his feet, and put a hand on Bug's fiancee's shoulder. "For Bug."

He ran up the beach towards Luke. He jumped into the hole next to Luke. They took it in turns hammering at the shell. It cracked, but didn't break. The thing inside moved furiously.

"Stop," a woman's voice called from above. "It wants blood. Blood will make it hatch."

Bug's fiancee held out her hands and let Bug's blood fall into the hole. It splattered on top of the off-white shell. The ground moved beneath them, shaking them off their feet, and a loud rumble emanated from below. The shell cracked like a windscreen in a car crash. Forks of lightning spreading out across the surface. A hole the size of a golf ball appeared and a rotten smell of sulphur filled the air.

Lucas and Luke pulled themselves out of the hole. Ruby and Eve joined them. They ran away from the hole towards the car park. Behind them the ground undulated causing waves to crash onto the shore. Lucas stopped as they passed the bodies lying on the ground. He looked at his own body and to the young boy. He knelt next to Ben. The boy looked peaceful, his hands were together in front of his chest. Lucas swept a piece of blonde hair out of Ben's face and then picked him up from beneath and ran, leaving his own body behind.

The sand bounced three times, like something was punching its way through and then it sank. A huge roar filled the air as from out of the hole emerged a creature with black scales and spikes like a dinosaur, hexagonal and sharp running down its spine. Two gangly, veined legs with sharp talons protruded from lower down its body. A large tail swung behind it, twenty feet in the air. Its head was the size of Luke, and its teeth were serrated and razor sharp like a shark. A foul-smelling liquid dropped from two fangs the size of Lucas's legs, creating a stinking, steaming puddle on the floor where the beach had been moments before. Its green eyes glowed, and it looked at them intelligently.

The four of them stood on the edge of the car park looking up at the Leviathan. Lucas held Ben's still body in his hands. "Now what?" Lucas asked.

"Wait for it," Luke replied.

"Wait for what?"

"For it to attack."

Lucas looked at him, his eyebrows raised, "If that thing attacks we're all dead."

The Leviathan cast a shadow that reached halfway across the car park in the low, early morning sun. The beast itself was a pitch-black silhouette that stretched forty-feet into the sky. It swayed as it got used to its newly found freedom and stretched out its limbs to their full length. If this thing was a baby, Lucas didn't want to know how big it would grow. Along the two legs at the rear, two further legs on either side of its body spread out from its back end as it exited the sand. Lucas watched as his body slid, along with the sand, down into the hole. Bug's final resting place was gone, along with his body.

"Trust him," Ruby said, from Lucas's other side. She looked paler than usual and her eyes had dark rings under them. "Trust him."

The Leviathan roared at the tiny humans beneath him. He couldn't yet talk as he had no body. Without a body, he wouldn't be able to carry through his work. It glared down with thunderous eyes and saw the child's body that Lucas held. Lucas met the beast's eyes.

"You want him? Come and get him," he said, not afraid.

It slunk lower to the ground, three forked tongues flicking from its mouth, tasting the fear, the blood and the humanity on them. It had been too long since it had walked the earth. It was the rightful owner, the king of all.

Lucas lowered Ben's body to the ground and then stepped in front of it. The others did the same. One of its taloned legs swept over them and they ducked to the ground.

"That's it, a little closer," Luke muttered. They huddled together, side-by-side in front of the body the Leviathan wanted, needed so badly.

The beast roared again, spittle flying from its mouth and over them. It attacked, this time with its spiny, razor-sharp tail which swung in a long loop over the shoreline. They ducked, except for Luke. He raised the sword in front of him and heard the shriek as the end of the tail careered off into the car park and landed with a dull thud. It was as long as the white Range Rover it landed next to. The impact shattered the bones in his right arm and dislocated his shoulder. He lay on the ground, groaning in front of the group as Ruby ran to him. She kneeled next to him, where he lay cradling his broken arm. The Leviathan shrieked and loomed over the mortal child who dared to fight him. Ruby held Luke in her arms as the shadow above put them in darkness. Its green slitted eyes looked at them both. It reared back its head ready to strike. Its long neck arched in the air and its mouth opened with long fangs dripping with venom. The Leviathan didn't notice Lucas and Eve as they rounded on it. Lucas struck first, the axe delving into thick muscle and flesh. Bug's fiancee went next. The sharp broadsword, with the red leather hilt sliced straight through muscle. The Leviathan's head, unbalanced by the lack of muscle, flopped forward like a man in prayer. Rank, ripe, rust coloured-blood erupted from its neck, covering them all in hot, wet mess. One stray tendon held the head to the neck, like a sailors knot holding a boat to shore. Lucas went to hack it with his axe.

"NO!" called Luke.

Lucas looked over at Luke and Ruby. The stinking juices of the beast covered them. "Wait."

Silence fell over the beach and the car park. From inside, the Leviathan started to hiss and gurgle. Silver steam rose from its still body. The scales and flesh started to constrict on themselves.

They stared on, covered in warm, thick blood that dripped from them, as the Leviathan shrank and devolved back into an egg no bigger than a washing machine.

Behind them, Ben stirred. Lucas ran to the boy, he lifted his upper body and cradled him like a newborn baby. His eyes opened. "Where I?" he said in a soft voice.

"At the beach," said Lucas, unable to think of anything else to say. "Your Grandad's been looking for you." He bent over the little boy and cried. Eve approached from behind and put her hand on Lucas's shoulder. Then she hit him hard with the hilt of the sword.

Lucas opened his eyes. He was lying on the ground next to the egg. Ruby, Luke, Ben and Eve were looking down at him. He reached to the side of his head with his hand, but felt no pain. What the fuck.

"Sorry," Eve said.

He sat up and across from him he saw the body of the well-to-do middle-aged man, his fancy shoes poking up towards the sky. Raising a hand to his face, he saw his cheap, digital Casio watch staring back at him from his wrist and the back of a hand he'd recognise anywhere.

"Thank you," he said. "Thank you."

"Lucas, if it wasn't for you I wouldn't have seen Bug again. We wouldn't have ended this, and this little guy," she rubbed Ben's hair, "wouldn't be here." Lucas could see tears in her eyes, but she looked remarkably calm.

They nodded in agreement. Lucas stood up. "Now what, Luke?"

"Grandad, Lisa and Petey are waiting for us."

"Where?"

"At the warehouse." Luke nodded towards the egg. "We need to bring that with us."

Lucas looked out over the car park. "That won't be a problem," he said, laying eyes on the white van. "What's going on, Luke? How did you know it would turn into an egg?"

"I'll explain everything, Lucas, as soon as we get to the warehouse."

"Okay, but we have one stop to make first, you can go on ahead."

Lucas, Eve, and Ben sat in the van's front. The back end was heavy from the weight of the egg, so Lucas drove slowly, although it was only a short drive to Gerry's house. He parked outside, and Lucas and Ben walked down the patio path, surrounded by bright flowers on either side, towards Gerry's front door. Before they arrived, the door swung open and Gerry ran out. He hoisted Ben into the air, ignoring the pain is his back. Lucas turned to leave.

"Who are you," Gerry asked, lowering Ben to the ground, but keeping hold of his hand.

"I'm a friend of Brookes," he replied, turning around. "Look after each other; not everyone gets to spend time with their grandad, especially one who cares as much for you as yours does," Lucas said, lowering himself to the same height as Ben. He ruffled his hair. "Look after yourself, champ."

Lucas walked down the front garden, a smile spreading across his face. He could see Eve through the window in the front seat. She was crying again. He got in and closed the door. Lucas started the van, and they drove in silence, until Lucas said, "I'm sorry about Bug, he was a great guy. He was my only friend."

"Thank you," Eve replied. Another moment passed as they drove past fields on either side. "The willow tree, do you think it's finished now?"

Lucas looked at her. "I don't know, but if you want me to take you down there after this is all over I will, I owe Bug that much. He loved you."

"Thank you."

14

Henry and Luke watched as Lucas, Ruby, Lisa and Petey hoisted the egg over the boiling vat of water. While Luke and the others had battled the creature, Henry, from the cold metal table Bug had laid him on, directed Lisa and Petey like a science teacher. Now he and his grandson sat next to each other watching, with their injuries bandaged.

The vats for making paint didn't need heat, but one vat was an old pasteuriser leftover from when the warehouse was used for cheese making purposes–that one would get very hot. Henry talked Petey through getting the vat up and running again, although Petey, the smart boy he was, didn't need much help.

They found an old pallet and a rusted lifter in the warehouse's corner and when Lucas arrived (without Eve) they rolled the egg onto it.

Now it hung in a silver chain-link harness above the boiling vat of water. Everyone left, except Henry and Luke, stood around the vat looking up at the Leviathan egg above.

"I feel like we should say something," Luke said, from the table he and his grandad sat at.

"Will this work?" Lucas asked.

"Yes, I'm sure of it."

Lisa moved forward and pressed the button that lowered the huge egg. It wobbled in the chains. They heard it hiss and bubble as it entered the water.

"That's for our friends," she said.

Outside they heard the sound of rain as it landed on the concrete of the warehouse's exterior. A cool breeze blew through from the wide open doors. The heatwave had ended.

SIX WEEKS LATER

I feel like I'm in that scene at the end of the Dark Knight Rises; you know the one where Michael Caine looks up from his newspaper in a cafe and sees Christian Bale with a brunette. They acknowledge each other with a nod and then the screen fades out.

I always pictured them in a cafe in Paris watching the world go by, happy that they'd saved Gotham and happy to be retired at last.

I'm not retired, far from it, but I have moved to Westford and have been a resident for three years; it feels like home.

I'm on a metal table outside the bar on Broad Leaf Square, no coffee for me; it's mid-afternoon and I'm enjoying a Glenffidich and ginger beer with lots of ice and lemon. No nice brunette either, but you can't win them all.

I've kept in touch with all of them and we plan to go en masse to Bug's grave every year on the anniversary. Luke and Ruby are still together, or were the last time I saw them. Lisa's on the verge of college a year early, smart girl that one, and Petey is a Youtuber which I'm still not sure what it means, but he's making some good money early for a teenager. Henry has started painting under his own name. Prettier landscapes than the one he used to paint. I haven't seen Eve since I dropped her off at the meadows. Ben's fine and he and Gerry are living the life I hoped they would. I take a drive-by there every now and again.

I went home; I saw my family. My grandad's gone. It happened quickly and I think he was ready to go. I hope wherever he is, he remembers me again. Fuck you Alzheimers. I can't say everything's great with my family, but it's better than it was.

Jess is still married to Mike and their kids are good. After the attack, the ambulance arrived and they found a pulse. She survived–just. I met Mike at the hospital and he seemed nice, if a bit of a jealous type. I didn't go back.

I'm pondering what to do with the rest of the afternoon, it's hot again, (not as hot as it was that summer) and the streets are full of kids and families when across the road I see him. His dreadlocks are gone, but it's him. He's with a skinny woman in a business suit. Eve. Bug's wearing nice clothes; a smart white button-up shirt and jeans. Nicer than the clothes I wear.

I slide down into my chair watching him from across the road. Wanting to chase after him, but knowing somethings are best left alone; I finish my drink and head to the next bar just as something loud like thunder crashes across the sky from above…

THE END

Read the first chapter of the next '*Westford Chronicles*' novel now.

VERMIN

It sounded like thunder, but when Jacob looked the sky was pale blue with a splattering of white clouds; it didn't look like stormy weather. Sam, his four-year-old son, was a little ahead of him on the yellow and orange leaf-strewn path. Jacob watched his eldest son as he bent down and picked a shiny conker from the grass verge under the big chestnut tree. The last leaves of summer clung to it as a light breeze blew. His youngest clung to his leg, clawing to be picked up; his big blue eyes staring at him. At the corner of the boy's eyes were little tears – not of sadness, but from the cold autumn air.

"Okay, buddy," he said and bent and picked him up. "Shoulders?"

Jack shook his head and wrapped his arms around Jacob's neck.

"Sam," Jacob said. "Wait for daddy, baby, okay?"

"Okay, daddy," Sam answered, rolling the conker in his gloved hands.

Once Jacob had Jack secure, he walked to Sam and knelt next to him. "What have you got? Is it a conker?" Sam showed it to him proudly. "Wowzers, baby, that's a big one."

The thunder crashed again. All three boys looked to the sky and saw something tracing a chem-line-like-trail across the blue. The roar grew as it soared across the sky. A white truck with the name of the cement company Jacob worked for steamed past on the road next to the path, and he jumped back in surprise. Jack screamed in his arms and tried to cover his little pink ears, and Sam put his gloved hands over his.

Jacob watched as the object's speed increased and it broke into bright yellow flame with another loud crash. It would land close by. The wind increased, and a cloud blocked out the low sun, making it seem later than it was. The three boys watched, like a slow-motion game of tennis with no returner, as the fire fizzled out and the object crashed into the woods near the quarry.

He scooped Sam into his arms so he had Jack one side and Sam the other and jogged to the opening in the hedgerow through the brambles and blackberries into the field leading to the quarry. He stopped and peered through the gap.

Just above the treeline of the woods, some one-hundred yards away, he saw the evaporating trail of the object and a thin line of black smoke coming from the middle of the woods. A plane crash? Jacob thought about taking the boys to explore, but the glow of the fire stopped him in his tracks – if it was just him, he wouldn't have even thought about it; he'd be halfway across the muddy field running to the orange, yellow and red leaves of the treeline. But, it was his weekend with the boys and he didn't want to be responsible for the boys getting injured; Julie, his ex, would have a field day playing the irresponsible parent card.

"What is it daddy?" Sam asked.

"I don't know, buddy, but I'm sure the police will be along soon."

They turned from the opening and carried on walking the mulchy path. Jacob lowered Sam to the floor, but Jack refused to let go. The smoke had drifted on the breeze, and Lucas smelled wood burning. Nothing to do with you, he thought. Get the boys home to the warmth and put on a spooky Halloween family film.

Sam had stopped walking and Jacob bumped into him. "Sorry, Sam. What's the matter?"

His son in his oversized grey coat, blue wool hat with googly alien eyes and bright red gloves pointed to the bushes ahead of them.

"I saw something, daddy, something in the bush."

"What was it?" Jacob replied, switching Jack to his other arm. The bushes rattled ahead. "Get behind me, Sam." He moved in front of him thinking it could be a badger, and the boy cuddled up to his leg. Whatever was in the bushes was scuttling and moving, causing the last remaining little orange leaves to fall and flutter to the floor to join their comrades from the summer.

"I want to go home, daddy."

Jack cried in his arms, while Sam hugged his leg tighter. A creature the size of an RC car covered in wet-looking, spiked-up black fur ran from the bushes and through the long grass; its tall tail sticking up like a shark's fin. The tail disappeared into the long grass of the green and brown leaf-stricken verge. Jacob thought he could hear the flickering of the flames from far away as they stood motionless, watching the verge. He knew a lot of the wildlife in the area, but he didn't know what he'd just seen. The tall grass parted as the creature made its way towards them. It was twenty-feet away.

"It's just a rat," he said, trying to convince himself, as much as the boys, he hadn't seen the glowing yellow eyes and extra spiny pink legs that sprouted from the thing's stomach. The creature moved fast with a sideway gait like a crab. Jacob picked Sam up from the path. Both boys were crying now.

"I don't like it, I don't like it, I don't like it..." Sam cried. Jacob turned from the verge. "Okay, baby, we're going, we're going." He went to step down the curb to cross the road, when another truck flashed past so fast that his hat blew from his head. Another truck from his work. When he got back to the office on Monday he'd have words.

"Shit."

The boys were really crying now. He had one in each arm, both with big fat tears running down their red cheeks.

He checked both ways and ran across the road. When he reached the other side, he turned back to see if the thing was still coming. The long grass was still. Behind the bramble bushes he saw black smoke, which was getting thicker. He squinted at the trees. The trunks looked like they were moving.

"What the fu–" he started, when the creature launched itself from the verge on the other side of the road. He glanced glowing yellow eyes and six thin black legs, just before it got hit by yet another thundering truck with his company's name on, and turned into red mist. Jacob let out a breath, rebalanced the boys in his arms and jogged onto the estate towards home.

The sky turned heavy with full grey clouds hanging low in the sky. The only colours were the vivid red, fire orange and banana yellow of the leaves on the floor and those still clinging to life on the trees.

Jacob ran along the freshly laid black tarmac paths with both boys held tight in his arms. His breath steamed in front of him. He rounded a corner and down a dark alleyway with blackberries growing amongst the wired-off, diamond fencing and rotting apples on the floor. The world was silent except for his sharp breaths and the snuffles of Sam and Jack.

"I can't... run... any... further," he said between breaths to the boys, stopping and putting them down. He leaned over with his hands on his knees. The boys clung to his sides as he waited for the heat in his chest to cool. He saw brown and mouldy insides of apples and the black stains of blackberries on the path, like blood splatter in the dark. They were only five-minutes' from home. Once he'd caught his breath, he scooped up the boys again and carried on.

He put them down as he rounded the corner and arrived at his gravelled drive. Tall ferns rose on both sides, casting the red front door in shadow. Yellow gravel lay on the black tarmac path, like stars in the night sky. Jacob reached into his denim jacket pocket and pulled out his keys. He had them in the lock when he heard a squark from above. Fuck this, what now?

He opened the door and pushed the boys into the small porch that smelled of feet as he turned his head to the sky. Black silhouettes of birds, some large like kites, others small like robins, flew in ragged lines blocking out the grey sky behind. Something warm fell onto his face and he touched it with the tip of his finger. When he pulled it away, he saw blood. The squawking increased as the birds got more frenzied above. He jumped into the porch and shut the door as a bird thumped into it with a bang. Another fell onto the roof of the car beyond with a dull metallic thud.

"What's going on?" he said to himself.

He helped Sam and Jack take off their coats and then entered the dimly lit living room. Scattered toys; colourful plastic dinosaurs and green toy army men littered the floor. Both boys ran inside and jumped onto the soft brown sofa. Jacob went to the front window and pulled back the curtains. Dark drops fell from the sky, grey light reflecting from the red. It was raining blood.

The blood soaked into the gravel on his drive. He saw a thick red puddle form on the road with pink froth and feathers floating on top as lifeless bodies of birds fell from the sky; hitting with soft whumps, muted by the double-glazed glass. He ran to the back of the room and opened the sliding patio doors. He heard the pitter-patter of blood hitting the plastic conservatory roof. Leaving the door open, even though the cold air from inside was already making the living room chilly, he sat down between Sam and Jack. They nuzzled into him and he wrapped his arms around both of them while he stared out the window at the birds falling from the sky and the red rain listening to the soft tap, tap, tap on the conservatory roof.

Both boys were snoring on the sofa next to him. The rain had stopped, and he had seen no birds fall from the sky for ten minutes'. He picked up his Samsung Galaxy and unlocked it with his fingerprint. No Wi-Fi or 4G. What was going on out there? He thought about calling Julie, but then thought, Fuck it, she wouldn't call me.

There had been no traffic down his cul-de-sac, which was strange. It had gone five, and the light was fading fast. Would the streetlights turn on? Jacob stood and looked out the window. There were no lights on in the neighbouring houses, and most driveways stood empty. Dark puddles, like oil, sat on the paths and the road. He went into the porch and hesitantly opened the front door. The air had a metallic taste mixed with the burning smell of wood. He peered around the corner up the street and saw an orange glow from the quarry. The fire had grown.

Jacob turned to his sleeping boys. He grabbed a cow print blanket from the other sofa and covered them with it. They could sleep down here with him tonight. Julie wouldn't be home till tomorrow – god, he hoped this cohabiting would be over soon. Not just because the sofa was uncomfortable, but because he was excited. A fresh start. A new life. His own time with the boys where he wouldn't have someone nagging or telling him what he already knew or what to do like a fucking primary school teacher. The initial shock had given way to the excitement of starting afresh. He was free – he was ready to move on.

He sat down on the opposite sofa, watching the boys softly snoring.

They'd be awake soon and wouldn't want to go to bed, but that didn't matter. How it looked outside, he thought it might be better if they were awake and alert. He tried the TV again, but without Wi-Fi he just got static. Picking up his phone, he relented and called 999. He hadn't wanted to waste their time, but felt there was now no choice.

Beep. Beep. Beep. Shit, he thought. That's never a good sign.

Bang!... Bang!... Bang!... The front door. The boys stirred but didn't wake.

"Jacob, Jacob? It's me, Mike. I saw your lights on, let me in…" Mike, his next-door neighbour. The streetlights came on with a warm orange glow that cast Mike in an eerie light when Jacob opened the front door. Mike brushed past Jacob and straight into the living room. Jacob glanced past him out onto the estate. The orange lights reflected in the dark puddles.

"Come on in," Jacob said and shut the door.

Mike paced in the centre of the living room. His dirty brown boots leaving red bloody stains on the cream carpet, which Jacob tried to ignore. Fuck it, wouldn't be his problem soon. He looked at the state of the house behind the sleeping boys on the sofa and where Mike stood. The sliding doors into the conservatory were smeared with dirty little handprints which shone up ghost-like in the reflections from the lamp above. Crumbs littered the carpet, as did trampled in stains of Play-Doh and slime.

She'd stopped cleaning when it looked like he was keeping the house. Then when he changed his mind and decided to move, (even though the separation was her idea) he'd expected her to start again. She hadn't. When it was her weekend away, he spent most of his time not playing with the boys but clearing up the mess in a house he would – not by choice – no longer be living in, while she went out.

"Mike, what's going on? Have you heard anything?"

"The TV, the radio, they both went down about an hour ago, just before the fireball. The internet was already down," Mike looked at Jacob. "I'm scared, man," he looked at the sleeping boys. "How are they holding up?"

"We were outside when that thing crashed – something chased us, but they're okay – we're okay."

"That's good, that's good," he said, taking in the house's mess. "Housekeeper on holiday?"

Jacob smiled. "Well since the separation, it's been kinda like me vs the volcano."

"Separation going smoothly, then? I saw her yesterday – she didn't say Hi. Can't say it surprised me, she always was – no offense – a bit of a strange one."

"None taken, haha, they say you don't truly know someone until you separate from them."

"Quite, quite, I'll tell you my story one day, but not today – slightly more pressing matters at hand wouldn't you agree?"

Jacob nodded and went to the window. Mike joined him and together they stared out into the artificial orange light of the autumn evening. The cul-de-sac was quiet. Eight of the eleven brick driveways were empty, and Jacob saw yellow lights in only two of the houses.

"Where is everyone?" he asked.

"I don't know, I've been home all day."

"What do you think is going on, Mike?"

"I'm a bit older than you, Jacob, but I can honestly say I have experienced nothing like this before – it almost reminds me of that radio broadcast of 'War of the Worlds' back in the 1930s."

"What should we do?"

"Wait it out; your boys are asleep – let them sleep. We can take it in turns to watch them, and then in the morning… we'll take whatever it brings."

Jacob reached a hand to Mike, who took it. "Thanks, Mike, I really appreciate it."

"Don't be silly – I'm all alone, my family left me, the best thing I can do is help you and yours."

"Still, it's appreciated, Mike. You can sleep first. I'll go get blankets."

"Deal."

The four boys hunkered down together in the messy living room, unaware of what was happening outside their safe four walls.

Vermin is available on <u>Amazon</u> now!

ABOUT THE AUTHOR

Jonathan Wheatley is a <u>professional copywriter</u> by trade and a novelist by night. Influenced by the likes of Dan Simmons, James Herbert, H. P. Lovecraft and Stephen King, his novels are a mixture of contemporary horror and historical fact. A treasure trove of general knowledge and a dedicated movie, book and TV buff, his books are filled with easter eggs to entertainment culture.

Born and raised in <u>Stamford,</u> Lincolnshire; when he finally puts down his pen and paper and stops reading, he is a dedicated family man. Father to Sonny and Harlan, he is often found sharing family memories alongside his sketches and photos on Instagram and Facebook. Jonathan wants to introduce writing and reading to a new generation and promote and encourage new writers.

The Priory is his first full-length novel, after previously publishing short stories and a serial novel on Wattpad and he is currently studying for a degree in Creative Writing and Literature with the Open University.

The Priory

Printed in Poland
by Amazon Fulfillment
Poland Sp. z o.o., Wrocław

58593646R00115